WICKED Saint

SINNERS AND SAINTS BOOK 1

USA TODAY & INTERNATIONAL BESTSELLING AUTHOR

VERONICA EDEN

WICKED SAINT

ISBN 978-1-957134-12-3 (Discreet Series Edition)

WICKED SAINT

SINNERS AND SAINTS BOOK 1

VERONICA EDEN

CONTENTS

AUTHOR'S NOTE

Wicked Saint is a dark new adult high school bully romance intended for mature readers. The Sinners and Saints series boys are all devilish bullies brought to their knees by a spitfire heroine, so if you love enemies-to-lovers type stories, you're in the right place. This mature new adult romance contains crude language, dubious situations, and intense graphic sexual/violent content that some readers might find triggering or offensive. Please proceed with caution.

If you like weak pushover heroines and nice guys this one ain't for you, but if you dig strong females and smug antiheroes, then you're in the right place! Hold onto your hearts, because these guys aren't above stealing.

Each book is part of a series but can be enjoyed as a standalone.

Sinners and Saints series:

#1 Wicked Saint
#2 Tempting Devil

#3 Ruthless Bishop
#4 SW (Book 4)

Sign up for Veronica's newsletter to receive exclusive content and news about upcoming releases: bit.ly/veronicaedenmail
Follow Veronica on BookBub for new release alerts: bookbub.com/authors/veronica-eden

ABOUT THE BOOK

GEMMA

HE STOLE MY FIRST KISS...

AND NOW HE THINKS EVERYTHING ELSE IS HIS.

I said no to the one person no one at this school dares to refuse.

Now I'm targeted by jealous girls, guys that compete to be the first to "break the prude", and by *him*. After one kiss, the king of the school hunts me down like I'm a conquest to win. He'll have to fight harder than that, because I'm no one's trophy.

They all want a piece of me, but I will not bend or break for them.

LUCAS

NO ONE REFUSES THE KING.

One case of mistaken identity and a hasty kiss turned my world upside down.

The new girl refused me. Not only that, she threw down the

gauntlet. That won't stand. No one ever says no to me. This school is mine and she'll learn her place as a loyal follower or her life is going up in flames.

I'll make her say yes. She'll be screaming it before I'm finished breaking her.

PLAYLIST

(Spotify)

Trouble—Ralph
Fuckboy—Dillistone
Ordinary Love—Yianna, Dillistone
All the good girls go to hell—Billie Eilish
Stupid—Tate McRae
New Girl—FINNEAS
King of Everything—Wiz Khalifa
Location—Khalid
There's Nothing Holdin' Me Back—Shawn Mendes
Tempt My Trouble—Bishop Briggs
Young God—Halsey
Waiting on the weekend—YUNGBLUD
Wow—Post Malone
Mad Love—The Pretty Reckless
Wicked Ones—Dorothy
Here—Alessia Cara
Molotov—Dillistone

PLAYLIST

Hard Pill to Swallow—Yianna
Survival of the Fittest—Ariana and the Rose
Cold—Mating Ritual, Lizzy Land
There's Nothing Holdin' Me Back—Shawn Mendes
Liar—Camila Cabello
Tongue Tied—Marshmello, YUNGBLUD, blackbear
Original me—YUNGBLUD, Dan Reynolds
Keeping It In the Dark—Daya
This Baby Don't Cry—K.Flay
Midas—Dillistone, LILI N
Circles—Post Malone
Young and Reckless—Charlotte Lawrence
Tables Have Turned—Ralph

To dreamers. Dare to dream big.

ONE
GEMMA

The minute I pull into the upscale, gated community of Silver Lake Forest Estates, my muscles seize.

Forging ahead is the only option. I focus on the GPS directions from my mounted phone. The cheery cartoon map is at odds with the anxiety slithering in my gut. I have zero interest in going, but here I am.

The sour taste of beer is still fresh when I think of the last party I went to.

It's funny how weird details like that linger when all you want to do is forget the whole thing.

Shoving the mounting dread aside, I grip my steering wheel and remind myself that this time isn't like before. I'm not joining in.

Get in, get out. That's the plan.

I'll get through this as fast as possible.

My body hasn't gotten the memo, stomach flipping in protest as I pass a sign for a pool and two tennis courts.

Despite not wanting to be on this errand, I have no choice. Mom had to guilt trip me into venturing into the fray to bring Alec home. Damn her wily, motherly ways of applying pressure to all my weak points.

If I didn't pick Alec up, I could kiss my use of our shared Honda CR-V goodbye and forfeit the keys to Alec's control. I don't give up control over anything anymore.

Just the thought of being at the mercy of someone else's decisions, even my family's, makes my fingers tighten on the wheel.

I can only guess what awaits me at Lucas Saint's house. The local golden boy is throwing a big bash tonight to kick off senior year. No one would shut up about it as I tried to navigate the halls of my new school.

A girl in my math class didn't clock my *leave me alone* vibe and told me his huge birthday parties always marked the start of the school year.

Catch me running as fast as possible in the opposite direction.

At least, until I was volun*told* to go pick up my twin brother.

Siblings are such a blessing.

I love being a taxi service, *said no one ever*.

The corner of my mouth lifts in a humorless half-smile.

Unlike me, it thrilled Alec to dive into the social scene. I guess it was his way of soothing the fits he pitched over moving away from our hometown. As soon as we started senior year at our new school, he tried out for the football team and made varsity for his agility.

He has no trouble fitting in with the crowd while I prefer to keep my head down and watch from afar.

The closer I drive to the party at the far point of the private lake, the tighter my stomach twists.

This neighborhood is way fancier than Ridgeview's east valley, where my family moved to in July. I drive by a rock climbing gym, for fuck's sake. What kind of rich people nonsense is this?

I roll my eyes as I turn onto the winding road that cuts back and forth along the incline. Silver Lake Forest Estates sits up on the mountain that divides the town of Ridgeview. Each house I pass is more extra than the last. The ones that boast lakefront property take the cake, with docks and boathouses large enough to count as a modest house.

This side of town is unfamiliar to me. I've only spent time getting my bearings and learning my way around my new house, where the middle and upper middle-class families are apparently peasants compared to the people living it up here on the west ridge.

A private security truck with the gated community's logo comes around the bend and heads in the direction I came from.

"*Your destination is ahead on the left*," the automated voice of the GPS tells me.

My stomach feels like the crunch of gravel beneath the tires as I pull up to the party, parking amongst Range Rovers and BMWs. The silver CR-V sticks out like a sore thumb.

The last place I want to be right now is some spoiled rich brat's party. This is *not* my scene at all. It hasn't been for over a year, not since I was sixteen.

Taking a second to give my quivering insides time to settle, I rub my belly and take in the luxury lakeside house. It looms high into the trees with a huge deck jutting from one side and a wraparound front porch. Kids from school swarm the property like rabid ants, clutching red plastic cups that slosh over while they dance and shriek over the music blasting.

God, I hate parties.

They only bring up bad memories and bile in the back of my throat.

My stomach gives another unimpressed roil.

"Let's get this over with," I mumble to myself.

As soon as I climb out of the car, I sidestep to avoid two streaks of dark hair and bare, bouncing boobs that dart past me in the inky dusk falling over the mountains.

I don't even bother snapping at them to watch it. Things are better for me if I don't engage.

The streaking girls are followed by two impatient meatheads from the football team. The girls giggle as they strip out of their matching cutoff shorts halfway down the long dock and the guys peel off their practice jerseys.

A muted scoff escapes me as the four of them dive into the lake, the girls' squeals echoing.

They aren't the only people in the water. Several other classmates splash around and huddle close.

Today's one of those cool early fall days in Colorado, not exactly ideal for skinny dipping.

A round of cheers from the deck draws my attention. I roll my lips between my teeth and try to push down the memories sinking their claws into me. I don't want to be here, but I need to pick up Alec.

Shoving my hands into the pockets of my jean jacket, I trudge up the stairs to the deck, keeping my eyes peeled for my brother. The sharp, skunky tang of weed cuts through the wood smoke of the fire burning in the outdoor stone fireplace.

I weave through the people milling around the deck. It's tough to look for someone and keep your head down at the same time.

Somebody tries to hand me a beer and I swerve away hard, balling my fists in my pockets while my nostrils flare.

I'm so busy getting the hell away from whoever tried to ply me with a drink that I plow right into the girl from my math class.

"Hey!"

Her soda—and whatever it's mixed with—splashes over the rim of her cup. I blank on her name and strain to remember the roll call Mrs. Ellis took this morning in math. Alana?

"Oh, new girl! Hey," Maybe-Alana repeats, her voice changing to a friendlier tone. She licks the excess soda dripping from her finger and hooks her arm with mine before I have a chance to move on. "You made it after all. Come on, let's go wish Lucas a happy birthday."

I dig my heels in. "Uh, I'm actually just here to get my brother."

"You have a brother?" Maybe-Alana ignores my disinterest and waves enthusiastically to one of the cheerleaders. "I think I saw Lucas inside. Let's check."

"Elena! Where you going, girl?" A bulky guy in a Silver Lake High School Coyotes football hoodie calls to us. "I thought you were my beer pong partner next?"

Elena. Shit. I'm glad I didn't call her by the wrong name aloud.

She flips off the football player and sends him a cheeky grin over her shoulder. "Later! We're on a mission."

We wade through the haze of cigarette, weed, and vape smoke blanketing the deck.

Elena's sleek black curls bounce as she leads me inside through a folding glass door. Except, it can't really be called a door when it's three panels wide and folds to open an entire wall of the kitchen.

"Damn," I mutter.

"I know, right?" Elena titters. "The first time I came here I thought it was Mount Olympus or some shit. But I was, like, ten. The Saints invited the whole fifth grade class for a swimming party for Lucas' birthday."

It's just as packed inside, maybe more so. There's a set of gold jumbo balloons in the number eighteen stuck to the wall. People dance in a writhing mass in the living room to music pouring from a speaker system attached to exposed beams in the vaulted ceiling.

For a second I freeze. My heart rockets into my throat and I'm sent to that night. A clammy cold sweat breaks out on the back of my neck.

Elena doesn't notice—or possibly doesn't care—as she babbles about knowing Lucas Saint since elementary school.

The interior is like a staged design out of an upscale magazine. I focus on that to claw my way out of my memories, back to the present. The kitchen has a massive island at the center with pendant lights that hang over the white granite countertops.

Rows of liquor bottles line the island along with stacks of plastic cups, set up as a self-serve bar. From Jack Daniels to Patron to Grey Goose, they've got it all. Pick your poison.

There's a farmhouse table by the windows where a rowdy game of flip cup is in progress. The groups playing shout nonsense at each other and I spot my brother amongst them, reveling in the fun.

A burst of relief spreads through me. I can retrieve Alec and get the hell out of here.

"There's my brother." I tug my arm from Elena's grip and jerk my thumb in his direction. "I'm just going to grab him and go. Um, thanks for showing me around."

"What? No!" Elena reaches for me, but I shuffle back. "Stay and hang out!"

"Another time."

I hold up my hands and back away. I don't have to tell her I'm lying. She's been nice enough, but I'm not looking to join in at Silver Lake High School.

Elena pouts, but is easily distracted by a group of girls that lure her on to the makeshift dance floor.

I hover behind Alec and watch the game with a detached fascination, seeing an entirely different game with other players unfold before my eyes like an out-of-body experience.

"Come on, come on, come on!" Alec howls as he jumps up and down for his petite teammate to flip her cup. "You've got this! Do it!"

He's the last one in the lineup, just like that night when we were sixteen.

My eyes slam shut. I take a minute to draw measured breaths through my nose, counting backwards.

"Alec," I say in a tight voice.

He ignores me.

Chewing on the inside of my cheek, I jab him in the side with my fingers. "We've gotta go. Mom wants us back before she leaves for her shift at the hospital."

Alec flashes a flat look over his shoulder. Aside from being identical in our dirty blond hair and green eyes, he stands five inches taller than me at five-foot ten. He shakes his head and ruffles the longer hair on top of his head.

Across the table, the other flip cup team shouts unintelligible gibberish, encouraging their final player to flip the cup from the edge of the table. Alec tenses and bangs out a beat on the thick wood.

The petite girl beside Alec manages to flip her cup upright and Alec wastes no time downing his beer. He's off like a shot flicking the plastic cup. It only takes him two tries before he lands it, sealing the win for his team while the opposite player is still flipping.

"Yeah!" Alec pumps his fists in the air.

The group around the table erupts in an uproar.

My body tenses and I shove my hands back in my jacket pockets.

"Alec! Alec! Alec!"

They chant it and slap him on the back.

It looks like my brother is already well known. He celebrates, wrapping his arms around the girl beside him and fist bumping a tall boy in a dark green soccer captain's zip up jacket.

"I thought they had us for sure," the soccer captain says, waggling his brows.

"Nah, man, not when I'm around."

A laugh rolls out of Alec again when someone announces another match.

"Bishop! Get over here!"

The shout came from across the room and it draws the soccer captain's attention. He disappears into the party.

I tug on the back of Alec's shirt. When he turns to me, I raise my eyebrows.

"Ready?"

His expression closes off. "For another game, you mean?"

"No," I say slowly, trying to keep a lid on my annoyance. "To leave. You heard me earlier."

Alec bumps my shoulder as he brushes past me. I hold back a grunt of frustration.

He's been tetchy with me since we moved. Alec was pissed when Dad broke the news a few weeks before we packed up and left Colorado Springs to relocate two hours north.

"Can you just come with me? Mom said—"

Alec whirls around. "You think I give a shit what Mom said? I'm not leaving. Fuck off, Gemma."

I grit my teeth.

A few people nearby watch with interest. High school kids are vultures for drama. They scent it like blood in the water.

My family issues don't need an audience.

I keep my voice level as I follow Alec. "It doesn't seem like you're unhappy here. You fit right in."

The ice in Alec's eyes twists my insides. I don't want to fight with my brother. It's my fault we had to move, which I hate.

I was ripped from my friends, too.

The ones I had left, that is.

Forcing out a sigh, I change tactics.

"Mom doesn't leave for her shift for another hour. If I text her to say we're stopping for burgers on our way home, can we go soon?"

Alec's expression shifts enough to tell me he's considering it. He can't resist food. We haven't kept up with our old after school ritual, so maybe I'm getting through to him at last.

"Strawberry milkshakes?"

The corners of my mouth quirk up. "Strawberry milkshakes *and* fries."

For a brief moment, we're not at odds.

Then a pair of strong hands yank me away from Alec by my hips. I'm whipped around and tugged against a wall of hard muscle.

Before I can react, the stranger's lips cover mine in a demanding kiss.

And just like that, there goes my first fucking kiss.

TWO
LUCAS

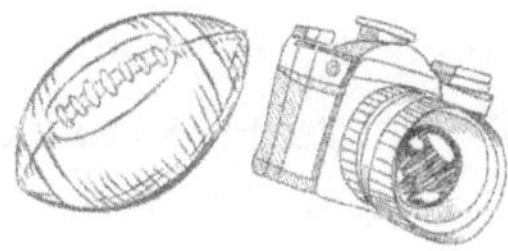

A cheer of coyote howls rises over the heavy beat of the music when I step off the stairs.

My house is packed. I grant people a happy grin that I don't feel, accepting the fist bumps, half-hugs, and slaps on the back with birthday wishes.

Smoke wafts in from outside when the contemporary glass panels are folded open to enter and exit. In the hall by the bathroom a couple of people lift their hands to their noses and snort bumps. All around me, people revel in the wild bacchanalia of a Lucas Saint party.

The old me would slide into the party vibe without any problem. But can I fake it so everyone believes I'm enjoying my birthday party?

Hiding a frown, I weave through friends and allow the

atmosphere to drag me under and bounce me around for a while.

When I come up for air, Carter's there.

"Yo, dude."

I bump my fist against Carter's and accept the shot he offers. "Burns."

"What's the count?"

Carter passes me a fresh beer after we down our shots. He's one of my closest friends and my teammate. We met in middle school when we tackled each other during football tryouts and from the first hit we'd stuck together.

I wipe the back of my hand against my mouth and swallow a sip of beer to chase the whiskey. "The count?"

My head swims a little. Everyone keeps handing me shots. I'm not trying to get fucked up tonight. My parents are out of town and I have Lancelot to take care of. I don't trust that anyone here would remember to feed him or take him out away from the trails where coyotes and cougars frequent.

The plump old pug dog waddles down the steps from the second floor, greeted by coos from the girls. He flops onto his back in front of one group and is rewarded with belly rubs. A fond smile tugs the corner of my mouth up as he stretches his back legs under the attention.

"How many girls have gotten you off tonight?" Carter asks.

I forgot he was standing there.

Carter pushes his black wavy hair back and shoots me a goofy smile. He's an easy-going guy. It's what I like best about him; he's always down to have some fun.

My smile doesn't stretch as wide as his.

I can't enjoy it like I used to.

"Ah, you know." I wave him off. "Can't kiss and tell."

"Bullshit, man. Last week you told me all about how Heather rode your dick in your Jeep at Peak Point."

I bite the inside of my cheek. He's not wrong, that did happen.

Carter laughs and cuffs my shoulder. "Just tell me the count tomorrow. I want to know if I won the betting pool with the other guys."

I snort, but I'm going through the motions.

Shaking my head, I say, "You guys are a bunch of jackasses. Go enjoy the party, you dick."

I leave Carter and hold back a sigh.

It's my senior year, I'm the varsity quarterback, and the whole school showed up tonight for my eighteenth birthday. People cheer my name when I walk by. Girls have been giving me the look all night, whispering promises in my ear with a gleam in their eyes as they palm my junk not-so-subtly.

I can have my pick of any hot piece of ass I want. Hell, all I need to do is shoot them a crooked grin and snap my fingers. I'm treated like a god amongst these pcople.

I'm living the high life right now.

And it all feels hollow.

One girl catches my eye across the room and mimes a blowjob with her tongue in her cheek. My dick should jump at the prospect of a bathroom quickie.

Instead of taking her up on sucking my cock, I hide a grimace in my beer as I down the rest of it and pretend I didn't notice her.

"Refill?"

Devlin tips his red plastic cup at me and quirks his lips into a smirk. Dark fringe hangs over his eyes. Everyone calls me the golden Saint but Devlin's known as the dark devil of Silver Lake High.

"Can't have empties on your birthday." Devlin steers me towards the keg. He nods to every girl along the way, doling out winks and blowing kisses. He's a huge flirt. Devlin gestures with his cup and points out a hot chick dancing with her ass pushed out. "If you don't come out of tonight hooking up with at least three of these girls at once, you've done your birthday wrong."

I snort and allow him to lead me to my next beer.

Devlin is a year younger than me and a junior at Silver Lake High. Our moms are sisters. He's been a built-in friend since we were in diapers. He's always around because his parents travel so much and the only company he has at his own house across the lake are his collection of cars.

Despite the slight age difference, he's got a couple inches of height on me. But I win with my muscular build.

He's leaner, all wiry limbs that grant him a lethal speed on the soccer field. I almost wish I'd tried harder to convince him to try out for football, even though the new guy is speedy as fuck. Devlin has always had a natural talent for whatever he picks up. Not that he gives that much of a shit about sports. Or anything, other than his precious cars, as far as I can tell.

Devlin lives up to his devil-may-care reputation. He only plays because his best friend is the team captain.

"Lucas!"

A chorus of people celebrate as we reach the keg. Someone shoves a fresh beer in my hands and Marissa drapes herself against my side. A hollow despair stabs me in the chest.

Marissa Hill is a cute little thing with pouty lips and a tight ass. I should know, I've been balls deep in it. She's been gunning for the head cheerleader spot since freshman year. Now that she has it, she's got it in her head that she and I will rule the school as our royal court.

I've been avoiding my on-again-off-again girl most of the night. I do a quick scan of the people nearby, hoping for some excuse to slip away from her.

She presses her tits against my bicep and bats thick fake

eyelashes up at me. Her brown hair is swept into a high ponytail with one of her oversized evergreen and white SLHS cheer squad bows.

"Where have you been all night, baby?" Marissa walks her manicured nails along my forearm. She pitches her voice low and seductive. "I've been trying to get you all to myself. I want to give you a special birthday present."

Marissa is a Coyote Girl.

It's what we call the groupie chicks that hang around the football players.

She was the first girl I kissed and the first I slept with. Ever since then, she's been climbing into my bed and hanging off my arm like I belong to her.

"It's my birthday. Everyone wants a piece of me tonight." I bark out a laugh and slam my cup against one of my teammates' when he toasts to me. "I'm just spreading the love."

Marissa's glossy pink lips twist. "You shouldn't ignore me."

"Riss." Defense faltering, I tuck her against my side. I'm keeping an eye out for a way out of this conversation. "We agreed to a break last month. It was your idea."

"That was before." Marissa hitches her shoulder. "I miss you."

My gaze travels down her body from her caramel-colored eyes to her tight white crop sweater that reveals her flat tan stomach. There's no denying she's sexy as hell. But no matter how many nostalgic memories I have of the first girl I thought I loved, I can't dredge up any desire for her now.

"Bishop! Get over here!" Devlin shouts at his best friend.

It's a weak distraction, but I turn my attention to Bishop instead of answering Marissa. She complains under her breath and rubs against me like a fucking cat in heat.

My jaw clenches in exasperation. *Jesus.*

Bishop leaves the group at the kitchen table and heads our way.

He is another junior, but he's allowed to hang out because he's Devlin's friend. Bishop is also the principal's son and has a mischievous streak a mile wide, so he's handy to have around in our group. He sidles up, hands stuffed in the pockets of his varsity soccer captain zip up.

Bishop surveys the handful of us huddled around the keg and narrows his eyes.

"No, no, no." He holds up his palms. "This just won't do. This is *Lucas Saint's* birthday." Bishop flashes us a grin and points to me. "There needs to be about eight hundred percent more shots going on. Especially for you, Saint."

Whoops and hollers follow Bishop's suggestion. Bishop and Devlin disappear for a few minutes, then return with a bottle of Jack Daniels and cups.

"Can you handle eighteen shots, or will you puss out on us?" Bishop presents me with a plastic cup and brandishes the whiskey.

"Fuck you, you damn sadist."

I snatch the cup while Bishop snickers. He pours shots for everyone.

"Want to do a body shot, babe?"

Marissa peeks at me through her false lashes. She pretends to lift the bottom of her cropped sweater higher, like she might show off some underboob. I think she's aiming for coquettish, but it misses the mark by miles and falls firmly under slutty.

I open my mouth, but my brain derails before reaching an answer. Goddamn it, the break was her idea and I'm getting sick of these games.

"To our golden boy, Saint," Devlin toasts, saving me from dealing with Marissa. I flash him a grateful look and he lifts a brow. "And to you seniors fucking off after this year."

Devlin ducks with unrepentant amusement when I swipe at him.

"Let's get fucked up!" Bishop howls like a coyote and downs his shot.

The rest of us answer his battle cry and down our drinks.

Marissa makes a show of letting her whiskey spill from the corners of her pouty mouth, the amber rivulets trailing pathways down her neck.

"Oops," she murmurs as she plasters herself to my body again. "I got all messy. Lick it up for me, baby." She rises on the balls of her feet to whisper in my ear. "And then we can go to your room and I'll lick you."

Incredulous, I watch her from the corner of my eye.

Part of me just wishes I'd give in. Even though I'm done with her bullshit, my life makes more sense when I go with what's expected of me. Play the quarterback position, date the head cheerleader, live the all-American dream.

It's easier to shut off and stick with the status quo.

But I can't.

"Marissa, come on..."

I gently nudge her back and wipe up the trail of whiskey from her neck with my knuckle.

I cast my attention around the party, looking for another paper thin excuse to slip away.

"Elena's trying to call you to dance." I give Marissa an encouraging push. "Go have fun. I'm probably going to swing out back for a smoke."

Thankfully, Marissa takes the bait. Her hips sway with exaggerated movements as she struts away from me. As soon as she's with her friends, she drops low into a squat and sticks her ass out, wiggling it enticingly.

"Christ," I mutter.

Devlin claps me on the shoulder. "Should've just let her

suck your dick. Then she'd get bored and leave you alone for the rest of the night."

"The break was her idea."

"It's always their idea when chicks want to free themselves of attachments."

I frown. "Her parents took her to Monaco over the summer."

Devlin gives a low whistle.

"Yup. She was totally trying to snag some guilt-free vacation dick." A contemplative expression crosses Devlin's face. "Or pussy."

"I don't care. I'm done with her anyway."

"Well, you're going to need to prove it in front of everyone."

"I've been looking all night, but nothing's caught my eye."

"What about that one?"

"No."

He scans around us and subtly points out another beautiful girl. "That one?"

I sigh. "No."

Our back and forth continues as we scope potential picks. Across the room, I spot a girl I can count on to get my current ex off my back for the night. She's my old faithful.

"There. Heather's perfect for this."

A mix of relief and heat trickles through me as I cross the room, eating up the distance in four strides.

She's talking to Alec, the new guy we appointed as our wide receiver. Her honey-blonde hair falls past her shoulders in soft waves that beg for fingers to sink in and pull on. It's shorter than when I saw in school. She must have gotten it cut.

My attention dips to her ass and I wet my lips.

Sorry, bro. Team captain status and my birthday trumps the new kid in line for pussy.

I grab her hips and spin her. The shocked squeak from her

barely registers before I crush my lips to her mouth. My arms surround her, fingers buried in the silky hair at the nape of her neck.

Her ass is divine. It fits perfectly in my hand.

She squirms and my arms tighten. Every time we fuck, we play hard to get as foreplay. It sets my blood on fire and my dick hardens in my jeans.

Wolf whistles chorus around us.

As I kiss her, I'm overcome by the urge to toss her over my shoulder and cart her to my bedroom. She smells incredible and I'm eating up the soft sounds that escape her.

God, my dick has woken the hell up. The apathy clinging to me has fled. I've regained a little of my old self. It makes me grin against her plush lips.

She's got me raring to go from one kiss.

I am going to fuck her so good she won't walk right at school on Monday.

All night long, my dick hasn't shown any interest in a girl. It's good to be back on top as I kiss the hell out of the fiery little minx in my arms.

THREE
GEMMA

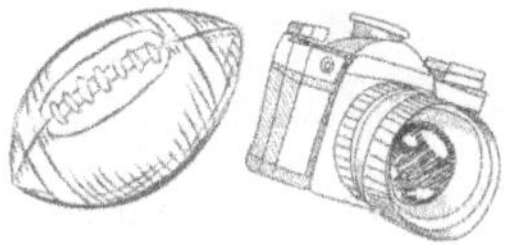

There's nowhere to go.

My body is trapped against his.

He has one big hand planted on my ass, squeezing it, and the other clamped around the back of my neck to keep me in place as he claims my mouth.

The kiss is ravenous.

My brain can't follow a straight path because the way his tongue pushes past my lips makes my toes curl.

When our tongues touch, his low growl vibrates through my body and triggers a piercing pulse of heat.

After what I've been through, I'm shocked by the answering excitement singing in my veins.

This is the opposite of what I pictured for my first kiss. The sweet, soft press of lips I imagined has burst into flames, scorched away by the reality of this wicked, possessive onslaught of heat.

As the caveman bastard's hand glides over my ass and digs *down* the waistband of my jeans, my brain finally catches up. I inhale sharply and bite the asshole's lip—*hard.*

It has the desired effect. He jolts back with a grunt, releasing me to press his fingers to his lip.

I hope it fucking aches.

"Is that what you do around here?" I spit, wiping my mouth with the back of my hand. "Just go around kissing every girl like you own them?"

Surprise crosses his face for a second before he blinks it away.

Now that he's not assaulting me with his uninvited kiss, I get a good look at him.

Oh *shit.*

The burglar of my first kiss is that damned football captain, Lucas Saint. I still haven't figured out how the gymnasium door opens without sticking, but I have learned that this guy is the king around here. The whole school worships him.

Lucas stands tall—taller than my brother at over six foot—with light brown hair and arresting blue eyes. He has broad shoulders, and those arms he trapped me with are sculpted.

His eyes flash and his mouth quirks into a sinful curve as he takes me in with a sweeping look.

"Sweetheart, every girl here is mine. And every girl in this town knows it."

Lucas touches his lower lip with his thumb. It comes away red.

I made him bleed.

Serves you right, dick. I cross my arms.

His amusement grows. He looks at me like I'm a dog performing a cute trick.

"They all throw themselves at me eventually." Lucas gives a carefree shrug. "You'd better fall in line, or we're gonna have a problem."

This self-important asshole!

I grit my teeth. I can still taste him.

"Not happening." To drive the point home, I return the once over he gave me with one of my own and curl my lip. "*Ever.*"

Lucas snorts and drapes an arm around my shoulders. I wriggle to get away from him, but he's strong. He contains me without exerting himself.

When I jab his side with my elbow, I come against hard muscles and the trim physique of an athlete. The hot puffs of his raspy laughter ghost across my skin.

He plucks at my hair and gestures at the giant blow up balloon decorations. "It's my birthday, you know."

I blink. "And?"

"Let's call that my birthday present." Lucas pinches my cheek and leers down at me. "Although, I won't say no if you want to give me something else. Eighteen's a milestone birthday, so you can give me something..." Lucas drags his fingertips down my cheek and traces the neckline of my t-shirt, "bigger and flashier than a kiss."

As I squirm, he holds me tighter. A frustrated breath hisses out of me. Lucas' nose presses into my temple and the entertained tilt of his mouth grazes my cheek.

"The way I see it, you owed me that kiss for coming to the party," he mutters.

"Fuck you," I snarl.

Lucas releases me and digs his fingers in my hair to keep me close. I could run, but I'd end up with my hair yanked for my trouble. His gaze trails over my body and he smirks. Lucas' entire aura is smug and cocky.

"We can do that, too, sweetheart."

The disbelief that crashes over me is so profound, it takes a moment to process the sheer audacity this guy has. A hazy red anger bleeds into my vision. I want to wipe that fucking smirk off his face.

How *dare* Lucas think I'm something he can have. He must be used to getting whatever he wants, whenever he wants it.

Well, tough shit, buddy.

I'm not the kind of girl who will jump at the snap of his fingers.

I grant him a sharp smirk of my own and relish the way he tracks my lips. I stomp on his foot with all my might, driving my heel down on his toes. Satisfaction blooms in my chest when Lucas bites out a surprised curse and lets me go.

"What the f—"

Before he can retaliate and use his strength to incapacitate me again, I dash out of reach.

Alec stands off to the side with an unreadable expression. I grab a fistful of his shirt and drag him behind me as I navigate through the drama vultures.

I shoulder past people that don't jump out of my way. Curses about spilled drinks follow me.

See if I care. I'm a girl on a mission to get the hell out of this party.

As we reach the big glass door, I glance over my shoulder. Lucas' gaze is pinned on me with a hunter's precision. There's something in his eyes that stirs an uneasiness in me.

My lips contort in acidic disdain. "Come on, Alec."

My brother trails behind me without a word as we leave the party behind us.

FOUR
LUCAS

It's not Heather.

That's the first thought that crossed my mind after she bit my lip.

The second thought persistently blaring in my mind is simple: *want*.

After the unfamiliar beauty breaks eye contact and disappears into the night, I rub my lip and stare after her. It's sore where she bit me.

A fire stirs in my belly and drives away the noise of the party.

Jealousy flares through me over her leaving with the new guy on the team. What does he have that I don't?

My interest sparks to attention as I suck on my split lip. A fog held me prisoner all night—one that crept in bit by bit over the summer—but now I'm alive again. The world realigns in crystal clear focus.

I'm driven by an incarnate instinct to go after that girl for another kiss until she changes her tune and screams yes for me.

Bishop stands closest, his sharp attention flicking between me and the open glass panel.

"Who was that?"

"New girl," Bishop supplies with a shrug. "She's Turner's sister, according to the file I swiped for you when he tried out."

My eyebrow lifts and I consider her beauty against Turner's features. "Twins?"

That makes me feel better, the jealousy ebbing away to a dull background noise. I want to make her mine.

"They're both seniors, so yeah."

I nod slowly and run my fingers over my chin as my thoughts mill in my head. The fiery kiss replays and my pants feel tighter. My stance shifts as I try to calm down.

"Anything else you know about her?"

"I don't know, she's kinda weird. I saw her in the office on the first day with her brother. She seemed like one of those angry girl types. You know, combat boots and a leather jacket paired with the school uniform." Bishop shrugs. "Want me to snag her file, too?"

Before I've even decided, I'm nodding. I clear my throat and run my fingers through my hair.

"Yeah." My voice is gruff. A horny, restless energy floods my veins and I want to slip away from the party to jack off with a head full of her perfect ass and sweet tongue. "Do you have a name? I can't go around calling her Girl Turner."

Bishop chuckles. "No, but I'll find out."

"Good."

I need to learn more. I have to know everything about her so next time I can convince her not to refuse.

"Lucas!"

A hand wraps around my forearm and I allow myself to get dragged back into the party. It's easier to let go and enjoy it when the cheer squad brings out a cake with sparkler candles. I don't even grimace at Marissa's Marilyn Monroe impression when she leads her crew singing happy birthday.

The whole time my mind is wrapped around a hot firecracker with honey-blonde hair and a sexy bite.

FIVE
GEMMA

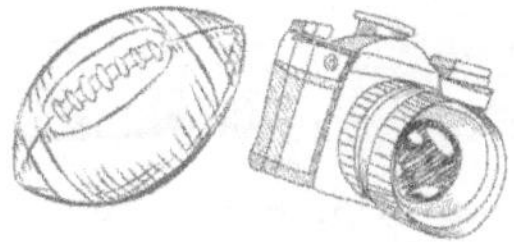

Saturday morning starts with me tripping over the miscellaneous moving boxes yet to be unpacked lining the hallway. I groan, rubbing my stubbed toe as I hobble down the hall.

Most of our house is assembled, but anytime we move we get complacent about what's not urgent. Since Alec and I were born, we moved three times around Colorado Springs.

Two months in Ridgeview and there are still random boxes in every area, some acting as makeshift tables while others are relegated to the corner of no return.

"Morning hun," Mom greets as she enters the hall. She turns her attention to the boxes with a determined air. "This weekend! Family goal: finish these boxes."

"Didn't you say to Dad there were some you never

unpacked from your first house when we were loading the moving truck?"

She waves me off. "Okay, updated goal: everyone picks one box. We'll keep going like that until we've finished."

A fond smile at her newfound resolve crosses my face. She probably found some Pinterest article on organization tips. Mom's always trying stuff like that. Big fan of the Marie Kondo method. Except when it comes to the miscellaneous moving boxes.

"You've got it, Mom."

"Fresh coffee downstairs in ten?"

"It's a date."

I was too chickenshit to tell her the whole truth about that night two years ago. Part of me wanted to confess it all, but then I put it off for so long in fear that she'd be mad at me for putting myself in that situation. All I told them was that a boy tried to touch me, glossing over who it was and the extent of it other than firmly stating I wasn't raped.

It wasn't the reason we moved. I told them I wasn't happy at school, so they fixed it. I no longer had to see him in the halls. They're great about helping and supporting me when I go to them. Then I struggled at the school I transferred to. I broke down when I couldn't take it anymore and begged for another change.

So my parents found work elsewhere and sprung this move on us.

The smell of caffeine greets me downstairs. I cling to the mug Mom hands me and hum.

"Did Alec say how his night was? What about you, did you meet any new friends?"

I choke on the scalding sip of coffee. My stupid lizard brain flashes to that bastard Saint and his grabby hands. *New friends.*

"Uh, he had a good time. Yep."

I gulp more coffee and skip over the party. And the kiss playing on loop in my head. Definitely not bringing any of that up. Despite her question about making friends, Mom and I don't chat *boys.*

Dad and Alec enter the kitchen like zombies. Mom waves them to the coffee.

"Morning, Dad."

He mumbles to me, incoherent until he's halfway through his first mug of the day. He slumps at the table, half-dozing. Alec fares the same, but I think he's hungover. He's not hiding it that well. I keep an eye on Mom and Dad's reactions to him.

Mom narrows her eyes, but she'll wait for him to say something about it. As we've gotten older, they like us to take responsibility for choices like that. Dad's favorite new saying from the last couple of years since we first got caught drinking is: *if you're going to pretend to be an adult you'll face the consequences like one.*

Once Dad comes to life via caffeine, he perks up. "How was the first week of school? Adjusting okay?"

They always say we can talk to them about anything. But I can handle it on my own. I can't run scared just because of some jerk's threat.

"Sure. It's fine. Books. Knowledge. The works."

Alec burns a hole in the back of my head as he fixes his drink. The clink of his spoon stirring sugar into his coffee jars me.

"That's good. You tell us if anything bothers you. That goes for both of you." Dad refills his mug and blows on it. As he passes me, he pats my head. "There're plenty of trails around this area. Who's in for a hike today?"

Alec moans under his breath.

"As long as we get some boxes done," Mom says.

"I'm in, Dad!" Alec winces at my bright tone on his way to

a seat. "I've been enjoying the new scenery to explore for photo ops."

"You should come, Alec," Dad intones. "Fresh mountain air is an excellent cure for the results of a rowdy night out. It's bracing. It'll do you good."

I hide my cough of amusement in my mug.

* * *

Lucas Saint is still on my mind on Monday and I'm fucking pissed about it.

I hate that I can't get that damn kiss out of my head. It's plagued my mind all weekend.

My hands squeeze the steering wheel. Frowning, I turn up the rock song on the radio and nod along as a pitiful distraction.

So what if it was a good kiss? I'm sure lots of people at Silver Lake High are good kissers—if I was interested in finding out. Which I'm not.

My lips purse because what's really goading my ire is that Lucas just takes without asking. He's every inch the spoiled king quarterback of this school.

"Whoa there, daredevil," Alec chides, gripping the handle above the door as I whip the car into the parking lot.

My nostrils flare. Okay, maybe I took that turn sharper than necessary. I need to get my emotions and thoughts in check.

"Deal with it, you big baby. You're alive, aren't you?"

Alec chuckles at my huffiness and taps the back of his hand against my shoulder. For a moment it's like things used to be, before my own twin brother hated my guts for something I couldn't control.

The moment passes and Alec's easy going demeanor fades. He clears his throat.

I swallow a disappointed sigh and pull into the first open

spot I find between a flashy red sports car and a sleek black Range Rover. With a quick scan of the cars around us, my stomach falls.

Our CR-V is a used model, but not a junker by any stretch. Most of the cars in the lot are souped up and expensive. The price tags are double and even triple the worth of our shared car.

Where are all the normal kids at this school who don't flaunt their parents' money?

Alec and I can't be the only ones.

The school looms on a hill above the student parking lot with stone columns to match the mountainside vibe of Ridgeview. The campus buildings are surrounded by pine trees that stretch into the sky. Coyote statues flank the sign in front of the school declaring it Silver Lake High School: Home of the Ridgeview Coyotes.

Before getting out, I tug at my evergreen and white plaid uniform skirt and adjust the blazer.

At my other two schools we didn't have a required uniform, and I was free to wear what I was comfortable in. I thumb the school crest embroidered on the black blazer, a gold shield with the school's initials surrounded by laurels.

I'm grumpy that my brother doesn't seem as bothered by the uniform. Then again, what's so different about putting on nicer pants than jeans? At least they're still pants. The worst he has to deal with is a tie.

We climb out of the car simultaneously with the guy in the neighboring Range Rover and I tense. It's Lucas.

He spots me before I can hightail it for the steps that lead up to the school. That irritating cocky grin returns.

"Hey, man." Alec greets as he and Lucas clasp hands, thumping each other on the back. "Dope party on Friday."

"Yeah." Lucas cuts his eyes to me over my brother's shoulder. "Wish you could've stuck around longer. We lit off fireworks over the lake."

"Sweet."

Behind us, another guy leans against the red sports car and crosses his legs at the ankle. His dark hair swoops into his eyes and his school tie is loose, hanging askew.

He lights up a cigarette despite the security guard in the booth right across from us. Curls of smoke snake out of his nostrils as he stares us down, slouched against his ride.

"Taking red out today, Dev?" Lucas asks.

The corner of the guy's mouth curls up and he shrugs. He runs his palm across the gleaming paint like a caress. "She was feeling neglected."

"The car?" I ask before I remember my vow not to interact with anyone.

Lucas' friend tilts his head at me. I purse my lips and flip my hastily done braid over my shoulder.

Keep quiet, Gem.

"You're new, right?" The grin Lucas shoots me is all predatory. "Alec is good about introducing himself around. But not you, huh?"

"I'm Devlin." The smoker with the fancy car offers his hand to shake.

I grant him a tight smile and don't take it. Lucas watches us. I can almost feel the press of his eyes skating across my skin.

"This is the part where you give us your name, sweetheart."

Lucas takes a step toward me when I don't answer.

"Gemma. Her name's Gemma."

I glare at Alec. He shrugs and goes back to ignoring me.

"Gemma," Lucas murmurs. "Now I know what to call you in my head instead of sexy." Heat flares in his eyes as he takes another step until his body almost brushes against mine. "Been thinking about you since Friday night. You been thinking about me, sweetheart? Was I in your dreams giving you more?"

My eyes widen at his brazen questions when my brother is right there and he just met me. Well, sort of. Friday doesn't count.

"Not for a single second," I lie, glossing over how he was on my mind five minutes ago when I was ranting in my head about his entitled attitude.

Lucas smirks like he can see right through it. He taps my nose with a curled knuckle.

"Guess I'll have to kiss you again to set you right."

"Try it." I show him my teeth. "I'll bite you harder this time."

With a sharp inhale Lucas grabs the edge of my skirt in his fist as he maneuvers me back a step until my shoulders hit the rear of my car.

"You're getting me all riled up. Keep talking like that, babe, and I'll have to tear into you right now. In front of everyone."

Protests scream in my rigid body. "Stop it."

"If they didn't catch the show on Friday night, they'll get a rerun. Everyone pulling in will see you begging for it."

I stare up at him, my face a blank mask. I force every ounce of self confidence and strength I have into it. On the inside my stomach ices over and I prepare to stomp on his foot again.

Is Alec really going to stand by and watch without doing anything?

My throat burns and I clench my jaw. I'm the only person I can rely on to protect myself.

Lucas traces my lower lip. I snap my teeth and he jerks his hand away before I can get him.

A cruel, raspy laugh rolls through him.

"Better watch it, kitten." Lucas' eyes bounce back and forth between mine, then they harden. He chucks me under the chin. "Don't make me get out the spray bottle."

A growl rumbles through me before I can control my reaction.

I look for an escape, but more people sidle up. It gives me the opportunity to shuffle several steps away from Lucas when the newcomers distract him. He tosses me a quick frown, but his friends demand his attention.

A glance at Alec confirms he's not even looking our way. Un-fucking-believable.

"Burns! What's up, brother?" Alec greets.

Alec bumps his knuckles against the guy he called Burns with familiarity and puckers his lips cheekily at the girls. Burns must be on the football team because he's stacked.

My shoulders tense. This is the crowd I want to avoid most of all. The *in* crowd.

The crowd I used to belong to, once upon a time.

Remaining quiet as the group talk, I form a new understanding of the dynamic.

I can see it in the way these people act around Lucas. The girls compete for his attention and Burns is poised to take whatever Lucas says as law.

He's the king around here.

Burns pulls out his phone and he and Lucas crowd around it, the girls elbowing each other to stand next to Lucas. Tinny moans drift from the phone's speakers and I roll my eyes. Lucas tosses me a smug look as his buddy high fives him.

"What a slut," one girl whines as she bats her eyelashes at Lucas.

Lucas laughs. "Maybe that's what I like."

His eyes fall on me again.

Whatever.

"That's Bishop's spot you parked in, you know."

I suck in a surprised breath.

Devlin is close to my back, able to loom over my shoulder with his height. Like a creep, he uses this advantage to intimidate me.

I narrow my eyes and take a pointed step away from him. The heat of Lucas' gaze bores into my skin again, but I won't give him the satisfaction of turning his way. Does he think he has some claim over me because of that kiss?

He's probably the caveman type that thinks that's as good as peeing on me to mark his territory. My nose wrinkles at the thought. *Fucking gross.*

"I don't see the name Bishop on it. Or any of the spots." I raise an eyebrow and shrug. "I guess he should've gotten here earlier if he wanted prime parking close to the steps."

Devlin considers me for a beat before he laughs. The amusement chases away the shadows that crowd his face and gives him a more boyish look.

"That's fair." Devlin stomps on his cigarette and blows smoke away from my face. "If he gives you shit, tell him Lucas said you could park there."

"If this Bishop gives me shit, I'll handle it myself." I cross my arms and tip my chin up. "I'm a big girl like that. I don't need the boys to tell me what I can and can't do."

Devlin's eyes move up and down my body, lingering on my gray tights, and his playful smirk grows. "Yeah, I bet, baby."

Something over my shoulder makes his eyes widen slightly. He shuffles back, tucking his hands into his pockets. I turn, prepared to thank Alec for getting his shitty new friends to back off, but it's not my brother who glares at Devlin.

It's Lucas.

My stomach drops.

The people surrounding Lucas mess around with each

other and talk about their weekends, but his fierce blue eyes are glued to me.

I'm done with this.

Ducking into the car, I grab my leather jacket from the backseat along with my camera bag that doubles as my school bag. Eager to put Lucas and his friends behind me, I flip the strap over my head and hurry along.

On the way, I toss the keys to Alec and nod to him. "Later."

When I reach the top of the stairs, I grit my teeth and cast a glance down at the parking lot.

I watch from afar, where I'm comfortable at a distance from the king's court. I need to avoid his radar if I'm going to white-knuckle my way through my last year of high school.

If I make a wrong move around him, he'll throw me in the proverbial high school gallows.

One more year and then I'm free to pursue my dreams. I pat my camera bag and head into school.

In theory, it should be easy to avoid Lucas' attention. He doesn't have any real interest in me, so he'll get bored and forget about this weekend in a few days when the next shiny thing draws him in.

I know his type. Intimately.

SIX
GEMMA

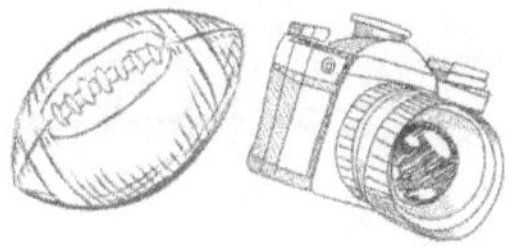

Adjusting to the new school environment is still a process.

At least my parents didn't take me out of one school in the middle of the year and toss me in another this time. That was rougher to get used to.

This time it's a fresh start with the other seniors getting accustomed to the daily schedules. The only difference is they spent the last three years learning the ins and outs of this school and they understand the innate social hierarchy much better than me.

They know who to go to for a fix, who to avoid hooking up with if they don't want to catch an STI, which teachers will let delinquent misdeeds slide and which ones are hardasses.

And which seats to avoid.

I find that out the hard way.

I'm late to study hall because I got held up after my class in the computer lab, enjoying my chat about Photoshop and Lightroom with Ms. Huang. I got lost on the way, the huge campus like a maze to navigate. The auditorium is packed by the time I make it several minutes after the second bell.

"Do you have a late pass?" A teacher in a tracksuit signals me forward with two fingers to the table in front of the stage, where she guards the hapless students of study hall.

Someone smugly mutters, "Busted."

Rolling my eyes, I trudge down to the stage, aware of all the eyes on me. The vultures are out in force today. It's the beginning of school, how exciting can it be to watch someone get a demerit over tardiness?

"I don't have a late pass. I'm sorry, I got lost," I explain when I reach the front.

The teacher squints at me. "I don't recognize you."

"I'm new."

"Where are you coming from?"

"Second floor computer lab in the north building."

"You mean the south," she corrects. Frowning, she waves me off. "Don't be late again without a late slip, please. Find a seat and work quietly."

Nodding, I step away and head for the first empty chair I spot rather than skulking back up the aisles to search in the back of the theater. I don't need to piss off the teachers into giving me a detention in my second week at Silver Lake.

I dump my bag on the armrest and catch the group in the row back watching with hawk-like focus. Furrowing my brows, I ignore them. What's their deal?

I plop into the seat and immediately shriek when there's nothing to catch me, the broken seat going vertical. I slide right off the cushion to the sticky floor and blink wide eyes at my surroundings. Hyena laughter echoes in the auditorium.

The group behind are the loudest.

I shoot them a dirty look.

"Five points for the squeal," a dude with a green beanie declares.

"All right," calls the teacher. "Settle down."

She shoots an unimpressed look at me. Like I'm causing trouble on purpose.

I struggle to my feet with as much dignity as I can muster, my cheeks hot. I smooth my hands over my skirt and freeze when I feel the unpleasant stickiness that followed me from the ground.

The shrieking from the girls in the row behind me increases. One guy's face is red from laughing at me.

I grit my teeth and carefully swipe my fingers over the wad of gum stuck to my skirt, shuddering.

"Eugh."

"Here."

A girl further down the row with hair the blue-gray color of a thundercloud offers me a napkin.

"Thanks."

I take it and clean what I can from my skirt.

"That seat's been broken for two years, but the school hasn't fixed it. You'd think they would with how much money they have, but no. Seat 143. Remember it, you don't want to run into the same problem again. People usually use it to dump their gum off instead of finding a trash can."

"Seat 143," I echo. "Got it. I appreciate it, thank you."

When I look up to make a joke about getting myself into a sticky situation, she's bent over her work, nail-bitten fingers sticking out of her baggy sleeves. She doesn't have the blazer, just the white shirt and the green plaid skirt.

I scoot a few chairs down and subtly check the integrity of

the chair before I take a seat. The catty group one row back cackle.

The teacher's level of caring has plummeted. She's absorbed in her phone.

"Those fireworks were epic on Friday," the guy in the beanie says. I sense his hat is against uniform regulations, the same ones I'm breaking with my boots. "And my boy got with Kira in the lake."

"Shut up, Kira was with me all night," a girl counters. She blows a bubble with her gum and pops it. "Zach wishes he could hit that, but I'm pretty sure she's dating Mallory now."

Beanie dude groans, but I can't tell if it's in resignation or envy.

They're talking about Lucas' party. My lips thin as I pull out the math homework. I'm skimming over the worksheet when my attention snags on their gossiping again.

"Saint's latest chick is hot as fuck though," beanie guy mutters.

I can't stop my shoulders from stiffening and clench my pen until my fingertips go white. Turning my head just enough without letting on that I'm listening, I nearly startle.

He's watching me. They know, or they heard, or they saw firsthand at the party.

"Please," bubblegum girl scoffs. "She'll be over in two seconds. Marissa said she hung out at Lucas' house, like, all weekend. They're totally going to be prom king and queen this year."

"Marissa's got a dope ass, but this girl right here," beanie dude pauses long enough to shuffle down the row until he's right behind me. He prods me. "This girl let Lucas get wild."

"I don't know what you're talking about." I turn around to block them out. "Do you mind? I'm trying to work on an assignment."

Hot air coasts over my ear and I flinch. His other arm comes over the seat, showing me his phone.

"Girl, I've got the proof right here. You like to get freaky."

"You shouldn't have touched Lucas." The bubblegum bitch snaps her gum. "Marissa will stomp your ass."

"I didn't touch him. He did all of that on his own. I was just standing there, minding my damn business."

"Thought you didn't know what we were talking about?"

I open and close my mouth. Beanie Dick laughs at me.

"Here." He drapes himself over the back of my chair. He presses play on the video queued on his phone. "Just watch. It's already all over school. If you're this much of an easy slut for Saint, I've got a fat sausage for you, sweetness."

Inhaling sharply, I pinch the inside of his arm hard, close to his armpit. He yelps.

"You bitch!"

Twisting around, I eye him up and down. "Don't touch me."

He rubs the spot where I pinched with a surly frown. "Fine, whatever. Just watch this."

He starts the video over and shoves his phone in my face.

Lucas and I fill the screen and wolf whistles sound from the speakers. The video shows his big hands digging down the back of my jeans and I'm mortified by the way I buck toward him. Before I bite his lip in retaliation, the video cuts to us kissing again, his tongue delving into my mouth and his hands all over me. Warmth creeps up my neck and pools in my belly.

It's not even halfway through.

This video—the one apparently circulating through the school of the stolen lip lock Lucas forced on me—is doctored.

It's obviously an amateur, too. Some whack-job with too much time on their hands and the assistance of a YouTube tutorial.

I sit in stiff silence and endure all forty-six agonizing seconds of the video. The moment where I bite Lucas and tell him off doesn't come. The edited clip makes it look like a steamy make out with the stock moans dropped into the audio track rather than showing the unwanted advance for what it really was.

They made it look like I was panting for it. The sleeves of my blazer pucker beneath my tight grip, no longer crisp as I hug my arms.

This clip is designed to blow things way out of proportion.

Okay, Gemma. Take it in, then pick yourself up. You're not the girl in that video.

My plan for this year is to coast by as an anonymous outsider. That goal doesn't change if people here decide they know me. They can label me however they like.

I still know who I am. That's all that matters.

I allow a breathy laugh of disinterest past my lips. "Man, you guys are a bunch of idiots if you can't pick out stock moans. What porno did you and your limp dick buddies pull that one from?"

Beanie Dick blinks his beady little eyes.

I barely keep the smirk off my face.

What, did he expect this to make me cry in embarrassment? If one second of this video clip were true, the girl depicted wouldn't give a damn about public consumption after kissing guys like that.

"This is the digital age." I pat his dumbfounded cheek and affect a pout. "Try harder next time."

A snort further down my row draws our attention. The nice girl who gave me the napkin coughs into her hand to hide the amused curve of her mouth. She flashes me an appreciative look, her eyes full of shining mirth.

She gets her chair kicked by the bubblegum bitch for her trouble.

"Who told you to laugh, Raggedy Anne?"

I glare at the mean girl.

The whole time the teachers don't intervene.

Thankfully, the bell rings before things go any further.

* * *

Last week I remained invisible during my lunch period, but almost every eye in the room turns to me when I step out of line with my tray.

I haven't made many friends here compared to my other schools. Part of me regrets my pact to keep everyone at arm's length. I used to have a lot of fun with my old friends.

It would be nice to have someone for moral support right now.

Brows drawn together, I start toward the table by the windows I think of as mine after sitting there alone last week.

I don't get three steps before Lucas' tall figure blocks my path.

I stare at his broad chest for a beat. His blazer is discarded. Damn, his uniform fits nice. It's tailored, unlike most guys here. The shirt is a perfect mold to the muscles beneath and highlights his athletic physique, the sleeves rolled up to the elbow to show off tan forearms.

Fuck, focus. You need to shut up, lizard hindbrain! Stop making me drool over his stupid sexy forearms.

"Hey, sweetheart. I didn't realize you had the same lunch period."

The faux-charm in Lucas' tone sets my teeth on edge.

I don't tell him I noticed him just fine. My hope that he'd

ignore me today flies out the window when he smooths his hand down my arm without asking.

No need to ask permission when you're the popular quarterback.

I suck on my teeth and contemplate the effectiveness of dumping my tray of food on him to make him leave me alone.

People give us a wide berth as they find their tables, but the chatter isn't as loud as usual. Everyone's watching this little show play out.

We're the lunchtime entertainment.

"Come eat with us."

Lucas tips his head, indicating the table behind him that's packed with his groupies. Including Devlin and that football guy, Burns.

"Oh, too bad." I hitch a shoulder and lay on the mock-disappointment. "Looks like your table's all full."

A cocksure smile curves Lucas' mouth. It's too smarmy and mars his attractiveness.

"You can sit on my lap."

"Yeah," I snort. "Don't think so."

"Come on," Lucas croons.

He runs his fingers over my braid, using it as a tether. I'm forced to lean in. My fingers press into the plastic tray and the items rattle.

"See everyone over there?" Lucas makes a sweeping gesture. It's full of beautiful people that I bet are just like Lucas beneath their pretty veneers. "We're where you want to be, sweetheart. I'm inviting you there. That doesn't just happen."

Gritting my teeth, I roll my shoulders back.

"I can open doors for you. Not just here, but anywhere in town."

Lucas' attention drops to my lips. His pupils dilate. He wants another go.

Kiss thief, I call him in my head. *Conman. Crooked burglar.*

"I'm not interested. Can you let me go eat now?"

His grip on my hair tightens. He grants me a challenging look.

"You're going to come sit with us," he commands.

My chin lifts a fraction. "How do you figure, when I just said I didn't want to?"

Lucas smiles down at me, but there's nothing sweet about it. The smile is all hunter, mean and precise. The smile of a hungry predator with its prey in reach.

"Because what I say fucking goes around here. If I want you to come sit in my lap, you'll do it. Do you need another reminder of who's in charge around here?"

Who the fuck does this guy think he is?

"Did a football hit you too many times in the head?"

A confused wrinkle appears on his forehead.

"No," I say slowly, so he understands. "I don't want to sit with you. I don't want anything to do with you."

Lucas tugs sharply on my braid. He literally pulls my hair, like the bullying boys that girls are always warned about.

A scoff of amused disbelief leaves me. "Did you really just...?"

"I'll give you one more chance, Gemma."

Lucas' playful demeanor and big-man-on-campus act has vanished. Now he's deadly serious as he stares at me.

"Or *what*?" Sheer astonishment at this whole situation bleeds into my voice.

"You don't want to know that. You're either with us or you're against us, and you don't want to be against us. Just accept it, like everyone else does, or you'll face the consequences."

With us or against us. Consequences. Lucas sounds like

some power-hungry mafioso rather than a high school quarterback.

"You've gotta be kidding me. I said no, you bastard." My voice raises. "Back *off*, or I'm going to dump my lunch tray on you! I don't think gravy stains will go well with your expensive tailoring."

He drops my braid, but I don't get the chance to move back before he grips my hips, his fingers digging at my skin through the material.

I mash my lips together to withhold a grimace.

"What is your problem? You can't just manhandle me into getting your way," I grumble. "Do you not understand what no means? That'll get you in trouble with the law someday when your power trip goes to your head."

Lucas rears back with a shocked look. Then his eyes narrow to dangerous slits.

"Jesus, I'm not a rapist, you little—"

I hoist my tray threateningly and he cuts off.

"Leave me the hell alone, Lucas! I don't want jack shit to do with you or your lousy friends!"

Hushed mutters breaks out around the room. A few phones are held up, capturing the drama as it unfolds. They've got proof of me denouncing their king.

It'll be all over Snapchat and Instagram stories within minutes, spreading like a fatal forest fire across the school, no doubt.

"You're going to regret that," Lucas promises in a rough, dark voice.

Those proverbial gallows feel like they're snapping around my neck and wrists.

But I won't bend the knee in fealty to this asshole.

Who would want someone like Lucas? Not me, that's for damn sure.

"See if I give a shit. Go ahead and throw a tantrum." I jerk my head back at my table. "I'll be over there enjoying my lunch."

Before the spectacle continues, I spin on my heel to end the conversation.

Lucas hooks his foot around my ankle as soon as I take a step and fucking trips me up. I stumble, but I don't go down. My water bottle is the only thing to topple from my wobbling tray. I meet the eyes of a few people nearby and can sense the hunger for blood.

No one's satisfied that I didn't crash to the floor face first into my lunch.

I bend to retrieve the water bottle and when I rise, Lucas is two steps closer, lurking right behind me like an imposing shadow.

"Bravo," I shoot over my shoulder. Lucas grinds his teeth, his hands balled into fists at his sides. "Real brave of a big, strong guy like you to actually trip a girl because she wasn't interested in your bullshit."

Squaring my shoulders, I stalk over to my table by the windows.

The nice girl from study hall is there. She grants me a half-smile and doesn't pause in digging into her sparse lunch of basic food groups. A half-eaten roll sits next to a scoop of peas, an apple, and a plain cut of chicken.

I nod to her and drop across the table on the opposite bench, purposefully giving Lucas my back.

It doesn't take away the weight of his attention zeroed in on me for the rest of the period.

SEVEN
LUCAS

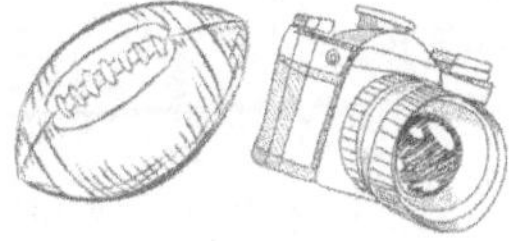

Fire roars in my blood when Gemma turns her back on me.

As she walks away, it takes every ounce of control not to grab her and drag her to my table. I let her go. For now.

It comes as a surprise when she still fights me. I expected her to fall over in fear, but she's not afraid.

If Gemma doesn't fear me, I can't control her. If I can't control her, then I'm not on top. That won't stand. It was my mountain first and she won't kick me off it with her blatant disregard for the way things work around here.

I stew through lunch, my gaze burning holes in the back of that uppity bitch's head.

Something about her pisses me off. I don't know whether it's her ballsy implication I'm some rapist over a moment of mistaken identity and a kiss, or that she keeps stirring trouble.

Not only do I still want a piece of her, now I want to take that prude down a peg.

I can kill two birds with one stone.

My mouth curves, but I feel no amusement.

I steal Devlin's fries and he grumbles under his breath, jabbing me with a pointy elbow.

"Buy your own, dick."

"If I bought my own, I wouldn't get the thrill out of stealing yours."

Devlin snorts and shoves his tray at me. His half-lidded gaze flicks over to Gemma's table and the corners of his mouth tense.

I silently agree with him. Gemma Turner thinks she's better than me. That she can just come in here from wherever-the-fuck and get by without playing by the rules.

This school is under my control. No one defies me.

It's always been easy to command the attention of those around me. Teachers and Coach Garcia call it leadership skills. People fall all over themselves to listen to what I have to say.

They expect me to play the part of their god, so I can't stand idly by while she runs around untamed. My rules apply to her, too.

The anger scorching my veins grows in intensity.

I will destroy her.

With a slight shift in my posture, all eyes at the table are on me. "Listen up."

Carter leans on his forearms, a wild grin spreading across his face. "'Sup, brother?"

I match his expression and nod to Gemma's table with her sad little girl squad of two.

"Open fucking season."

The handful of football team members whoop and break

out in chatter. Devlin quirks a brow and glances between me and Gemma.

“We’re going to play a game.” I rifle through my wallet and slap a fifty down. “Place your bets now.”

“What’s the game?” asks one of our bulky defensive line players.

I wait a beat, tilting my head and smirking. “Break the prude. Anything goes.” I point across the lunchroom. “First to get Gemma Turner—with proof—wins the pot.” I prop my elbows on the table and rest my chin on my laced fingers. “Destroy her. No mercy.”

Laughter breaks out and I settle back to survey what I’ve set in motion. Carter lets out a howl and drums his palms on the table. They act like a pack of jackals let loose on the hunt. Money is laid down and big claims made over who’s winning.

But I already know who will win.

It’ll be me.

I’m going to break Gemma Turner by making her mine.

EIGHT
GEMMA

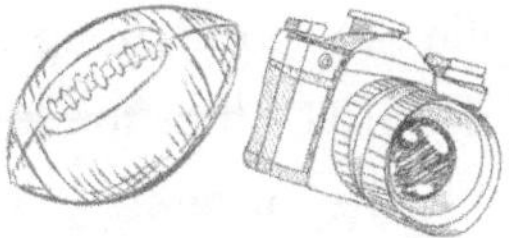

This school has gone fucking crazy in a matter of days.

Carter Burns followed me from my car one morning, leering at me the whole time. I arrived at my locker to find a small mailbox super-glued to it beneath a sign that said *Peak Point Blow Job Requests, C/O Gemma Turner.* Carter gave another guy a high five and told me he liked his cock sucked extra sloppy.

People slut-sneezed and called me a Coyote Girl—whatever the fuck that was—as I went from class to class, their snickers trailing after me as I rolled my eyes.

A pretty girl in second period sat on top of my desk yesterday and showed me her Instagram post. It was a still image taken from the video of my kiss with Lucas, except instead of Lucas she photoshopped it so I was kissing her instead. She got the lighting spot on. The caption had my actual phone number and said *txt Gemma Turner 4 a good time* with a slew of saucy emojis. The photo had over 250 likes and several comments within minutes. My phone buzzed in my bag and dread speared through me.

Players from every team at school howled as they flicked the edge of my uniform skirt, phones at the ready to snap a photo. The third guy that tried that met my fist in his gut and my sturdy boot on his toe. Lucas had seen the whole thing from several feet down the hall, leaning against a locker with an unreadable look. I flipped him off and stormed to class.

It was only lunch, and I was ready to kick the wall. This was insanity. How could teachers let this kind of shit fly?

I hadn't found any faculty around during these incidents, and a large part of me was too stubborn and prideful to go crawling to the administrative office to file a formal complaint—even if it meant stopping the torment.

The last time the principal's office got involved in one of my problems, there had been a humiliating investigation that I didn't want to relive.

"Are you going to eat, or keep doing that angry pacing?" Blair asks.

She's my sole ally.

Blair tucks her blue-gray hair behind her ear and takes one of the protein bars I emptied onto a bench in the courtyard where we're spending our lunch period.

We're not hiding. We're just...getting a break from the shit that's been my constant since Monday. I'm desperate for the week to end so I can escape this psychotic hell hole for a couple of days.

I drop beside Blair on the stone bench. It's cold against my butt and I wrap my leather jacket tighter around my body.

"Who decided skirts were a good uniform choice," I groan.

Blair snorts. "Men."

"Ugh."

"Mood." She tears into a second protein bar. She nudges a few packets my way. "Eat. You can't plan retaliation and world domination on an empty stomach."

"I'm more of a pacifist." I release a heavy sigh. "Are all the students here always so rabid for the drama? The mob mentality is fucking eerie."

Blair hitches a bony shoulder. Part of me feels bad for making her skip lunch with me. I've guessed it's one of the few solid meals she gets from her threadbare appearance and secondhand uniform. I have another box of protein bars in my bag I'm giving her.

"There's never been something this big." She studies me. "I think you're the first person to really stand up to those jerks that run this place. The rest of us nobodies have kept our heads down."

"What the hell," I mutter.

Slipping my phone from my pocket, I flick my nail against the edges. I've mostly had it off. Whenever I turn it on, there's a bombardment of new messages from random numbers. I stopped reading them when the dick pics started coming.

"This is harassment. This isn't a prank. He started all this shit."

I turn the phone on anyway and block out the incessant buzzing of new notifications.

"Have you told your parents?"

"No. I..." I push out a sigh and clench my phone in a white-knuckled grip. "I've had to change schools twice. When I was sixteen, a friend that I thought liked me, he..."

Blair puts a hand on my shoulder and squeezes. "You don't have to tell me."

"I just don't want them to worry anymore. I can handle this."

My eyes close as the memories of my nightmare flood my mind. His hands holding me down, touching me while I beg him to stop. I feel silly for not explaining the rest of the story to Blair. I wasn't raped, but I'm still haunted by dreams of his hands all over me, pressing my face into the mattress as he ground himself against my backside and tried to pull my pants down.

A shudder rolls through me and I swallow the surge of bile.

"What about the cops or something?" Blair nods to the cell phone in my hands. "At least to stop the shit on your phone." She claps her hands together and intones in a mystical voice, "Dick pics be gone."

"I can't believe people are gullible enough for this amateur shit. Don't they notice it's the same angle as the other video?"

"People are fucking stupid. And teenagers are gremlins. They'll believe any rumor and bad photo edits for a juicy scrap of entertainment."

"That's a bleak outlook."

The laugh that escapes Blair is grim and bitter.

I'm stronger than people think. I can endure this.

Despite my resolution, I'm feeling the pressure of being hunted by the whole student body. They follow Lucas Saint's word like mindless lemmings and every one of them decided they hate me.

All because I stood up for myself against Lucas.

* * *

I purposefully started parking in random spots at the edges of the student parking lot, much to Alec's annoyance. There's a familiar shout as I'm walking to the car.

"Goddamn it," I hiss.

A grip on my messenger bag strap halts me and a strong body collides against my back, sending me stumbling forward. Lucas steps around and blocks me from going anywhere by stalking into my space, caging me between him and the muscled meathead behind me.

I lock my jaw and glare at him. "What do you want?"

Lucas has a smug aura. Hands snake around my stomach, roaming wherever they please. I tense and turn my head to see who it is. Carter Burns winks back at me.

"Think you can take both of us at once?" Lucas muses. His chest brushes against me as he threads his fingers in my hair. "The guys on the team want to settle a disagreement that's been going on in the locker room after practice."

"Do you want the front or the back door, bro?" Carter buries his nose against my skull. "You smell sweet."

A low growl makes Lucas' chest vibrate. It's hardly audible, but I *feel* it. He slides his touch down the side of my face and wraps his fingers around my throat in a controlling gesture. His eyes bounce back and forth between mine.

"Can you do it?"

I blink when I realize this question actually expects a response.

"Fuck no," I say with a hard laugh, but my voice shakes.

Lucas gives me a shark's grin and leans close to press his lips against my ear.

"Does the thought scare you? What if we want it? I've shared girls with Carter before. Want me to make you bounce on my cock and then hold you still while Carter fucks your mouth?"

His breath is hot and it makes me shiver.

As much as my hatred for him burns in every cell of my body, I picture the dirty ideas he puts in my head. The thoughts send a sick pulse of heat throbbing between my legs. His thumb prods the corner of my mouth. My stomach turns over, though I don't know whether it's in excitement or dread.

"Go fuck yourselves, pigs," I push out through my teeth. Carter's hands still explore. "Stop those hands and let me go, Burns, or your balls are toast. If you touch me freely, I'll touch you right the fuck back, but I don't think you'll like it as much."

"Your kitten's got claws, Saint."

Lucas laughs, but there's a darkness clouding his eyes that triggers a deep instinct in me to fear what he could do to me.

He pulls me free from Carter with ease and swings me around. With his cool gaze locked on me, he herds me backwards until I hit a car. I glance down and in my peripheral vision I see the funny contradictory bumper stickers Alec and I slapped on the back in one of our many squabbles.

Lucas traps me against the car by planting his arms on either side of my head. Carter props his body beside me, missing the momentary look of annoyance Lucas tosses at him before he redirects the full weight of his attention on me.

"What do you think, sweetheart? In the back seat right here, or should we make the trip all the way to Peak Point?" Lucas hums and hovers his mouth over mine with scarcely enough room to breathe. "You're cute when you blush."

The hardness in his expression makes me squirm, pressing my legs together. I'm getting turned on by the champion king of my tormentors, wet from the awful way he looks at me. What the fuck is wrong with me?

"You like an audience, though. I think you'd enjoy it more if we did it right here. Let's make the car rock and fog up the windows like in Titanic."

He presses his hips into me and I can feel his erection. My breath hisses between my lips. He lowers his head a little more, closing in on kissing me.

"Hey. Come on, hasn't it been enough, yet? It's getting a little old and I'm not down to watch you make out with my sister."

Lucas stills as Alec walks up. Carter frowns and pulls away from the car. Chills swallow me as Lucas peels his body away, leaving me cold and empty inside.

Alec works his jaw, glancing between all three of us and shoulders past Carter to unlock the car.

"Come on, Gemma."

Alec hops into the driver's side. I swallow down the confusion and guilt, avoiding Lucas' gaze as I get in.

"See you tomorrow, sweetheart," Lucas promises.

I slam my door and jab the lock button as Alec reverses and speeds off.

An awkward silence blankets the car as Alec navigates through the rolling hills on our way home. Finally, it becomes too much and I attempt to break it.

"No practice today?"

Alec grips the wheel hard enough for his skin to stretch over his knuckles.

"Game day," he grunts. "I need to run home to drop stuff off, then I'm heading back."

"Oh." I haven't kept up with his schedule much. An ache echoes in my chest to feel my brother so out of reach when he's right there across the car. "Thanks for, um. Back there. With Lucas and Carter."

Alec twitches his shoulder. His face pinches angrily, but I don't know whether it's meant for me, Lucas, or himself.

The last time Alec caught me in a compromising position like that, his best friend was on top of me and we were all drunk at a party. He listened to Matt's story instead of mine, but at least he dragged me out of there. I thought that night would go so differently. Matt and I hadn't kissed, but we'd been flirting for weeks and holding hands. I thought he'd be my boyfriend soon.

I'd been so wrong. That wasn't what he wanted me for.

My throat is tight when I swallow and stare out the window at the passing pine trees.

"Why did you stop them?" I have to know. I twist my hands in my lap. "You don't need to stand up to your friends for me."

Alec slams his fist against the wheel and I jump.

"Damn it, Gemma." Alec sighs. "I don't know. I just *did.* I don't...like it."

"Well, you don't have to." I run my fingers through my hair. The memory of Lucas's hands lingers. "Just let it happen. I can handle whatever they want to throw at me."

Alec frowns.

"I don't care about what anyone thinks of me. None of it's true."

"It's still not easy to listen to the shit they're all saying about you." Alec grimaces. "Again."

I bark out a hollow laugh. "Yeah, I bet that's a real hardship for you. Is it screwing up your game day headspace?"

"Fuck, Gemma, it is!"

I scrub my face and blow out a breath.

"Look. I'm telling you I'm strong enough to do this by myself. I know how much you want to be involved and just enjoy your last year before college. That's all you, I don't give a fuck about these people. I don't want to give in so that the same people who spread rumors about me try to be my friend in another month when it dies down."

"That's not how it used to be. You used to care a lot about your friends' opinions. It's not like we ran with different people, we were all together."

"Yeah, well..."

That wasn't going to happen again.

"Now I'm a loner chick. I'm all badass and shit." I wiggle my boots as I stick one foot up on the dash. Alec chuckles and shakes his head. "If you try to step in, not only will you ruin the *great* cred I've built up," I point out sarcastically, winking at my brother, "it'll cause a rift for you with your team and their friends."

Alec doesn't look happy with that answer. Stubborn brat. He can't have it both ways—either he's pissed at me or he's the protective brother, but I'm getting whiplash from his hot and cold act.

"If joining in with the social scene is what you want so badly, then go for it. Don't let me and my problems hold you back."

"That's fucked up. I can't just let you—"

"*Let* me? Oh, fartbreath," I say in a sage tone, using my favorite nickname for him, "you don't get a say in what I do."

"But it's all too close to what happened before. I don't like the reminder."

"Wow." I cover my eyes. "You're right, I'd totally forgotten about that."

He grunts at my cold sarcasm.

I snap my fingers. "That must be terrible on you. Poor you."

"Gemma..."

"Save it. Noble brother isn't really your schtick." When Alec grumbles, I take pity on him. "I promise, I'm fine. Sticks and stones, right? It rolls right off my back. None of that crap is true, so I'm not letting the rumors get to me. If you are, well, that's an Alec problem, not an Alec-and-Gemma problem."

"Fine," he agrees as he pulls into our driveway.

"Thanks anyway, though."

I reach over and ruffle his hair so it's wild and messy before darting out of the car when he shouts my name.

For a little while I'm able to put Lucas Saint from my mind.

NINE
LUCAS

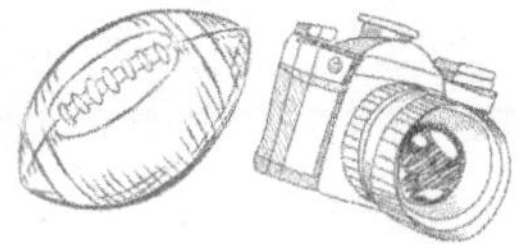

"Dude, that pass was insane." Carter makes an appreciative sound and mimes throwing a football as we walk with Devlin and Bishop down the hall. "Your arm is going pro. I've got good money riding on it."

"Just his arm?" Bishop chimes in, giving me a skeptical once over. "What about his left leg?"

"Surely his hair can make the pro league," Devlin agrees.

"Shove it." I mash my palm over Bishop's face and give him a playful push. "Or I'll never bring any of your sorry asses to live the high life with pro cheerleaders and bottle service."

Carter makes a dramatic show of crocodile tears, leaning on Bishop. The four of us are entertained by his antics.

Up ahead, I spot Gemma's honey-blonde hair piled into a

messy bun. Headphones dangle from her ears as she crosses the hallway and my mouth quirks up in anticipation.

I take her in from head to toe and give into the urge to capture her. I want to taste her sweet lips again and I don't know if I can hold out any longer.

That kiss has stuck in my head on repeat. It's at the top of my nightly rotation when I jerk off. I don't know if I'm intrigued because this is the first time a girl has refused to fall on my dick because I looked her way, or if I'm still high on the thrill of chipping away at her for revenge.

Either way, Gemma has become my fucking obsession. She owns so many of my thoughts. I can feel her beneath my skin whenever she's near.

I meet my friends' eyes and nod towards my conquest. Carter lights up. He's gone hard for taking Gemma down a peg.

Bishop and Devlin fan out, flanking my approach. People who see us are quick to scoot out of the way, parting the path to Gemma.

Coming up behind her, I snatch her, lifting her until her toes barely graze the ground. The headphones fall out and dangle from her bag. She lets out a delicious little yelp. I want to get her alone and hear her make that sound again.

Against her ear, I whisper, "Caught you, sweetheart."

Gemma bucks, but I'm stronger. I swing around to the bank of lockers and drop her with enough force that she lands hard on her feet. Before Gemma catches her balance, I turn her around and press her into the metal.

Two blotchy pink spots color her cheeks, but she meets me with a fierce snarl that calls to the fire in my gut.

"You dickhead," she growls. "How many times do I have to say it until you get it through that thick skull! I don't want to talk to you!"

"That's not nice," Bishop comments.

Devlin stands next to him, messing with his phone. "Hunter...catches...target," he mumbles as his thumbs move across his screen. "And—posted."

A savage grin stretches on Bishop's face at whatever Devlin captured of the scene unfolding.

"What's not *nice*," Gemma grits, "is your boy here. You're all psycho."

Her body jerks, aiming to slip away. I block her before she can escape. I lean in and hold her chin.

"You liked it before. You can't deny the way your body gets excited when I'm near." I brush my thumb over her chin, grinning when she tamps down on a shudder. "See that. Now, these lips are just begging me to kiss them. What do you say?"

"Wow, now you know how to ask? Thanks." Gemma's green eyes shoot daggers at me. "*No*."

I bend closer anyway, intent on kissing her. A small noise escapes her and she digs her fingers in my shirt. I don't know if she expects to hold me back or drag me in.

"Get to class!"

My head pops up. The French teacher—an ancient crone with a beak nose—lurks by her classroom door.

While I'm distracted, Gemma wriggles away, evading me by the skin of her teeth. I grab her upper arm before she can go far.

"Don't fight it, baby. You'll be mine by homecoming."

Gemma shrugs me off and straightens her school blazer. "In your fucking dreams."

The itch to have her lingers.

The guys snicker as she stomps off. Carter wolf whistles at her back.

"Damn, that ass is fine." Carter bites his lip and thrusts his hips in her direction. "I just want to hold her still and drive my cock into her tight little pussy. Think she's a screamer? She's gotta be, right?"

I can't stop the growl that rips out of me and before I know it, I have Carter by the collar against the locker where I just teased Gemma. Devlin's hand on my shoulder pulls me back from the thick haze of jealousy crashing over me.

Carter stares back at me with wide eyes, his palms up.

"Chill, bro," he says. "I'd give you first dibs."

My stomach clenches. Carter's always scooped up my sloppy seconds. While other guys complain about that shit, it's never bothered him. Hell, once Marissa dated him for a while when we were on one of her self-imposed breaks.

It's never gotten to me like it does right now. The thought of Carter touching Gemma, even after the other day when we cornered her in the parking lot, drives a spike of ice into my chest.

I don't know what's come over me or why.

Releasing Carter, I step back and run a hand through my hair. Devlin raises an eyebrow at me.

"You cool, man?"

"Yeah." I force a chuckle. "Let's get out of here. I feel like cutting next period."

Bishop whoops and slaps me on the back. "Nice. I've got a sweet ass joint rolled. Let's go hit that."

This time my laugh feels genuine as I join my friends in mischief during the middle of school.

TEN
GEMMA

The computer lab is comfortable. The dimmed lights and glowing computer displays are like a second home. On the wall Ms. Huang has enlarged prints from National Geographic, abstract digital art from students, and a corner for open sharing where students and teachers can post up images from their portfolio.

I consider the last of my image selections for the ongoing project Ms. Huang assigned.

A few other students are in the lab, though they're trickling out. I'm usually the only one that stays a while after school to work on my project.

Ms. Huang pauses behind me and bends over to study my choices over my shoulder.

"You have a great photojournalistic eye, Gemma," she compliments.

"Thanks."

A smile breaks out on my face and I bite down on my lip. I listen to my gut after going back and forth between a photo of an older man on a hiking trail and a landscape, selecting the picture of the man. Ms. Huang hums approvingly.

The older man's fitness is on display as he's mid-hike. I like the way the soft overcast light highlighted the craggy wrinkles on his face. There's an air of adventurous spirit gleaming in his happy, crinkled eyes.

"I like that one. Great moment."

"I don't like to disturb the subject too much. I pretty much just observe and let the scene unfold before me until the right moment to press the shutter." I eject my SD card from the computer and put it back in my camera. "It really works out for my people watching habit."

Ms. Huang chuckles at that. "Great work, Gemma. I'm looking forward to seeing your project when it's completed."

She moves onto the next student working after school and I lose myself in editing my images, my personal meditative happy place.

* * *

By the time I leave, the sun kisses the horizon and the light is fading fast in the parking lot. I stayed longer than I meant to, but I made good progress on my photo project.

There's almost no cars left in the student lot. My CR-V sits by itself at the back. I'm distracted as I stroll up, going over a list of photo ideas on my phone.

I halt in my tracks after I unlock my car.

There's a flat tire—wait, no, shit! All of my tires are flat!

I drop into a crouch to skim my fingers over the deflated tires.

"There's no way."

I drag my teeth over my lip and check for slashes. The valve caps are still in place, so no one stole them. Some asshole simply unscrewed the caps and let out the air to strand me.

I groan and scrub my face. "God, really?"

The one thing we don't keep in the car is an air compressor. We have a way to fix every other problem. There's a spare tire, but that still leaves me with three flats.

I thump my fist half-heartedly on the side of the car. Footsteps draw my attention and I bolt to my feet.

Lucas walks by, his hair damp and curling across his forehead. He must have showered after practice. His t-shirt stretches over his shoulders and his bicep as he hitches his equipment bag higher. Every nerve ending in my body wakes up at his approach.

I tell every single one of those stupid fuckers to shut up.

Lucas looks my way, disinterest evident in his vacant expression as he takes in my situation.

"Hmm, is this what it looks like when the whole school hates you?"

Lucas tips his head to the side and flashes his teeth.

I chew on the inside of my cheek. I won't ask him for help. I have my phone, I can just call Alec and see if he's done with practice, too.

"Do you want a ride?" Lucas surprises me by offering.

"I—"

I clamp my mouth shut and mull it over. Does Lucas want something from me? Is it another trap?

The breeze stirs the trees surrounding the lot, their

branches creaking and groaning. I shiver and tug my jacket tighter around my shoulders.

"Yeah, okay. Fine."

Lucas stares at me with narrowed eyes for a minute, then he bursts out in sharp amusement. He shakes his head and drags a hand through his damp hair, his attractive grin at odds with the way he's laughing.

"Too fucking bad. You had your chance."

I jerk my head back, though I can't say I'm surprised he's taking another opportunity to bully me. I cross my arms as he jogs to his car.

Within a few minutes, he revs the Range Rover's engine and leaves me alone in the dusk blanketing the lot. I curse him quietly.

The overhead lights flicker on, but my car sits between two pools of light in the growing darkness.

The security booth is empty, the guard done for the evening.

I send a text to Alec.

Gemma: Are you done practice yet? I'm at the car. The air's been let out of all 4 tires. [Frown emoji] [Frown emoji]

A few minutes later, his response has my stomach sinking.

Alec: WTF??? That's my car too. [Knife emoji]
Alec: I'm hitting the weight room. I'll catch a ride with one of the guys. You're on your own. Better get it fixed by tomorrow.

I squeeze the phone and groan in frustration.

"Stupid jerkface brother," I mumble.

Plan B. I open the door and plop my bag on the seat. I dig

through my wallet and find the roadside assistance card. After going through the automated prompts, I prop the phone between my ear and shoulder. I lean against the side of the car and debate turning it on to sit in the warmth rather than freezing my ass outside in this stupid uniform.

The low rumble of an engine echoes in the distance, probably another athlete heading home after practice. A loud screech of tires follows, coming closer. People at this school are such stupid daredevils, but I don't have time for some asshole's nonsense right now. I've got classical holding music in my ear and I'm cold.

The car stops behind me. Then there are hands on me and I shriek. The hands grip hard enough to bruise as I'm wrenched away from my car. My phone clatters on the ground. I do my best to struggle free, dropping my dead weight and trying to throw off my attacker.

The psycho is strong as fuck and all I get for my trouble is a grunted curse.

"Let me go!" I yell, hoping someone at this godforsaken hell hole of a school will hear.

Soft fabric drops over my head—a t-shirt, maybe? Either way, it's black and I can't see shit. I try to calm my breathing so I don't spiral into a panic. The heat of my air trapped in the material blindfolding me is humid.

My attacker lifts me from the ground when I stop struggling and my fear amplifies again, skittering across my skin in distressed chills.

When I hear a car door open, I cry, "No!"

I can't leave the scene! That's always what the crime shows say. If I'm taken without my phone, there's no trace of me to follow. I dig my nails into the muscular forearms wrapped around my waist like iron bands.

"Jesus, Ge—!" he growls and cuts himself off, jerking me around and forcing me into the unfamiliar car.

"Just let me go," I plead. "The cops will find you. They always do."

As I keep babbling, I pat down my pockets for any clue I can drop that Alec or someone else might find and know that I'm in trouble. I come up empty and tears sting my eyes. My chest heaves with a ragged breath.

I'm being kidnapped and no one will know how to find me.

My assailant wrestles my hands into my lap, squeezing my wrists until the bones jolt with pain. A whimper escapes me as he tightens a loop of plastic over my wrists, binding me with a zip tie. In the struggle, my elbow catches on the center console. I turn my head from side to side, trying to squint through tears and the t-shirt covering my head for any information.

The monster crowds into my space, dragging his fingers up my legs. I didn't wear tights today because I ran out of clean ones. He teases his touch beneath the hem of my skirt, stroking the tops of my thighs.

I grit my teeth, forcing out a vicious growl as I clamp my legs together, twisting my ankles around to lock my legs. This fucker has another thing coming if he thinks I'll let him rape me so easily.

He disappears with a muttered curse.

My throat burns like a fire has razed it. My breath comes in harsh pants as the door slams. Am I alone?

The car is running, the radio set to the local alt-rock station. I hear the muffled thump of a car door closing before another opens behind me. I twist my head to the side to listen better. The monster dumps off a sack or something in the back seat, then he gets in and we're on the move.

I count in my head as I drag breaths in through my nose.

Every muscle in my body is wound tight with tension. If I bide my time, I'll have another chance to catch this guy by surprise.

I just have to wait.

The car isn't in motion for long before the makeshift blindfold is whipped off. I blink at the dim boxy interior of a Jeep. It's an older model. It's nice, restored to perfection to look like new. We've left school, the hills of town rolling by the window.

My bound hands sit in my lap, the plastic digging into my skin a little.

Gathering my courage, I tip my head far enough to the side to face my kidnapper. Once I do, my insides go from icy cold to boiling hot fury in a matter of seconds.

Lucas. Fucking. Saint.

I suck in a slow inhale, the rage building in my chest. The fear I felt with his hands all over me—up my skirt, incapacitating me, tying me up—turns into a brittle wrath, cracking as it overflows from my whole body.

"You've got to be *fucking* kidding me, Lucas!"

My shout makes him draw in a surprised breath, but he recovers quickly and tosses me a smug look.

"That's a good look on you, sweetheart."

"What, fucking pissed?"

"No. Tied up. Helpless." With one eye on the road and one on me, he leans over and hisses in my ear. "At my mercy."

"You kidnapped me, you psycho!"

His pompous smirk stretches. "I'm stealing you for a joyride."

"My parents like me home by a certain time," I lie.

Lucas snorts.

"They won't be expecting you. Alec gave me the passcode to your phone for fifty bucks and a girl's number I know. It was a steal." He holds it up, wiggling it. "You just texted your mom to not worry about you. You're hanging out with a friend." He tucks it in his pocket and tips a sly look at me. "She said have fun. She seems sweet."

My stomach sinks.

"Were you also the one who let the air out of my tires?"

He lifts a brow, but doesn't answer.

I fall back against the seat, unclasping my legs and stretching out the stiffness from holding my entire body ready for attack at a moment's notice. A small sound gets caught in the back of my throat as I stretch. Lucas watches me, shifting into a more relaxed position with one hand on the wheel. He rubs his fingers over his mouth as his gaze flicks over me, then back on the road.

"Fuck, you really do look good like that. It's getting me hard."

"You're sick and insane."

He snorts and drops his hand on my thigh, squeezing it. I try to kick him off and scoot closer to the window. The searing rage rises again.

"I can't believe you! You don't even think, you just keep doing whatever you want like there are no consequences to face! I could file assault charges against you for this!"

Lucas reaches for my thigh again, easily capturing it when I only have so far to go. He traces a circle on the inside of my knee. My effort to throw him off is fruitless.

Lucas lets out a sinister, pleased laugh and spreads his hand over my bare skin, always taking and taking and taking.

"It won't stick. My dad's a lawyer and this town loves me."

"*Loves* you? How could they! You're fucking crazy—you go around kidnapping and tying up girls for your own messed up amusement!" A ragged sound leaves me and tears fall from my lashes. "I need to file a damn restraining order against you so you stay the hell away from me once and for all."

He mulls that over for a few minutes, his jaw working. I

sniffle and bring my restricted hands up to awkwardly wipe my face. I make sure he's paying attention when I smear the snot on his center console. His lip curls.

After a few minutes of caustic silence, the debilitating fear that gripped me ebbs away. Lucas still might hurt me and make me miserable, but he's not going to rape me and chop my body up in tiny pieces to scatter through the mountain range.

Well.

I hope.

He's an asshole, but my instincts are relaxing. The only thing left is anger rather than true terror. That has to count for something.

"Why don't you switch schools? There's two others in the district."

My teeth gnash as I sort out how to answer that.

"Why should I have to? Maybe you should quit your little mind games. I'm clearly not giving in."

"Yeah, clearly." Lucas grumbles something and squints at me. "Why can't you just give in?"

"That's not me." I lift my chin in defiance. "You don't get my surrender."

He hums and goes back to tracing patterns on the inside of my thigh. This time I don't bother trying to divert him. I catch glimpses of the last colors of the sunset as the car climbs higher in elevation. I don't know where Lucas plans to take me.

"Where are we going?"

"You'll see. Just sit there and look pretty."

My gaze narrows and my brows pinch together. "Fuck you."

Lucas purses his lips, then licks them. "I wouldn't say no."

"Ugh!"

Fed up with him, I wriggle around until my body is turned away. I glare in silence out the window, ignoring him.

Lucas lets out a raspy chuckle and drums his fingers on the steering wheel to the beat of a song I like on the radio.

Gritting my teeth, I focus on the lights flickering on in the valley below.

* * *

It's fully dark when I jolt awake.

My neck is slightly cramped from sleeping propped against the cold window. I wince and blink, trying to get my bearings. The car has finally stopped.

I can't believe I fell asleep listening to Lucas sing along to the radio as he coasted around winding mountain roads.

"Where are we?"

My voice is groggy. My hands are no longer bound. I rub my wrists, my thumb tracing the slight indentation from the plastic.

Lucas reaches over and strokes my head. I'm too tired to push his hand away. I have no idea what time it is.

"This is my secret lair." He gives my hair a light tug. "It's where I'm going to trap you forever as my prisoner."

I shoot him a poisonous look. I wait a beat, then swipe for him. He snorts as he lurches back to his side of the car.

Lucas hops out of the Jeep and grabs something from the back. I find the door unlocked and slide down.

It's my house. He took me home.

He knows where I live?

I wave off the thought, worrying my lip with my teeth as I hug myself. Not only did he bring me home, the CR-V is in the driveway. The tires look good as new.

I swallow as Lucas comes around to my side of the car. I gesture at my CR-V. "How?"

Lucas hitches a shoulder. He hands his bundle to me—my bag. My phone sticks out from the side pocket.

"Alec and Devlin took care of it after I executed my prank."

I grant Lucas a suspicious look and take out my phone to inspect it for damage after that fall in the parking lot. He didn't have time to go through it in the midst of kidnapping me and he didn't text and drive. I make a mental note to change my passcode and make it something Alec won't guess. There's some gravel wedged in the lip of my case and a smudge of dirt on the screen, but it seems okay.

At least, until I unlock it and it opens to a text conversation with a new contact—Lucas. My teeth clench so hard that I go lightheaded for a second.

Gemma: Gemma Turner is Lucas Saint's property. [Kissing face emoji] [Peach emoji]
Lucas: And don't you forget it baby. [Black heart emoji] [Eggplant emoji]

Fucking bastard. There's also a photo sent from my phone. I tap on it to see it full size. My stomach bottoms out.

It shows me sitting in the Jeep, blindfolded by a Silver Lake High Coyotes t-shirt wrapped around my head and my wrists restrained by the zip tie. The flash gives the picture an illicit quality, casting me in harsh contrasting light, the shadows made darker, where sinister thoughts lurk.

In my school uniform and leather jacket I look like something naughty and forbidden with the skirt riding up like that, exposing more of my bare thighs.

Heat floods my face, prickling across my skin and throbbing in my ears.

I rip my gaze away from the incriminating photo to find

Lucas watching me with an intense expression. He wants a reaction.

If he spreads this photo around the school, I'll kill him.

God, if my *parents* see this photo, I don't even want to think about what they'll do.

The front door opens before I formulate a scathing response to the final prong of Lucas' elaborate prank. We turn and my mom comes out, bundled in a puffy jacket and teal scrubs.

"Hi kids," she greets with a cheerful smile.

I press my phone to my chest to hide it from her. My heart thumps. Lucas guides me up the driveway with his hand at the small of my back.

"Hey, Mom." I curse at the quaver in my voice. Maybe she won't notice. "Um, sorry I'm home so late. I, uh—"

"Did you enjoy your dinner date?" Mom asks. "Alec said not to expect you for dinner."

I falter, tripping when my boot catches on my ankle. Lucas said he texted her from my phone that I was hanging out with a friend. Lucas wraps his arm around my waist, steadying me.

"Careful, sweetheart."

The smarmy amusement in his voice rakes across my irritation threshold.

Lucas shakes my mom's hand when she offers it to him.

"We had a great time, Mrs. Turner. Thanks for letting me take her out on a school night."

Lucas turns on the charm that has everyone calling him the golden Saint. I glance between them with my brows raised high. He rubs my arm, like he's trying to caress me and keep me warm from the biting chill in the air. Then he drops a chaste kiss on my temple—right in front of my mom—and pinches me when I turn into an ice sculpture, stiff and brittle.

Lucas murmurs against the side of my face, "Didn't we enjoy ourselves, Gemma?"

He terrorized me all night, kept me at his mercy, and, with the help of my brother as his accomplice, had my parents believing he took me on a date?

That. Fucking. Asshole.

Fuming, I leave Lucas in the dust and go inside without saying anything when his deep voice calls after me.

Lucas Saint fights dirty. I'm going to have to sink to his level to fight back.

ELEVEN
LUCAS

Lancelot circles my legs as I head upstairs after dinner.

He gets underfoot and I almost trip. I hoist the chubby pug into my arms, snorting at his bug-eyed fruitless wriggling.

"Easy, buddy boy," I soothe, giving his belly scritches. He warbles happily, stretching in my arms. "Right there? Hah, yeah, you're a good boy."

I let him down outside my room.

There are no responses to the teasing texts I sent Gemma. I pull up the photo of her tied up again. The swirling obsession is shifting, growing as I fixate on the photo, taking in her thighs and bound hands.

The success of kidnapping her burns fresh and hot in my gut, signaling a shadow that lives inside me. The thrill of besting her as I wrangled her into my Jeep is addictive. I want to do it again.

In a way, it's better Gemma didn't roll over and take it when I demanded she fall in line, like other girls might. The challenge of going after her will make her submissions that much sweeter when I break her.

For now, I push Gemma out of my head.

A stack of new sketchbooks sits on my desk beside a strategy playbook. I grab the top one and flop onto my bed. Lancelot jumps up with a grunt and settles at the foot of the bed.

Sticking headphones in and starting up a chilled out playlist, I lose myself to sketching. I start with a few drills to warm up, then make up building designs.

Drawing after school relaxes me. It's my favorite way to unwind at the end of the day, just me and a sketchpad and my dog.

If it were up to me, I'd quit football in a heartbeat to have more time to practice. I only got into it recently, so my lines aren't up to snuff yet. A YouTube artist I follow calls it mileage. The videos I watch online feature artists that are years ahead of me, people that knew what they wanted back when I still enjoyed football because it was a fun way to hang out with my friends.

The shelves in my room are packed with trophies from every year since I was in little league, barely able to throw the ball.

I'm stuck in the sport. At this point, it feels like everyone expects me to dream about going pro.

Over the summer, I hinted that I was thinking about quitting the team. I had no desire to play varsity, didn't care about being the quarterback, and was the wrong choice for team captain. My parents didn't pick up on my hints.

Whenever I bring up quitting, they tell me I should stick it out because I've played for ten years.

It's important to see commitments through.

Mom had ruffled my hair and handed me my freshly cleaned jersey. Dad was proud of me for my achievements. When I asked what happened if I had other aspirations, Dad missed my point entirely. He'd said as the team captain, my friends relied on me.

I didn't ask to play football forever. My parents tossed me in every sport they could when I was a kid. Football stuck because it was where my friends were.

So what if I'm good at it?

I have other plans for my life. Ones I don't want to shove aside because I have a talent for throwing a ball. It's bullshit.

When Mom knocks on the open door with my jersey, I salute her with my pencil and put the finishing touches on the sick contemporary house I imagined.

"You look so handsome in this jersey," Mom says as she hangs it on the door, smoothing her hands over the material. "I'll miss seeing your number 14 after this year."

Number 14. I always say I'm lucky twice because of my number.

I hum and shrug as inspiration strikes. I zone out as I add a cool walkway.

"Dad put some brochures on the table for you downstairs." Mom perches on the bottom of the bed and pets Lancelot. He rolls onto his back and paws at her to keep going. "He said he could take a Friday off so the two of you could go visit campuses."

I sigh and tug an earbud free. "Let me guess. Colorado State, Utah, and Washington?"

Mom smiles and nods.

Of course. All schools with nationally ranked football programs. One of them Dad's alma mater.

I don't tell her about the bookmark on my laptop for Oak Ridge College. Or the brochure in my glove box. Or the filled-in application hidden in the bottom drawer of my desk.

My grip tightens on the sketchpad in my hands. Mom hasn't ever asked to see what I'm drawing, even though it's all I do in my free time around the house anymore. I've practically lived on the back deck and the dock filling up sketchbooks with my newfound hunger to learn.

It's like a drug, discovering I'm skilled at more than football.

It'll open the doors to my dreams.

"Thanks, Mom. I'll talk to Dad about it."

Mom gives me a kiss on the head, ruffling my hair like I'm still a kid.

"I can't believe next year you'll be in college."

I shrug, helpless for how to react when she gets like this. Mom leaves and I stick my earbud back in, turning the music up. I flip to a clean page and start a new drawing.

They won't let me quit the team. If it makes them happy, I'll finish the year. But I'm doing college on my terms.

It's been a hard lesson that I can't have everything I want. But I'll snatch anything I can take without a second thought. It's the only way I exert some sense of control in my life.

TWELVE
GEMMA

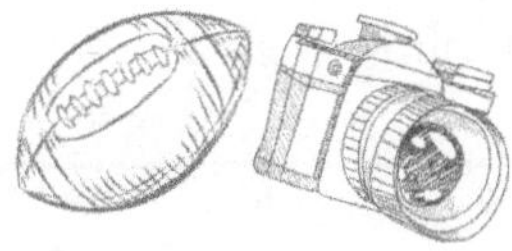

After Lucas' little kidnapping *prank*, he leaves me alone other than texting me.

It seems most of the student body has grown bored with me, too. The relentless tide of their ire follows the whims of Lucas' mysterious ceasefire.

It has me on edge. A couple of weeks pass and nothing happens. I wait for Lucas and the goons that follow him around every corner, tensing when our paths cross.

Last weekend I was in town taking photos. I ran into him unintentionally. He sat outside a coffee shop with a small sketchbook open on the table. He had sunglasses on and his head was bent over his drawing. When I first spotted him I thought I could slip away unnoticed, but the next time my gaze skirted in his direction he was gone.

Then he snatched me around the waist, capturing me once more. My usual reaction was quelled when he growled in my ear not to make a scene or he'd make my brother's life hell next. That shut me up quickly.

To onlookers, Lucas seemed like he was being sweet on me. In reality, he whispered such filthy things in my ear as he trailed his hands over me that my face turned beet red. I was powerless against the heat of unwanted desire coiling around me like a rope. Lucas kissed me on the cheek and grazed the waistband of my jeans. Then he was gone and I was alone.

He can come after me all he wants, but I'll be damned if he ruins anyone else's life because he wants to get to me.

Lucas is an inescapable force of control and power. The people in this town light up when he's around. Am I getting pulled into the orbit fooling them all?

* * *

I trudge back to class from my bathroom break in a funk.

My head has been such a mess since last weekend that I can't pay attention to Mrs. Ellis drone on about math. She doesn't pause as I enter the room and return to my seat behind Elena, the girl who latched onto me at Lucas' birthday party at the beginning of school.

My eyelids grow heavy and I hunch over my notes. Hushed whispers and a stray titter catches the edge of my attention, but I ignore it. A nap sounds fabulous right now. If I just rest my eyes for a few minutes, all will be right in the world.

"Work on the equations on the board for the rest of the period and pass your homework forward," Mrs. Ellis announces as she finishes up the lesson.

Chatter breaks out amongst my classmates as the rows collect worksheets.

Elena twists in her seat and gives me a knowing look as I surreptitiously wipe the back of my hand over my mouth to check for drool.

"There's a party after the game this Friday. Think you'll go?" Elena prompts, holding her hand out for my worksheet.

"No. I don't even plan to go to the game."

I bend over to get my homework out, keeping my attention on her. My hand grasps at air and I frown, leaning further. Maybe I kicked my bag in my sleep and scooted it beneath the seat.

A wrinkle appears on Elena's forehead. "You won't even go to support Alec and cheer him on?"

"He doesn't need me to do that kind of stuff. He's happy enough just to have fun playing."

I grunt and sit upright before I topple out of my chair and make an ass of myself. When I peer down, my bag isn't there.

"What the..." I check the other side of my desk. My heart skips a beat. "Um, this might sound weird, but have you seen my bag?"

"Huh?" Elena looks up from her phone. "You had it when you came to class, didn't you?"

"Yeah, it's a messenger bag. It's not here."

An unpleasant tingle skitters across my nerves as Elena asks a few of the people around us. None of them are as helpful or kind as her.

"Is it a big bag? You girls like those big ass bags," one guy comments.

"You probably didn't have it with you in the first place," the girl to my left says without looking up.

Blood rushes in my ears as my heart pounds faster. My stomach imitates a carnival ride. I think I might be sick.

Their snide dismissal grates and I'm reminded that I'm still not welcome here.

"I wouldn't just misplace my bag. It's got my wallet, my homework, and my stuff."

My camera and three lenses are in it, too, but I leave that out. Not knowing where my bag went sends my thoughts spiraling, and an itch digs its way under my skin—I need to get up and tear through the school to find it. I know it was there when I returned from the bathroom. The only other time I wasn't paying attention was when I fell asleep.

Shit.

I think someone stole it. Glancing around, my suspicion only grows when I catch a few people's intent gazes. It's like they're waiting for me to blow up.

At the front of the room, Mrs. Ellis thumbs through the stack of worksheets.

"Gemma, do you have yours?" she asks.

"I, uh..." I feel the stares of Elena and the others. It'll only make me seem crazy if I start throwing around accusations about my missing bag. I lie instead. "I don't have it with me."

"It's not like you not to hand in your work, Miss Turner."

"I know. I'll, um. I'll have it tomorrow for a late mark. Sorry."

She levels me with a disappointed frown that sits uneasily. I'm not the most studious person, but I'm not a slacker, either. I do my work.

"Very well." Mrs. Ellis checks the time and takes a seat at her desk. "Your assignment for tonight is on the board."

Once the bell rings, I'm out of my seat like a shot.

"I'm sure it'll turn up," Elena calls.

A sick weight makes my stomach heavy. I cram my hands beneath my arms to keep them from trembling with the nervous energy bubbling over.

My bag isn't in my locker. I knew it wouldn't be, but I had

to do something. I head for the office to check the lost and found.

It must have been stolen when I was napping in class. I could kick myself for letting my guard down. Lucas is behind this somehow—either directly or indirectly, his influence is definitely at work.

I was stupid to think he was done with me.

As I enter the office, I collide with someone as he's entering at the same time. I catch myself on the doorway.

"In a hurry?"

It's Lucas and Devlin's friend. The junior who is the varsity soccer captain. His angelic features distract me from my dilemma for a second.

"Connor, is that you?" Principal Bishop calls from his open door at the back of the hive of administrative offices. "Come in, your mother wants us to grab lunch together before the appointment."

He's the principal's son? Brows raised, my gaze swings back. Connor winks at me and slips by, casting a solemn glance at the secretary desk. As he steps through to his dad's office, he shuts the door behind him with a bang.

Shaking my head, I hurry over to the circular desk at the center of the room run by office aid volunteers and a rotation of secretaries.

"Devlin?" I blink. "I didn't expect you to be here."

Devlin props his chin in one hand and gives me a cheeky smile. "Why not?"

"I...I don't know."

"Don't tell anyone," he leans over and gestures me closer, "but office aid is the best elective. I get to flirt with the staff, eat donuts, and sneak into Principal Bishop's office."

"Uh, that's great." I tuck my hair behind my ear. "Has anything new come into the lost and found?"

"Misplace something?" A sly grin stretches his lips. "Or are you looking for good shit to steal?"

My lips press into a thin line.

"My bag is missing. It's a messenger bag. Brown leather."

Devlin shrugs and waves at the box in the corner.

"Have at it. I just got here." He reclines in his chair and kicks his legs onto the desk, crossing his ankles. "Want me to make an announcement?"

I dig through the box, setting aside designer sunglasses, outerwear, and a few cell phones. For a second, a brown bag catches my eye, igniting my excited relief like a rocket, but when I drag it out, it's just a backpack.

With a sigh, I drop everything back in the box.

"No luck?" Devlin spins in his chair, his dark hair fanning with each rotation. He tips his head upside down to meet my eyes. "What a shame. I'll keep a personal eye out for it. Devlin's on the case."

"Thanks anyway."

As I turn to leave, I find Blair in the doorway with a slip of paper pinched between her fingers. Her pretty brown eyes turn to slits when she zeroes in on Devlin.

"I was called to the office," she says.

Devlin sits upright. There's a cruel shift in his expression, his brows lowering and the corners of his mouth ticking up.

"Davis. You were caught stealing from the kitchens." He twirls a pen around his thumb in a repetitive motion. "Put your paper in this tray while I fill out your ISS form."

"Suspension?" I yelp. Surely this school can afford to spare some extra apples. "That's not fair."

Devlin flicks a disinterested look my way. Blair stalks into the office and crumples her paper before dropping it on Devlin. It ricochets from the desk and hits him in the chest. Grumbling under his breath, he swipes the paper ball and smooths it out.

"Better run along, Turner. You have a bag to look for, and —" Devlin pauses and points up. The second bell rings. "— you're late for class."

"Can you write us late slips?" I cross my arms and stand beside Blair. "We have study hall together this period."

A muscle in Devlin's jaw jumps. Where the hell did this severe attitude come from? When I see him around Lucas, he's usually carefree and relaxed. There's hardly anything that gets to him.

"It's fine, Gemma, just go ahead," Blair mumbles. She cuts a hateful look to Devlin as he fills in the suspension paperwork. Sighing, she nudges me. "I'll see you later, okay?"

"Okay..." Something tells me not to leave, so I retreat with slow steps. "Keep an eye out for my bag, will you? It's *missing*."

The emphasis I put on the word has Blair's brows shooting up. I shrug helplessly. She nods and waves me away.

As I exit the office, I hear Devlin's words to Blair.

"The next time you cross us, I'll make you regret being born, Davis. Don't try your petty pickpocket bullshit again, or I'll have you kicked out of school."

I pause outside the door and glance back. Blair's teeth are bared and Devlin looks ready to shoot fire from his eyes. The tension between them crackles in the air, reaching all the way into the hallway.

Part of me wants to hang around to give my friend back up, but a teacher strolling through the hall sees me standing there.

"What are you doing out of class? Move along."

I have no choice but to make my way to the auditorium. The sick roil still makes my stomach feel like lead as I go there without my missing bag.

I need to find it.

* * *

I check everywhere.

As the minutes tick by throughout the day I grow more frazzled. Classes drag as my knees bounce. Cruel laughter and whispers follow me everywhere.

Between every class I stalk through the halls of the huge campus and confront anyone who looks at my twice. No one has answers.

All I earn for my trouble is more frustration and rude snickers.

By last period, I break down and check Instagram. If the whole school knows, then that means there's a clue and I *need* to find my bag.

Sure enough, I have a bunch of tags when I open up the app in the bathroom. My stomach tightens and drops like cement through water as I tap on a few of the notifications flooding my feed.

@brightgem give me $50 & a blowjob for ur bag.

Saw this gutter troll digging through the trash. Hear she's buds with Raggedy Anne #yikes #silverlakehs #theyremultiplying. In this photo: @brightgem.

@brightgem found what you're missing right here baby. #8inches #nolie [*wink emoji*] [*eggplant emoji*].

This last one is a photo of a guy's abs and the trail of hair leading into his low waistband tugged down to tease his junk.

A disgusted scoff drops from my lips. In a last ditch effort, I clear my notifications and navigate to Lucas' account.

(What? I'm not a stalker like him. I've looked once or twice. Just to see who I was dealing with. You can tell a lot about a person by their social media habits.)

There's a new photo. A selfie. He's smirking at the viewer with nice backlighting leaking across the photo. *Morning light,* I note with narrowed eyes. The caption reads:

@GoldSaint: *All things lost will be found again. To catch a kitten, set a tasty lure #herekittykitty.*

Bastard. He's a goddamn monster. This is all a mean joke to him, but that camera is more important to me than anything.

With a bitten off sound, I swipe out of the app. I've seen enough. I wait in the bathroom until the final bell rings, then shove the door open to get the hell out of this cesspool of heartless greed.

"There goes the crazy angry chick."

Ignoring the group of douchebags, I shove the doors open with my backside, burdened by a stack of books from my locker. Students shoot me open looks as we head en masse for the parking lot.

If I can't find my bag...I don't even want to think about it. I have to find it.

That camera is my lifeline.

Blair caught up with me later in the afternoon and helped me retrace my anxious steps. She reminded me not to let these assholes get to me, but the advice fell flat when she was gritting her teeth from being slapped with an in school suspension for taking an extra carton of milk.

I hike my heavy stack of books higher as I go down the steps to the parking lot. Right about now I'm regretting parking at the very back corner. My biceps burn with the effort of holding my stuff.

I'm a little winded by the time I reach the car. A little groan of relief passes my lips and I rest my load on the bumper.

Thankfully Alec has the car keys. If they'd been in my bag that would have made a sucky situation even worse.

It's bad enough as it is.

My heart hangs heavy with a well of emotion that makes my throat scratchy. I suck in a deep gulp of air to hold back the tears threatening to burst free.

After the short break, I readjust my stack of books so I can put them on the hood. As I round the back of the car, I stop with a sharp breath.

Lucas leans against the CR-V.

He holds up my bag with a lazy smirk.

"Looking for this?"

Tears prick my eyes as I release a watery gasp.

The crash of emotions is hard to pick apart between the annoyance at his existence and the balm of relief to find my bag safe and sound. My shoulders sag and I close the distance between us.

"Give me that. How did you even get it?" I shake my head as soon as the words leave my mouth. "Never mind. I don't want to know. You're an asshole, by the way."

A laugh puffs out of him. "Hello to you, too."

I grapple with my cumbersome books and finally squat to dump them on the ground. I pop back up and blow hair out of my face.

Lucas doesn't offer up my bag. When I grab for it, he holds it out of reach. My gut twists and I pummel his chests with a fierce yell.

"Don't drop it!" I lift my hands, trying to reach. "Come on."

Lucas wraps an arm around my waist and tugs me against his body. He's warm and I can smell the forest-clean scent of his aftershave. His fingers dance over my back, sliding beneath my school blazer.

"Give me a kiss and you can have your things back."

A bolt of indignation shoots up my spine and I grunt as I try to claw my bag away from him. He holds it higher and I grow more pissed.

"Damn it, Lucas!"

He chuckles, low and smoky. Every shift brings the hard curve of his pecs and the firm planes of his stomach against me. His bicep ripples and bunches as he adjusts his hold on me. Fuck, why does he have to smell so good?

"Give me a kiss," he demands.

"That's coerced consent. It's not real consent." Tired of stretching, I rest my hands on his shoulders. He stares into my eyes and I gulp. Reflexively, I spit out, "Fuck you."

Lucas chuckles again, his mouth curving into a cocksure smile. He releases me and has no trouble keeping me at arm's length as he paws through my bag.

"I know you're behind this."

"Prove it."

I grit my teeth. Damn him.

"The Instagram post."

"Oh yeah? I heard my friend's cat was missing. That has nothing to do with you, kitten."

"If you pull this shit again, I'm not going to turn the other cheek," I promise through my teeth. "You're pissing me off. I'll get you back."

"I eagerly await sweet retribution from you."

He's not even paying attention to me.

"Don't—" I cut myself off when he pulls out my camera. I chew on my lip, struggling with how to get my stuff back without giving up a piece of myself. I don't want to let him know how much that camera means to me, though I suspect he must have some idea. Maybe he figured it out from Alec. "It's fragile."

"And expensive," Lucas comments in a distracted tone. "I looked it up."

The energy racing through my body is hard to contain. I force myself to stand still while Lucas fiddles with the settings. He points it and snaps a few frames.

"I suggest you reconsider your refusal," he says as he clicks through the pictures he took. "I let Alec into my circle, but I can shut him out just as easily."

I suck my lips between my teeth and cast a glance to the side. He's serious. I guess Lucas has no qualms about destroying my brother to get to me.

"Or," Lucas drawls, setting my camera safely on the hood as he turns back to me. The corner of his mouth lifts in a lopsided smile. "I'll just kidnap you again. This time I really will keep you to myself instead of going easy on you. Maybe when I'm done, I'll drop you off in the mountains to find your own way home."

"Easy on me?" My question comes out as an incredulous laugh. "God, you're infuriating."

I still haven't forgiven Lucas for kidnapping me. He's such a crazy asshole.

In a blink, Lucas traps me against the car. He won't let me escape this time without a kiss. I swallow and lick my lips. His eyes fall to my mouth and he mirrors the gesture.

"You're really going to force me?" I whisper.

Lucas grunts and narrows his eyes. He pushes his hand in my hair, twisting the strands around his fingers. Then all at once he steps back.

When he makes no other moves to trap me, I dart to my camera and cradle it to my body. Lucas remains quiet as I check it for any signs of tampering. Everything seems in order and nothing else is missing from my bag.

For the first time since it disappeared, I feel like the tension in my muscles unwinds. It leaves me with a heavy exhaustion as the build up of adrenaline burns off.

Lucas tucks his hands in his pockets and regards me with an unreadable expression. With his tailored uniform, he looks more like a model than a high school student. His hair flops over his eyes when he tilts his head forward.

The beep of the car locks disengaging makes me startle out of the trance. Alec must be close.

I open the back door to stow my belongings, keeping my camera on me. Lucas hovers behind me, his body heat seeping into the back of my blazer. I look over my shoulder and bite my lip.

Lucas props one hand on the roof to support his weight, towering over me.

"I'm not your trophy to win, Lucas. So give it up already." His jaw tics and the corners of his mouth turn down. I scoff and cut my gaze to the side. "I'm never going to want you."

"We'll see about that, sweetheart."

When I look up, Lucas is gone.

Alec walks over and gives me a *what are you doing* look when I just stand there. "Get in, or I'll leave your ass here."

On the ride home my limbs jitter restlessly. Alec shoots me a dour glance when my knee bounces. I chew on my thumb and stare into the middle distance as my thoughts race back and forth, caught between how much I hate Lucas and how much I underestimated him.

I thought he would lose interest in me eventually.

Was I wrong?

THIRTEEN
GEMMA

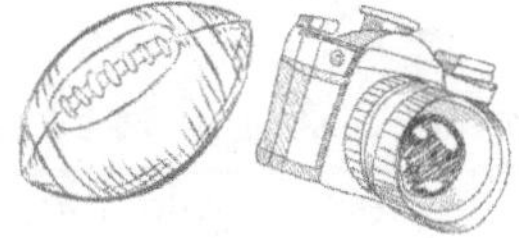

When my last period of the day lets out, instead of heading for the exit, I make my way to my history teacher's office. They called my name on the intercom as the bell rang to see him after school.

A sea of black blazers, silk ties, and plaid skirts fight me as I navigate the halls against the flow of traffic, the other students antsy to leave school.

I have so much homework to do this weekend. I make a mental tally and organize the list into efficient chunks to tackle.

Lucas has been texting me all day with disgusting pick up lines and it's getting old. I scroll through my phone and another pops up at the top of my screen.

Lucas: The school skirt is hot on you. It would look better on my floor.

Stupid jerk.

A beam of sunlight catches my eye through a window and I pause to admire it. The natural light of golden hour is my favorite to shoot. I'm itching to get outside to see what I can capture through my lens.

"Hopefully this won't take long," I mumble as I head into the locker room.

Coach Garcia's office sits in the hall between the girl's and boy's locker rooms. I pause outside his door.

The lights are off inside. I try the door, but it's locked.

"Then why the hell..."

Trailing off, I furrow my eyebrows and retrace my way to the deserted locker room. It shouldn't be empty. Blair is on the girl's track and field team. She told me once that it's always packed right after school with girls from her team and the cheer squad squabbling to get changed for their practices.

I jump when my phone buzzes with a text. It's from Lucas again.

Lucas: Let's play a game today. You run and I'll chase you. Loser has to give me a kiss. (That's you [black heart emoji] [smirk emoji]).

"Asshole." I put my phone away and linger by Mr. Garcia's door.

It's eerie in the empty room, every step echoing. I get the irrational feeling like I'm in a horror movie and my heart rate kicks up a notch.

I spin on my heel to head for the exit. Fuck this. Mr. Garcia can hit me up tomorrow for whatever he needed to see me about.

The lights cut off, sending my heart swan diving into my stomach. I let out a strangled sound, plastering myself against a wall of lockers. I cover my mouth with my hand and try to adjust my eyes as fast as possible to the darkness.

Some jerk is messing around. That's all, I tell myself. *Horror movies aren't real.*

A shadow moves in front of me before I can pull out my phone to use as a flashlight and my skin crawls with an automatic fight-or-flight response. With the hair on my arms raised to attention, I hold my shaking fists in front of me, balled tight to throw a punch.

"Hello?" My voice cracks. "Who's there? This isn't funny."

Taking my chances, I skirt the edge of the room and make a run for the door. The handle won't budge.

"What?" I hiss, yanking on the locked handle. "Are you kidding me right now?"

My heart pounds in a heavy *thud-thud-thud*, clanging against my ribcage. Panicked, outlandish thoughts dash through my head. I'm going to be some mentally unstable whack job's victim and make the news. I can see the lead-in now: *cult member uses corpse of eighteen-year-old high school student, Gemma Turner, to paint Satanic symbols in the locker room at Silver Lake High School.*

"Not today, Satan," I whisper.

Someone grabs me and a yell erupts from my lungs. I fling my arms and legs in wild arcs as I'm lifted from the ground, throwing all of my strength into aiming a blow at the assailant.

"Satan will have to take a number," Lucas rumbles against my ear. There's a smile in his voice. "Caught you. Give me a kiss."

It takes a second for my mind to connect the dots. A pathetic wheeze leaves me.

I kick one last time and thrust my elbow into his side. The angle's wrong and it ends up as a glancing blow that makes him snicker.

Lucas sets me down. After whirling me around, he presses my back to the lockers, looming over me as he plays with my hair.

"Looks like we're locked in here."

I can only make out some of his features—the edge of his jaw, the sharp ridge of his nose, his brow bone. Even without seeing clearly, it's simple to discern how amused he is.

"So get your buddies to let us out. I'm sure they're all laughing it up outside the door. I've got photos to take for my assignment."

"Hmm, no." Lucas drags his nose over my cheek. "I have a few ideas for how we can pass the time. I told you the rules of this game."

We're locked in a stalemate. I have nowhere to go with Lucas trapping me against the locker. I try to shift and he moves his hands to my shoulders, keeping me where he wants me.

He takes my bag and sets it aside.

"I have you all to myself now."

The deep quality of his voice promises dark delights if I give in at last.

Lucas traces my neck, giving it a light squeeze when he wraps his fingers around it.

"No catty retort today? Has my kitten lost all her bite?"

I bare my teeth as he slides his knee between mine, ruining my leverage to stomp on his foot when he kicks my legs further apart. Lucas trails his lips over my cheek, the soft touch at odds with his hold on my throat and his other hand sliding down to my waist.

He nips my cheek and I hit my head against the locker when I startle.

"What do you think you're doing?" I protest, clenching the hem of my skirt at my sides in case he tries anything.

Lucas is so close that I can feel the vibration of his smug chuckle. It pulls a string in my stomach, unravelling a desire I have trouble fighting. His other hand explores my body, wrenching a few buttons open on my shirt to expose my collar bone.

Cool air hits the top of my breasts. When he grazes his nails over my bra, I clamp my legs around his thigh and growl.

"Lucas, back off."

My hands fly to his wrist, trying to tug him off my neck. He won't move, so I dig my nails into his skin.

"Why do you fight me so hard, sweetheart? If you keep that up, I won't make it good for you. I'll have to punish you for being bad."

Those words should turn my stomach and piss me off. Instead, heat spirals down my spine and pulses between my legs. Lucas catches the slight hitch in my breath and his hot exhale ghosts over my lips.

"So that's what you like, huh, baby?" He squeezes my neck harder, to the point it's almost a challenge to breathe. I swallow and my throat moves against his hand. He can feel it. He presses his wicked grin into my cheek. "Oh, yeah. You like that. Is that what you've been wanting? I should throw you over my lap, flip that sexy skirt up and slap your ass until it's raw and throbbing."

Fuck. I don't mean to squirm, but he moves his leg and it connects with my aching center. I grit my teeth and try to tamp down on the cry that threatens to tear out of me at the contact.

A rough noise leaves Lucas and his hand drops to my hip, directing me to repeat the same motion. Surrounded by darkness, the confusing desire he stirs in me is easier to embrace.

With my air caught in my throat, I give a tentative rock of my hips, grinding on his thigh.

I make a small whimper and he answers me with another growl.

I'm afraid to say anything. Reluctant to break this weird spell entrancing us. It makes me feel dirty, but it feels too good to stop.

"You get off on me hurting you. That's why you haven't given up." He bends his head and sinks his teeth into the juncture of my shoulder and my hips jerk in response to the rush of sharp pain mixed with heady pleasure. Heat throbs in my clit. "I bet you've been dreaming up ways to piss me off. Antagonizing me so I can't ignore you."

I want to deny it. He's the one terrorizing me. But I can't find my voice. I can only gasp and rock against the pressure he gives me. His erection prods my stomach, the firmness weirdly fascinating.

"How many times have you wished I'd hunt you down, slide between your legs, push your underwear to the side, and fuck you until you screamed? Did you dream about it in class?"

"N...o—nngh."

A pleased hum answers my attempt to deny everything he's saying.

My breaths come out labored, his tight grip on my neck controlling how much air I get. A moan echoes in the locker room and I think it came from me. The pleasure builds, coiling in my gut and making my legs tremble as I ride Lucas' firm thigh.

If we keep this up, I'm going to come.

"Gemma," Lucas rumbles, his breath teasing my lips.

He's leaning in to kiss me. He stops short and a frustrated sound almost escapes me. I bite it back at the last second, my hold on his wrist flexing.

It hits me like a breaking wave.

I want to kiss Lucas Saint right now. I need it.

I wait for it, straining against him. But his kiss doesn't come. I blink my eyes open—I don't remember closing them—and peer up at him in the dim light. My eyes have adjusted to see better. His face is barely illuminated, but the lust in his gaze is intense and I want to taste it.

Licking my lips, I tip my head up. He stares at me for another beat, and then in a rush his lips crash over mine in a hard kiss.

The last of the tension snaps in a flurry of heat. I don't just let him kiss me...I kiss him back, moving my lips with his, melding my body to his.

Lucas digs his fingers into my hip as we grind against each other. His tongue swipes over my lips, then presses into my mouth. I'm powerless against the harsh way he claims me. The kiss is even more addictive than the first time.

It's like being dragged down by a strong undertow, overwhelming and rolling over my body with relentless force. There's no escape, no choice but to hold my breath and ride it out.

My knees go weak. Does Lucas have to be so good at kissing? I'm not going to give him an award ribbon.

Every last scrap of my resistance falls away.

I'm lost to the rush. The rise of delicious heat pulls me close to the edge. I need more.

I must make a noise, because Lucas nips my lip and adjusts our position so I'm hiked up on my toes with my legs spread wide enough for my skirt to ride up indecently. He angles my body so that when his hips roll against me I can feel his cock pressing against my underwear. A hot flush moves over my whole body. A cry I've never made before gets stuck in my throat. It's desperate, like a wild animal.

Lucas curls one hand around my thigh and drags it higher on his hip as he deepens the kiss. The hard ridge of his cock grinds perfectly against my throbbing clit. I think my underwear is probably soaked. An instinct calls to me, begging me to jump up and wrap my legs around his waist. My inner muscles clench as the ache demands more.

The darkness makes me braver. I give in to what I want and bury my hands in his hair to pull him closer.

"Fuck," he bites out when he pulls back before recapturing my lips.

I'm nearly there. Small cries of need tear at my throat and I tighten my fist in his hair, thrilling at the way he hums into my mouth. I'm about to come. He flexes his grip on my neck and I rock my hips with more force.

So close, I just need—

Lucas rips away from me.

It takes a second for my brain to catch up with the moment. I pant and stumble for balance against the lockers. My skin prickles with heat and the cold metal of the lockers makes me shiver.

"What's wrong?"

I'm breathless, my legs shaky and my vagina tingly from the almost-orgasm. I take a step forward. Lucas takes a step back and I halt.

My defenses fly back up and I collapse against the wall of lockers. It's not because my legs feel like jelly, but I only tell myself that weak excuse to feel better about the mess of emotions fighting for my attention.

"Lucas?"

Intense desire fills his eyes. Instead of finishing what he started, he backs away into the shadows.

The click of the door reaches me and an indignant huff passes my swollen lips. I press my fingers against them. My body calls out for Lucas, my insides twisted and needy with the way he made me feel. After a beat, I re-button my shirt with hasty movements.

Of course it was another one of his mean pranks.

How could I not see it?

Worse, how could I kiss the guy who has been the champion of assholes to me? The guy who stole my first kiss and laughed about it?

The humiliation burns. I played right into his game.

I scrub my mouth with the back of my hand, ignoring the way it feels after kissing Lucas.

The only one to blame for this is yourself. Not your body. You gave in. You let it happen.

You wanted it, my mind supplies.

Why did I like everything he did? Is something wrong with me?

Releasing an angry breath, I close my eyes and touch my throat.

FOURTEEN
LUCAS

Like the first crack in a wall, I've slipped through Gemma's defenses.

I can feel it in the way her gaze tracks me in the days that follow the locker room encounter. It's only a matter of time until she breaks. I've left her to stew. It was obvious how much she needed me to keep going when I pulled back and left her hanging on the cusp of orgasm.

One part of me reveled in the look that flashed across her face. I did that to her, broke down her high and mighty attitude until she was a shivering mess in my hands. Her surrender was beautiful.

Another part of me struggled to walk away. The lust on her face was like a siren's call, drawing me back in to finish her off, to burn myself into her body so no one could satisfy her other than me.

I want her to come crawling to me.

Holding control over her is empty if she doesn't want me to take charge by submitting to me. She'll beg me to give her more.

There's no way she'll refuse me now. I'm in her head like she's in mine. I don't plan on leaving.

Now that I've tasted her, I need more of her perfect mouth and her sexy little sounds. Her fiery attitude and her stubbornness make her surrender that much sweeter. Gemma is an addiction. One that I might overdose on, because I need another hit.

My resistance lasts four days.

The plan to wait her out goes up in smoke.

Instead of Gemma muddling through seduction to get me to dick her down until tears of pleasure stream down her face, she does the opposite of what I expected.

The first inkling that something is wrong niggles at me as I pass Gemma at lunch.

She doesn't pretend to avoid me only to secretly watch me, as she has in the last several days. She doesn't jump into my arms, either. No, instead she meets my gaze head on as she exits the lunch line. There's a self-assuredness in the tilt of her mouth, the determined furrow of her brow, and the brightness dancing in her eyes.

Gemma heads for the table she shares with her weird friend, confidence swinging in her steps. My attention falls to watch her ass. My palms tingle with the desire to touch that perfect ass again.

It's not until the end of the day that I understand why she met me head on at lunch.

I walk out to my Jeep to grab my equipment bag for practice. The weather is nice today, bright and sunny, so I took my prized baby out to show her off rather than my usual ride.

Maybe I drank too much over the weekend or my head isn't screwed on right today. But as I scan for the classic white Jeep Wrangler, discomfort crawls over my skin.

My Jeep is missing.

I swing my gaze back and forth in a faster sweep, searching for my car.

What the fuck? Where is it?

For a second, I can't breathe. My heart pounds in my ears as my nerves spike with a nasty jitter.

"Where the fuck is my Jeep," I snarl to myself, whipping around to look in the rows I've passed.

People call my name, trying to get my attention. Their words go in and out of my ear at the edge of my perception. The only thing I can focus on is killing the asswipe that stole my Jeep.

Rushing over to the spot I *know* I parked in, all I find where a white fucking 1990 Jeep should be is a square of paper. I rub my fingers together as I glare at the note. With a grumble, I retrieve it. I unfold it, accidentally tearing an edge with the force of my actions.

A smiley face drawn in black marker stares up at me.

My stomach twists, followed by a rising surge of outrage. It heats my skin as it builds. The paper shakes like a leaf in my clenched grip.

When I find out who did this, I'm going to kill them. They're dead. This douchebag's life is officially *over* as soon as I find them.

No one fucks with me or my Jeep.

I restored it piece by piece last year. The pride that blooms in my chest when I drive it around isn't because I have a sweet ride—it's because I rebuilt the classic myself. My sweat and blood went into it. Other than Lancelot, it's the most important thing I own. Someone knew that and knew exactly how to cut me deepest.

A few guffaws echo around me and my glare snaps up. They're asking for my fist in their face. Maybe they know or saw something. After I punch them for laughing, I'll beat answers out of them.

It'll feel good to burn off the angry energy surging through my body by punching the shit out of something. Better a face than a brick wall.

I snarl as I turn around and spot a couple of stoners toking up on the hood of a car. They give me lazy smiles and hold up lopsided peace signs.

"Did you see the Jeep that was parked here?" I hardly recognize my voice as I stalk up to them.

"Hell yeah, man. Sweet ass ride," one says, his eyelids drooping.

"Did you see *where it went*," I force out through my teeth, enunciating harshly.

The other stoner shrugs and scratches the beanie swallowing his head.

"It was like magic, dude. One second it was there and the next it was rolling away."

My head cocks and I blink. As I form a fist, my knuckles crack. I grab the closer one by the lapel of his school jacket, the fabric bunching as I yank him closer.

"Details. Now." I do nothing to stop the crazed stretch of my mouth that makes the stoner's eyes widen. "Talk fast."

"I don't know, man! It was hilarious though."

The wheezing amusement breaks off into choked coughs when I give him a rough shake.

"If you don't want me to smash your face, you're going to tell me where the fuck my Jeep went!"

"Chill, man," says the other stoner. He scrambles to pull out a phone and tosses it to me. "Look. See, it's sick, right?"

I catch the phone one-handed, earning a drawn out *ooh* from their appreciation of my dexterity.

Before I look at the phone, Devlin and Bishop jog up to me. They're in their practice jerseys and soccer cleats.

"Lucas," Devlin snaps. "You need to get to the football field *now*."

I don't have the patience to parse the pinched expression on his face. Bishop looks antsy, which is weird for him. With a feral growl, I release the stoner and follow my friends.

I toss a look at my empty parking space.

"My phone, man!"

Rolling my eyes, I throw it at the guy. He yelps as it clatters to the ground. I don't give a shit if the screen cracked. Not my fucking problem.

"Now, Lucas! I'm serious."

"Okay, I'm coming," I grumble as I follow them.

We make our way to the football field. There's a crowd of onlookers gathered around the sidelines blocking our way. Normally a handful of people watch our practice from the bleachers, but this is at least twice as many people.

I rub my brow as I push through to get to the field. Coach is fuming, stomping back and forth, waving his arms in big arcs with his clipboard clutched in one hand. The team stands around with dumbfounded expressions. He throws the clipboard down on the ground, his face red and his eyes bugging when they land on me.

The magnitude of the ire he directs at me makes me fall back a step in confusion.

"Saint!" Coach screams.

I have no idea what's going on until I scratch the back of my head and glance away from him. Then I see it and my blood runs cold.

I found my missing Jeep.

What. The. *Fuck.*

My stomach flips over, relief mixing with an anxious squirm.

My Jeep sits on the football field in the middle of the torn up grass, deep tire tracks arcing in uneven donuts. The damage from the joyride stretches at least thirty yards.

I take a few steps toward it, drawn by disbelief.

My number is painted in black on the hood. The giant number 14 suddenly makes my usual saying seem stupid. Nothing about this scene can be described as *lucky twice.*

On the windshield there's a message painted in huge block letters. It reads: King Midas of Ridgeview, beautiful destroyer.

I lace my fingers behind my head and force out a brittle exhale. My stomach feels like a nest of snakes coiling, writhing, and twining in a constantly moving mass.

"Saint, what the hell were you thinking?" Coach grabs me by the back of my collar as he yells. "Destroying school property—we'll be lucky if we can fix this before the game this weekend. Do you think this prank is funny?"

The cloud of confused discomfort lifts enough for me to take in the way everyone's looking at me. They really—?

I can't hold back the sharp laugh that punches out of my lungs. Everyone thinks I did this myself. They know me even less than I thought, seeing only the persona I wear like a knight's armor around these people.

Why would I do this? It's stupid. Too easy to get caught. Pranks are only worth it when you can get away with it.

Of course the school's golden Saint would be cocky enough to proclaim himself King Midas.

I cut a glance to Devlin and Bishop, hovering with the mix

of people watching. A few people have their phones up, likely recording it all. Devlin raises his eyebrows and gives me a little shake of his head.

He doesn't know how it happened or who did it.

"I can't believe that you would do something so stupid and reckless—this could end our season early! The *championship*!" Coach rants in my ear, his spittle flying. He jabs a finger at the car. "Get that off my goddamn football field or you'll be off the team!"

The vein throbbing on Coach's temple stands out against his purpling face. I'm worried about his blood pressure if I don't get this under control fast.

Holding up my palms, I plaster on a sheepish expression. "I'll take care of it. I'm sorry this happened."

Hopefully the school won't press charges for any damages. Dad would take care of it, he's pretty friendly with the police force. He'll use lawyer-speak to spin it like the harmless havoc of youth. He won't be happy with me, though. Not if it means ending my football career early.

I kind of wish that could happen, minus the blame for this bullshit prank.

My day gets worse when I can't find my keys in my backpack. I shove my hand into every pocket, eyes narrowing by the second.

"Saint," Coach growls in a warning tone.

"I know, I know! I swear, Coach, I'll handle it." My mind is completely focused on getting out of this unscathed. I drag a hand through my hair. Where could my keys be? I turn to Coach Garcia to convince him. "Don't bench me, Coach. I'll do double time to make it up to you. And I'll pay for the sod replacement for the field. We'll be ready for the game."

"Fine." Coach's lips work and he crosses his arms. "Make it happen, Saint, or I'll have no choice but to take this up with

Principal Bishop." He addresses the team. "Suicide sprints. *Now.*"

Their groans have me hiding a grimace. I wish Coach didn't take his anger out on them. This could fuck with our plays if they resent me for a week of grueling practice.

Whatever. I don't have time to deal with that right now. I jog over to Devlin and Bishop, dragging them away from the crowd watching the drama. Some of them compliment me for doing it. My jaw tics and I huff.

"My keys aren't in my bag," I mutter.

Bishop's brows jump high. "Someone seriously got the slip on you."

"Don't rub it in." I rub a hand over my face, pinching the bridge of my nose. "Either of you have any ideas?"

"Spare set?" Bishop suggests.

"No, I think I know someone who might know," Devlin interrupts. His lips press into a thin line as a shadow falls over his face. "Go check the girls' track team."

"Why?" I don't give a shit about the girls' sports teams, so I don't follow his logic. "I need to get a ride to my house to grab my spare keys."

Devlin grips my shoulder. "Seriously. That little bitch with the sticky fingers is on the track team."

"Gemma's friend with the blue hair? The one who picked Eddie's pocket to prove she could?" A thoughtful look crosses Bishop's face. "She's kind of hot in a guilty pleasure way. I'd totally do her in the backseat of my car at her trailer park."

A vicious growl escapes Devlin and he shoves his best friend. Bishop and I both stare at Devlin. He's so carefree that it's odd to see him react so strongly to anything.

"I keep telling you, bro." Bishop slaps Devlin on the back as he steers him toward the soccer field. "You have to let me know when you want to call dibs."

"Shut up."

Devlin gives Bishop a shove.

I have no choice but to head for the girls' track and field practice. It's better than driving all the way home. Coach will work himself into a damn frenzy with the time that would take.

Devlin turns out to be right.

As I approach the area where the girl's track team are doing drills, I find Gemma hanging out nearby. She has two textbooks open as she writes in a notebook. Her honey-colored hair hangs over her shoulder in a thick braid, loose strands framing her face.

Gemma tucks her bottom lip between her teeth, appearing lost in thought. She looks beautiful in the late afternoon light.

I want to fucking destroy her as I stalk over to her.

It takes her a second to look up once my shadow blocks her light. I fold my arms and tower over her.

Once she peers up at me, shielding her face from the sun and squinting one eye, I get fired up.

"What did you do?" I hiss, reaching down and wrenching her to her feet.

Gemma yelps as her things topple to the grass.

"What the hell?" Gemma whisper-shouts, clawing at my arms.

It does nothing to make me release her. My fingers dig harder into her upper arms.

"How did you do it, Gemma?" I demand, bringing my face close to hers.

She gapes at me. She's a damn good actress. I almost believe her act.

"You're squeezing too hard." Gemma pushes my chest, but I don't let go. "Lucas. That hurts."

"You deserve it."

"Quit being such a caveman."

I growl in her face. "You like it when I hurt you, remember?"

Gemma grants me a grunt in return, a little angry sound that stirs something in me, yanking on my impulsive instincts. My grip on her biceps flexes and I eat up her wince as retribution for the shitty afternoon I'm having. It's a step in the right direction.

She's so goddamn stubborn. She makes my veins burn with fire. I'm going to consume her until there's nothing left that isn't mine.

"How the hell did you get my keys, huh? Who helped you?" I'm trying to make sense of how she pulled off her stunt with my Jeep. There's no way she did it on her own. "I only saw you at lunch."

"I don't know what you're talking about."

"Gemma, I fucking swear if you don't tell me, I'll—"

"I did it all alone."

She spits it out in a single breath, then clamps her lips shut. She stares at me hard, but her eyes slide to the track team for a fraction of a second. It's long enough for me to guess her friend helped.

Devlin did call her sticky fingers.

I lift my eyes to the track and field team. A few of them have drifted our way. Even their coach has half an eye on us. Gemma's friend finishes a sprint and her attention locks on Gemma.

"Are you sure you worked by yourself?"

Gemma tips her chin up. "Are you calling me a liar?"

"You're not a liar. You're a fucking demon."

I grasp her chin in a punishing hold and force her head up. I seal my lips over hers and kiss her with a fierce intensity, biting her lips until they open for me.

She whimpers, lurching in my hold with nowhere to go.

Gemma's smart, though. She relaxes and offers her surrender for me to take.

I devour her mouth in front of our audience. No one will deny Gemma Turner is mine.

Gemma's body shakes when I tip my head to the side and kiss her deeper. As soon as she starts to kiss me back, I rip my mouth away from her.

Against her lips, I declare in a snarl, "I own you now. You are mine whenever I want you. If you deny me, I'm going to rip you apart on the spot for touching my Jeep."

Gemma's pulse thrums beneath my palm where I hold her jaw and neck. Her eyes are wide and full of fear. Good.

I press my forehead to hers and narrow my eyes to slits of steel.

"You just destroyed any shred of hope that I'd give you mercy. You're *mine*," I repeat, "until I've bled you dry."

Gemma's throat bobs against my hand with her gulp.

"Go get my keys. Right now."

Releasing her with a shove that makes her stumble, I stuff my fists into my pockets to keep from snatching her back for another wild kiss.

Gemma keeps her eyes on me, like I'm a threat. She's right to look at me like a predator prepared to annihilate her at any second.

"Keys, Gemma."

A small noise gets caught in her throat as she drops to her knees, pawing through the bag I stole once. As she stands, she brushes grass from her black tights. I have half a mind to bring her with me when I get my Jeep, toss her in the back and rip her tights apart to get to her.

She'll learn that I'm in charge.

My keys dangle from her fingers and I rip them away from her. She jumps and hugs herself, eyes moving between me and the people watching. Her cheeks are pink and with a shaking hand, she pushes the loose strands out of her face.

I grab her chin and force her gaze back to me.

"I always get what I want." I pin her with a possessive, dangerous look, willing her to understand. "Don't test me again."

It takes a few seconds, but she lifts her eyes to me. They're shiny with emotion. Staring at me with her bottom lip sucked into her mouth, she nods in agreement.

Gemma Turner has finally recognized that no one denies me. And she won't escape.

FIFTEEN
GEMMA

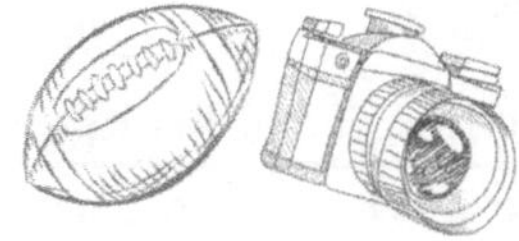

Lucas Saint will take everything if I let him.

I can't let him.

I have no idea what I'm doing anymore. I wasn't going to let him win or get to me...but I can't deny that the kisses are insanely good. He has a talent for breaking through all of my defenses when his mouth is on mine, making me forget for a second why I hate him as I'm swept away on the tide of his kisses.

I'm stuck between anticipating him and fending him off.

After Lucas came for his keys, he attacked me with a kiss whenever he found me at school. Every morning I strengthen my resolve, staring myself down in the mirror as I coach myself to stay strong.

And every day he breaks through and makes me crumble against his body.

I should hate him with every fiber of my being.

But I don't think I do.

My head is so messed up.

There might not be a point in fighting him, other than my pride. Everyone in school already thinks I'm with Lucas. Social proof flies around via mass text, Snapchat, and Instagram all day. People record our kisses and slap stickers and captions detailing their precious Saint's latest conquest.

I overhear bets running for how long I'll last before the next girl gets a turn.

How long until the prude breaks.

That's what they think of me. Even now that the students have backed off a little, it's a double-edged sword to be Lucas' fixation. Instead of being open about it, the bullying from other girls continues in sneaky ways. I'm cornered in the bathroom and told to move on by girls I've never met. They're eager for their turn.

Carter Burns is the only one bold enough to keep proclaiming dibs when Lucas finishes with me. He's only so brave, though. He waits until Lucas isn't around to corner me.

Carter makes my skin crawl. Unlike Lucas, who makes me question my sanity because he's gotten in my head and refuses to fuck off, the way Carter looks at me makes me uncomfortable.

He poses a different kind of threat.

My only safe haven from the absurdity is at home.

I'm doing the dishes after dinner when Alec whips me with a dishtowel.

"Hey!"

Alec dances away when I flick soapy water at him.

"Butt face." I hold two fingers up and wave them between

my face and his. "I'll remember that. I'm watching you. Expect payback."

Alec snorts and props his elbows on the counter behind him. Our parents are watching Netflix in the living room. Other than my Lucas drama, everything feels like it used to. It's a normal family night at home and it makes me smile.

"It's good to see you're making friends." Alec draws me out of my thoughts about our Rockwell-adjacent evening.

"What do you mean?"

"Lucas and everyone. You're getting along with everybody." Alec shrugs and grabs an apple from the bowl next to him. He crunches into it and speaks with a full mouth. "It's a weight off my shoulders. I was worried."

I roll my eyes. "Yeah, you really stood up for my honor or whatever."

"Yeah, well..." Alec has the decency to look sheepish for being a dick. "I'm glad I don't have to stress about you now."

I press my lips together. What I told him before still applies. I don't want to ruin things for him at this school.

If I tell him everything Lucas has done to me, I doubt he'd be so relieved.

"Whatever," I mutter, switching the water off. "I'm going upstairs to chill."

Alec hums and wanders into the living room as I make my way up the staircase.

I pull my hair down from a messy bun and braid it, flopping onto my bed.

A text from Lucas pings on my phone. Grimacing, I open it, like the masochist I am.

Lucas: Tell me what you sleep in at night. I want to know how I should picture you when I jerk off thinking about it. Do you go commando? [wink emoji] Or do you have a cute little sleep set that would drive me crazy? I'm coming to your window tonight to find out.

Ugh. Goddamn pervert. I throw my phone facedown on my bed.

I hate that he can get to me even when I'm in my room.

Every inch of my walls are covered in photos I've taken since first discovering my interest in photography. Behind my bed I have a string of fairy lights and square prints that I update every month. I trace my fingers over the ones I've added since moving to Ridgeview.

Two of them have Lucas in them. I didn't mean to snap photos of him, but he does draw attention to himself. He's impossible to ignore.

I'm a photographer—of course I can begrudgingly acknowledge that Lucas is attractive. The planes of his face probably fit the golden ratio. His face is...aesthetically pleasing.

And it pisses me off.

Pursing my lips to the side, I peel off the prints featuring Lucas from the wall and toss them in the drawer of my nightstand. I grab a pillow behind me and cover my face to muffle my groan.

Stupid Lucas.

I stew like that until I fall asleep.

* * *

I startle awake. It's dark and I'm disoriented.

I think I fell asleep with the light on, vaguely recalling the comforting orange glow of my lamp. Mom or Dad must have checked on me before going to bed. They always turned my light off after I fell asleep when I was little and afraid of the dark.

As I lay there, the dream comes back in starts and stops.

There was an intruder that climbed in through my window. Lucas. It was him and he was torturing me. Touching me. Kissing me.

Blinking a few times, I squirm my legs beneath the covers. My skin prickles and heat throbs between my thighs. I bite my lip and snake a hand down my body, the light touch sparking along my nerve endings. My chest heaves with my muffled gasp. I'm so sensitive.

I dip my fingers into my damp underwear and trace my folds, arching from the bed.

As I touch myself, my dream fills my head.

I lick my lips and circle my fingers faster on my clit, seeking the satisfaction of release that Lucas hasn't given me.

My hips rock up and I pant.

I wanted that kiss in the locker room to go further. I wanted *more.*

"Ah—"

I bite my lip hard and turn my face into my pillow to muffle my cry as my orgasm ripples through my body, the tingling pulses erupting from deep in my core. My limbs flop against the bed.

Blinking at the ceiling, I exhale. I can't believe I dreamed about Lucas. I can't believe I *masturbated* while thinking about him!

I cover my face with my arm.

I shouldn't want him at all. He's a monster.

But...I do want him.

Even if I know it's wrong.

This feels like I'm playing with fire. It'll give me a bad burn if I'm not careful.

SIXTEEN
LUCAS

Having Gemma in my web unlocks something inside me. I'm no longer fine with watching her from afar.

When I see her heading into the lunch room, I bump my fist against Carter's shoulder and dart ahead to catch her.

She's walking with Davis, talking animatedly, her hands moving. It makes it easy to get what I want.

I grab Gemma, tugging her against my body.

A breath knocks out of her and she tips her head back to look at me upside down.

"Lucas." My name is a stubborn sigh.

"Sweetheart." I grin. "Come sit with me."

Her eyes narrow, but she doesn't complain when I slide my arms around her.

"I don't think so."

"Yes. I say so."

Without waiting for an answer, I lift her from the ground and carry her toward our usual table.

"Lucas!"

Gemma's body wriggles and I have to tamp down on the spike of desire spiraling to my dick.

Wolf whistles chorus around the lunch room. I plop down and settle Gemma in my lap. Her face is pinched in a frown.

"What's wrong?"

"This is obviously out of the question." She maneuvers in an attempt to slide away. "Can you at least let me off your lap? Jesus."

"Nope."

The mutiny in her stare is too cute, all flustered and combative. A calculative look passes over her expression.

"I'll stay here on one condition."

"Shoot."

Carter takes a seat across from me with a dopey grin. Devlin hangs back a few feet. He's in Davis' face.

"I'll start sitting with you...*if* Blair is allowed to come, too." Gemma nods to her friend, getting distracted by the sight of her friend and Devlin. "I don't want to leave her alone."

"Sure, whatever." I play with Gemma's hair. "As long as I have you here with me."

Gemma clambers from my lap. I hook a finger in the back of her skirt before she can move away. She shoots me a flat look. Smirking at her, I crook my finger in a come hither motion.

She sighs and bends down while I wrap my arm around her thighs. I steal a quick kiss that leaves me wanting more.

"Now you may go."

Gemma affects a faux simpering tone and bats her lashes at me. "Oh, can I? Bless, what a noble master."

"Don't be like that, sweetheart."

Gemma rolls her eyes and goes to talk to Davis. Once Gemma walks up, Devlin's expression closes off and he comes to the table, dropping beside Carter. Gemma appears to be convincing Davis, motioning toward the table with a pleading look on her face. She succeeds and the girls come over.

Gemma tries to sit next to me, but I wrestle her into my lap again.

"Back where you belong," I rumble into her ear.

Gemma shivers and darts a glance from me to her friend. "*Lucas*. Goddamn you."

Unrepentant, I kiss her cheek.

Davis takes a seat next to us with a stony expression, her shoulders stiff.

"Isn't this cozy," Devlin says lightly.

"Get used to it," I say with a shrug. "We're changing it up."

Devlin's eyes cut to Davis, then slide away. He and Carter get up and head for the lunch line.

"Aren't you going to let me up?" Gemma asks.

She's not exactly comfortable sitting in my lap. Her body hunches in on itself to make herself smaller and she's gripping the table.

"Not a chance." I stroke my palm down her back. "You're right where I want you."

"Well, I want to go buy lunch, so..."

Gemma lifts her brows. I grant her a sardonic tilt of my mouth and wave my hand. Gemma gets up and tugs on Davis' sleeve. The girls go to the lunch line and I trail after them a few minutes later.

Back at the table Gemma tries to take her own seat again. That lasts two whole seconds before I drag her back onto my lap. She sighs in annoyance, but her body relaxes slightly. Good. She's accepting that I'm going to get my way and she should accept it or remain uncomfortable.

"Don't be fooled. I'm not giving in here. I just don't want to waste the pointless energy fighting you right now." She makes a dismissive gesture with her hand. "You're such a caveman. People get it, grr I'm your plaything. No touchie. You don't have to put me in your lap to get the point across. It's not like I'm your girlfriend."

That won't do. I trap her against my body. Leaning in, I brush my lips against the back of her neck and get a thrill from the way she shudders.

"People have seen us do worse than this," I breathe against her skin.

"No thanks to you," Gemma mumbles. "You're a damn exhibitionist. I guess it makes sense. Quarterback. Popular. You love the attention and want people to know how good you have it."

A chuckle rolls through me.

"What we've done isn't even close. When I have you, sweetheart, no one gets to see but me."

I hear it when Gemma swallows at my words. She has no snarky comeback for me.

For a while Gemma talks quietly with Davis, only interacting with me and sometimes Devlin. I think she's trying to play it like I don't have her seated on my lap, acting as if things are normal. She ignores Carter and everyone else at our table.

Carter and I get lost in strategy talk.

I steal one of the potato wedges from Gemma's plate. Gemma growls under her breath and clamps her hand around my wrist. Actually growls.

It's fucking adorable.

"What, you don't like to share?"

I offer her the rest of the wedge and after spending a long second weighing her options, she parts her lips and lets me feed her while she glares at me. It pulls heat into my gut.

"You're infuriating."

"There's my girl."

"Don't you know better than to steal fries from chicks?" Devlin quips as he spins his fork half-heartedly in a plate of pasta. "Her fries belong to her. And your fries belong to her, too."

"My sister's a psycho for fries," Carter agrees.

Devlin props his elbows on the table and pins Davis with a look that promises trouble. He pinches Davis' tray, dragging it across the table out of reach.

"Is this all you can afford, sticky fingers? No fries for you. Just the free lunch program for poor people."

The only indication that Davis hears Devlin are the tight lines around her mouth. Gemma goes stiff in my lap, though. I stroke her thigh beneath the table to soothe her and keep her attention on me.

Devlin picks up a limp piece of broccoli from Davis' tray and scoffs at it before popping it in his mouth.

"It tastes like sadness and food stamps."

Carter cracks up, smacking Devlin's shoulder as he chews and stares Davis down. Gemma scrambles from my lap, elbowing me with a sharp blow to the stomach when I try to keep her where she is. Davis scoots down to give her room to wedge between us.

Gemma's about to fight back. Davis might take it lying down because she knows how our group gets, but Gemma isn't one to stand for it.

Devlin picks up random things from Davis' plate and drops them on the floor. Davis balls her hands in her lap.

I level him with a look, but don't intervene.

"Hey, Devlin. Can you fucking not?" Gemma snaps, poised to fight.

Devlin doesn't acknowledge Gemma and tips the whole

tray off the table. The clatter echoes above the cacophony of chatter in the cafeteria.

"You're used to eating from the garbage, so what's the difference eating off the floor? You shouldn't be here. You don't belong."

Davis shoots a hard-eyed stare across the table as he ruins her lunch. He smirks and returns to eating his pasta.

"Not all of us are born with that silver spoon in our mouths and a no limit credit card," Davis snipes.

Devlin's brows shoot up before he quickly covers, pulling his mask back in place.

Gemma bristles and I grab her around the waist before she dives across the table to deck my cousin for being a little shit.

"What is wrong with you?" Gemma shouts. She turns to her friend and nudges her tray closer. "Here, Blair. You can have the rest of mine." She tosses a dirty look at Devlin. "I've suddenly lost my appetite. The smell of pompous asshole is lingering like a rancid fart."

Davis snorts and takes a potato wedge from Gemma's plate. "That's exactly what it smells like. Old Spice and privileged manbaby tears."

Gemma cracks a smile that I want to kiss. "Can I buy you another tray? They had pizza today. Want some?"

"No, it's fine."

"Are you sure?" Gemma jabs a thumb at Devlin. "We should make him buy you more for trashing your food."

Devlin's lip curls and he moves down the table a few seats to flirt with the girls at the other end. Gemma frowns at him.

It's sweet that Gemma stands up for her friends. But Devlin's got a point. Davis isn't one of us.

"Careful," I warn, tossing a sidelong look at Davis. "Not everyone here appreciates when criminals hang around. My Jeep hasn't been right since your accomplice touched it."

Mentioning Davis' involvement in the stunt with my Jeep makes Gemma's eyes go wide. Her gears turn frantically in search of something to get my attention off Davis. She bounces her gaze between my eyes and then fists the lapel of my blazer, dragging me down to press her soft lips to mine.

As far as distractions go, it's an obvious attempt. A bit sloppy for Gemma's style, but I won't deny a kiss.

For a minute I sit still and let her move against me. When she gets desperate, her tongue swipes against my closed lips and I can't hold back. I lock my arms around her and take my fill, slipping my tongue into her mouth. It doesn't sate my hunger for her, only stokes the flames higher.

When I release her, she's left with a stunned expression.

The bell rings to signal the end of the period. I'm not ready to say goodbye to Gemma yet. As she and Davis go to dump her tray, I follow and lift her up in my arms. She makes an aborted sound of surprise and kicks her legs.

"What are you doing, caveman? I get it, you're stronger than me!"

I exit to the busy hallway with Gemma, carrying her around school. Other students catcall us and slap me on the back like I've won a prize.

The raging green monster roaring inside my chest is impossible to fight. The thought of her leaving my side right now is something my entire body bucks against.

I've never been this possessive over any of my girlfriends before. It's a little crazy.

"I'm sick of everyone else getting to look at you all day," I decide, hauling her body against my chest with ease. "I'm not letting you out of my sight. You're coming with me for the rest of school." I pause to give her a wolfish smile. "I'm in the mood to kidnap you again."

"What?" Gemma blushes a pretty rose color. She writhes like an angry snake. "You're so annoying! Lucas, let me down!"

"Nope." I sidestep the clapping onlookers and drop my lips to her ear. "You belong to me, so I say where you go."

Gemma's jaw works, her bottom lip pouting. I doubt she's aware of her expression, but it makes me lose sight of logic. I want to shove her against the wall of lockers and drive my cock into her as I attack that sexy mouth.

"People can't belong to others," Gemma mutters.

A growl rips through me. I let her drop to the floor and herd her against a locker with nowhere to go. Cupping her face, I bend to speak against her mouth.

"When I say you're mine, I don't just mean you're my girl, sweetheart. I mean I want to own you all the time."

Gemma's lashes flutter as she peers up at me with a stubbornness that I'm growing fond of.

"Do you understand how much I want to sneak up to your window at night to watch you sleep? To slip into your bedroom and touch you? I need to keep an eye on you all the time. If I don't, I'm going to give into this urge I have to take you away and hide you at my house. I'd keep you chained in my room and never let you leave."

Gemma's throat bobs. "You're...crazy."

A hollow laugh punches out of me and I swipe my thumb over her lip.

"Maybe. You make me that way."

I let that sink in for a beat before I kiss her with all the ferocity I held back. She trembles. I love the dazed look in her eyes when I pull away.

She can fight me all she wants with her words, but her actions don't lie. She is attracted to me. She likes it when I kiss her.

"Now. Let's go before I'm late for class."

SEVENTEEN
LUCAS

Bringing Gemma to class with me might not have been my best idea.

It was worth it for the cute look of worry as she sat beside me through two classes. Coach didn't care that I brought a...*guest* to world history, but on our way to the north building one of Gemma's teachers spotted her. They served her detention on the spot for cutting class.

Still, I didn't feel guilty.

Gemma was pissed at me. She socked me in the arm and stalked off while I snickered.

I sent her a few texts, but the only response was an absurd amount of middle finger emojis.

After practice, I hung around to see her in detention. I

planned to give her a ride home, since I saw Alec leaving school with a hot chick riding shotgun.

Gemma refused to talk to me. Stubbornness came off her in waves as she bent her head to hide her face from me when I sat on the desk in front of her. I tucked her hair aside, and she shot me a vicious look.

"I'm done being your little play thing for your personal amusement," she hissed.

My brows pulled together. I left her alone to fend for herself, knowing her brother already left school.

I thought that would be enough of a lesson not to give me attitude, but she ignored and avoided me for a couple of days. It got old real fucking fast.

Agitation rippled through me every time I thought I clocked her honey-blonde hair weaving through the halls, an itch niggling at me with the urge to make Gemma understand the beast she unleashed within me.

When the itch becomes too much to ignore, I recruit Bishop to help me leave Gemma a surprise.

She asked for it, so it's my duty to deliver the punishment she earns.

I wait near her locker between periods, leaning against the wall with my arms crossed. My eyes have been on her all day, but I've kept my distance, far enough not to alert her. She appears at the end of the hall.

Davis is with her. They giggle about something and Gemma waves her hands. That easy smile tugs at me, but I remain where I am, waiting for Gemma to open her locker.

As she opens the locker a flash of red lace pops out first. I smirk at the strangled sound that escapes her. Before she can slam her locker shut to hide what I planted, a strip of condoms and handcuffs fall out, the metal clattering against the floor.

Gemma goes rigid. The locker inches open, revealing the lacy lingerie in its full glory.

"Um," Davis says, tugging on the ends of her blue hair.

"Shit." Gemma drops to the floor to scoop up the condoms and handcuffs. "This—these aren't mine. I don't know how or who—"

"Damn, Turner, you really do like to get freaky!" Carter strolls up and props his weight against the bank of lockers, plucking the condoms from Gemma. "This ain't gonna be enough for us, though."

Fuck. I grit my teeth and it takes all of my self control to remain where I am.

Carter leers at Gemma as she snatches the foil strip away from him.

"You're a pig, Burns," Gemma snaps as she shoves everything into her locker and slams the door shut.

Her entire face matches the red lace for color. She plants herself in front of her locker and crosses her arms.

"Oh, come on, baby girl." Carter touches Gemma's face and she snarls. I ball my hands into fists. "Saint can't have you every day. You can take a night off from his dick so the rest of the team can sample you. I'm first in line."

"Fuck you," Gemma growls, slapping him.

The corner of my mouth lifts at the loud echo of her palm meeting his cheek. It silences the raucous laughter and chatter in the hall.

That's my girl.

Carter might be one of my closest friends, but I will end him if he touches Gemma again.

"Fucking uptight bitch." Carter holds his face. "Fine, Saint can have your wild ass. Bet he needs the cuffs to tie you down so you don't bite."

"Damn right." Gemma takes an aggressive step toward

Carter and he backs up from her threat. "I'd bite your goddamn dick off, Burns."

A chorus of low *oooh*'s travels through the hallway.

"Whatever."

Carter flaps his hand dismissively and leaves.

Davis touches Gemma's shoulder and speaks too low for me to hear. Gemma's eyes land on me and the fire searing my veins rises.

Time slows and the other students milling around the hallway fade away.

We're locked in a stare, the tension of an elastic band threatening to snap. Her chest moves with each heavy breath. My hands flex, the muscles in my arms shifting.

With a violent tug on my resolve, I spring away from my post and turn my back on her. She curses in my wake as I leave for my next class.

* * *

"What the—*holy shit*!" Gemma yelps when I catch her later in the student lot against the side of her CR-V.

Her hand instinctively darts out to defend. I grab her wrist before she can hit me and step closer until our bodies are flush. I rub the soft skin of her wrist with my thumb as I lift an eyebrow.

"Ready to play nice?"

Gemma blinks in disbelief. She tests my hold on her and sighs when escape proves to be fruitless.

"Not in your wildest dreams, you entitled bastard."

My mouth curves and a rough laugh leaves me. I squeeze her wrist, raising it above her head until she has to lift onto her tiptoes to avoid the strain. She winces as I place a lingering kiss on her cheek.

"Be a good girl, or I'll have to keep punishing you."

"You're sick, Lucas." Gemma turns her face away and pushes out a ragged breath. "Damn it. I'm seriously going to file a restraining order or a harassment report if you pull that shit with my locker again. Asshole."

"Which part did you not like? The lingerie? The cuffs?"

Color fills Gemma's cheeks and her eyes flicker to the side.

"Ah." I drag my nose against her cheek. "Then I'm sorry for making you face that desire in school. If I'd known the idea of me restraining you got you so hot, I would've kept that a secret for myself. Mmm." My teeth graze over her soft skin, grinning when she shivers and makes a small sound. I grip her wrist harder. "I like the idea, too. Did it make you wet?"

My other hand skates down her side and teases the hem of her skirt. She doesn't have tights on today. Gemma squirms.

"Lucas..."

"What about right now, hmm? If I filled you with my fingers, would your tight little pussy soak them?"

Gemma licks her lips and makes another quiet whimper. She glances over my shoulder, where other students stroll to their cars and shout to each other. We're hidden away between the cars, her CR-V parked in a back corner.

Releasing her wrist to hold her chin, I draw her attention back where it belongs. My lips seal over hers, making her melt against me with a filthy kiss. Gemma shudders and grips the material of my shirt beneath my school blazer.

While I have her distracted and pliant, I slide a foot between hers and kick her legs apart. I swallow the noise that leaves her, muffling her feeble protest. I kiss her deeper as I slide my fingers up her thigh.

"Lucas," Gemma says in a rush after ripping away from the kiss. "What are you—?"

She cuts off when I reach her underwear. I hold her wide-eyed stare as I tease my fingers over her, tracing up and down her pussy.

"Hmm, you're not wet enough if I can't feel drenched panties." I slip past the waistband of her underwear and bite my lip when she gasps. She's so warm and soft. I glide my fingers over her folds, releasing a dark chuckle when she tries to clamp her legs shut to trap me. "Too late, baby. This is your punishment for ignoring me."

"Lucas!" Gemma pleads, tugging on fistfuls of my shirt. She looks around and whispers, "This is—we can't—not here!"

Gemma bites down hard on her lip to muffle herself when I rub her clit. Her eyes flutter, then snap open again. She shakes her head at me, her words fleeing.

I grin and nod, kissing an uneven trail across her cheek as I move my fingers against her. She tries to fight me, but I know I'm making her feel good.

"You're fucking crazy," Gemma mumbles, burying her face in my neck.

"I know." I make her look at me again. "Don't hide from me."

"I can't! You can't expect me to—*nngh*!"

I adjust my hand to cup her pussy. She's getting wetter by the minute, making sweet sounds as I tease her. I push a finger over her hole and watch the conflict dance across her face.

The minute she surrenders with a tiny nod, I slide it inside and kiss her hard. She opens for me right away, her tongue meeting mine. She's hot and tight and *wet*.

I muffle a groan into her mouth and add a second finger. Gemma's grip on my shirt flexes, her nails digging crescents into my pecs.

My cock is hard, straining in my pants. Heat pulses through me along with a crashing wave of possessiveness. I'm claiming

Gemma right here in the parking lot, against her car, students milling around as they leave.

The only thing hiding us is my body covering Gemma and the cars we're wedged between.

I curl my fingers and Gemma gasps, the hot puff of air hitting my neck as she tears her mouth from mine.

"Lucas." It's a wrecked whisper.

She lifts her eyes to mine. They glisten with the wetness of tears. I swipe a thumb beneath her eye to catch a tear and suck it into my mouth. A shuddering breath rattles out of her as she presses her hips against my hand, seeking more.

"Hey."

Gemma freezes, eyes wide with the terror of being caught, but I don't stop. I keep pumping my fingers in her without missing a beat as Devlin walks by the row of cars we're in. I don't break eye contact with her, twisting my fingers. She swallows around a restrained moan she can't quite contain.

"What's up, man?" A wild grin crosses my face as I block the sight of what I'm doing to Gemma from Devlin as I call out to him. "Beers on the boat later?"

"Yeah, sounds good. I'll meet you at your house." Devlin's voice drifts away as he moves on. "Later."

Gemma's lip wobbles and more tears fall. I fuck her faster with my fingers, eating up the flush in her face, the shine of wetness in her eyes, the way she shivers and parts her lips for me.

Her pussy clenches on my fingers and a deep rumble resonates in my chest.

"That's it, sweetheart. Are you ready?" I whispering to her between kisses. "Are you going to fall apart on my fingers?"

Gemma mewls.

"Come for me, baby."

Her body tenses and she wraps her arms around my neck.

"Fuck, fuck, fuck," Gemma grits out in a choked whine.

As I thrust my fingers inside her, she shudders around them. She gasps against my mouth.

"All of your sounds belong to me and me alone. No one else gets to hear them."

Gemma nods and presses up to kiss me. I give it to her, twisting my fingers again. She seizes up as her orgasm hits. I want to keep going until she's a delirious oversensitive mess, wringing orgasm after orgasm from her until she can't come anymore without sobbing.

I reel my urges in. Soon. But not here in the school parking lot.

"Good girl," I rumble as I slow my movements, savoring how wet she feels.

Gemma breathes harshly, resting back against the car. She's flushed and wrecked and fucking *gorgeous*.

I pull my hand from beneath her skirt and flick my tongue over my shiny fingers, tasting her. A hungry groan leaves me and I lean my weight into her body, pressing my cock against her.

I stroke her face as I touch her lips. She darts her hooded gaze up at me. I pet her lip and nudge inside her mouth. She hesitates, then closes her mouth around my finger and sucks her own taste, tongue curling around my finger.

Another groan leaves me and I tear my hand free to kiss her. When we part, I rest my forehead against hers.

"You're mine, sweetheart. Don't forget that."

EIGHTEEN
GEMMA

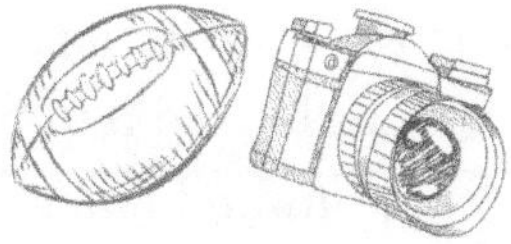

"Gemma?" Ms. Huang stops me as I'm packing up after class.

"Yeah?"

She smiles and tucks her short black hair behind one ear. "Could I ask for your help with a photo assignment? Usually I have two students from newspaper and yearbook club take photos, but they're both absent."

"Okay, sure." I sling my bag over my shoulder. "I have my gear with me and I'm free."

Ms. Huang lights up with a relieved look. She claps her hands together.

"Wonderful! It's nothing major. You'll be covering the boy's football team practice after school today. The school paper needs your files by tomorrow morning for their story if you can meet that turnaround time."

By some miracle I keep my face blank.

I know I just agreed, but I should refuse. Make up some important appointment I just remembered.

"Sure." My voice is robotic. Foreign. "No problem."

Inside, my shoulders sag. Once I leave the room, I let out a big sigh.

"Of course," I mumble.

Hitching my bag higher on my shoulder, I head off to my doom. I stop by my locker and drag my feet the closer I get to the football field. At least there will be other people around. And I won't have to get close. The telephoto lens is the greatest invention ever for avoiding social interaction.

Parking myself by the fence surrounding the field, I set down my things and busy myself with my camera settings while the football team jogs warm up laps.

It's not until Lucas runs by and our eyes meet that I admit I've been afraid to be alone around him since he touched me in public. I sink my teeth into my cheek as he grants me a smug look.

"Hey."

That's all he says, voice deep and amused. One word and my insides dive-bomb for a crash landing.

Lucas' buddies chuckle and give him playful punches.

Lucas demands attention without asking for it, making me track him as he rounds the bend of the track. It's like I'm hypnotized by his muscles bunching with each stride. He makes running look easy. His legs pump effortlessly and his skin glistens with a sheen of sweat.

He looks like a damn god. It's no wonder everyone worships him.

The rest of us are lesser beings. We should be thankful he graces us with his presence.

Heat blooms in my face and I will it away.

Come on, Gemma, I think, *can't get flustered over a boy jogging.*

Except I am. God, I so am.

I shake my head at myself.

The pack circles the bend in the track again, Lucas leading the bunch. His attention flashes to me and the corners of his mouth curl up as he picks up the pace. He shoots me a wink.

"Let's go!"

The guys all answer him with yells that must make them feel like they can take on the world. They follow Lucas as he runs off.

Alec is the only one that overtakes Lucas in the straightaway. He pumps his arms in the air and I lift my camera to snap the frame. A fond smile curves my mouth as I check the back of the camera.

My brother's so competitive. He can't let the captain beat him in a race.

I settle into a rapid-fire rhythm of capturing action shots. The team completes two more laps before they move onto the field for practice. After running some drills, they start a practice scrimmage.

I don't think it's warm enough, but Lucas peels off his shirt. Half of the guys follow for a shirts and skins game.

What? Don't they have like—practice jerseys for this?

Lucas seeks me out. He blows me a kiss and flexes for the camera, showing off tan skin, broad shoulders, and sculpted abs. He adjusts his shorts, the indent of muscles at his hips visible.

Oh my god.

Lucas peeks at me with hooded eyes and cocky smugness. I press the shutter and let out an unsteady breath.

It's impossible to deny his physique and athleticism as the game gets underway. Lucas snaps the ball in a spiral through the air and calls out plays. The ripple of muscles in his arms and shoulders as he throws the football is alluring. I lose track of how many shots I've taken, absorbed in documenting the grace and strength of his body as he moves around.

I take a break to scroll through what I've captured so far. There are almost 350 pictures on my memory card.

One image on the card calls to me. I zoom in on it. I already know I'm going to make it a black and white. Lucas is about to throw, arm poised as he skillfully grips the ball.

Those hands were on me. Touching me. Making me come.

You're mine, sweetheart. Don't forget that.

Heat bombards me, my skin buzzing with a hot-cold feeling. When I raise my eyes to the practice, Lucas is watching me.

It's like he knows all the thoughts spiraling through my head.

I gulp and fuss with my leather jacket, wrapping it tighter around my body.

The fire doesn't leave my body. It only burns hotter because Lucas keeps looking over at me.

He doesn't even have to pay attention to the game. His team is winning. He's that good.

I make a feeble attempt to distract myself, playing around with the shutter speed and aperture. It doesn't work for long. I blink through the viewfinder when Lucas moves into the foreground.

Lifting my head, I find him jogging over to the fence with a gleam lighting up his eyes, making them appear bluer. That sparkle spells mischief.

"Enjoying the show?" Lucas is barely winded. The shine of sweat and his messy hair pulls at my belly. He motions for my camera. "Can I see?"

"Um."

It's difficult to find composure being so close to Lucas while he's shirtless. Mashing my lips together, I flip my camera to show him the back, clicking through the last few photos. They're of Lucas. Most of the images on the card feature him.

I couldn't help myself.

Lucas seems pleased, but then a shadow falls over his features. It's visible for a scant second before he brightens again.

The flash of emotions tug at my instincts. I want to know more about that Lucas. Why did he look almost...sad to see himself throwing the football?

"You got my good side."

"That's because your bad side isn't on the surface." I take my camera back and set it down on my bag. My hands rest on the fence. "I guess I'm the only one that knows about that side."

Lucas purses his lips to the side and squints at me. He steps up to the fence and cups my face. Before I know what he's planning, his lips are on mine.

He kisses me in the middle of practice, stinking and sweaty.

And I give in.

I lean into the kiss, my fingers flying up to curl in the damp hair curling at the nape of his neck. Distantly, I'm aware of the other guys on the field howling like wild coyotes. A whistle blows.

Lucas laughs into my mouth and I dig my fingers in his hair.

He pulls back, his breath a hot puff over my lips. "Come with us after practice. We're going to the lake to hang out."

"Oh. I, uh—I don't know."

Lucas caresses my face. There's a beat where I'm torn between the face of my entitled tormentor and the guy that makes my head foggy when he kisses me.

"I should really—"

"Come on," he murmurs. "It'll be fun."

I cling to reluctance for another minute. He gives me another kiss that steals my breath away.

Then I'm nodding before the daze clears.

"That's my girl."

"Saint! Get your loverboy ass back to practice!" Coach shouts, interrupting the moment.

Lucas winks and jogs away. As I watch his back, I wonder what the hell I just got myself into.

My whole plan this year is to avoid and fly solo. Hanging out with Lucas and his friends is the exact opposite.

* * *

The sky is ablaze with the fading afternoon light over the lake. Music thumps from the dock's fancy speak system. I'm sitting next to Alec out of some misguided sense of seeking a security blanket so I don't vibrate out of my skin.

This isn't my scene anymore. I don't have any interest in fitting in with the girls in bikini tops and chunky cardigans with cut-off shorts and flirty shirtless football players. Everyone is drinking and swaying to the beat as they giggle.

It pulls up the uncomfortable memories. It's not as bad as the first time I came to Lucas' house to pick up Alec, when it was crowded with people and everything was happening in excess. But it doesn't totally go away, either.

Lucas disappeared inside a while ago and now I'm floundering for a reason to be here. I should've said I couldn't come.

My palms prickle, an itch irritating my skin that I can't satisfy no matter how many times I scratch my palms raw.

I'd much rather chill with Lucas' sweet pug dog that trots from person to person to see who will pet him. I click my tongue to call the dog over for the third time since we arrived.

He's a chill, pudgy little dog that helps keep my freak-out at bay when I stroke his fur.

Further down the dock, Carter has been messing around with the girl he's trying to get with, teasing her about throwing her overboard. Something about the way his hands keep sliding down her sides makes me think of Matt and my breath grows short as my throat dries out.

Elena Morales from math plops next to me, her sleek black curls bouncing.

"Come on, Gemma. I love this song!" She grabs my hands and for a second I have to work hard to quell the instant urge to snatch them back. Missing my startled expression, she pulls my arms like a marionette while she rolls her body in time with the music. She laughs and falls against my shoulder. "Girl, loosen up. It's a party! Let's get lit."

She can hardly get the words out before she holds up a blunt, cracking herself up.

I offer a feeble smile and scoot closer to my brother. Alec flashes me a look with his eyebrows jumping up, subtly motioning to the cute girl perched in his lap. Sighing, I hold up my hands and shift away.

Fine, I get it. Twin sister hanging around like a shy toddler clinging to the only familiar person. Total cockblock.

My bad.

Carter appears in front of me and offers a hand up. "Come dance with me."

"I'm good."

"C'mon, we'll have a good time. We're going to get a contest going. Let's show everyone else up. I know you've got moves. You've got that vibe."

Carter runs a hand up my arm. My whole body screams *no.* I shrug him off with a violent movement and turn back to Elena.

She's the only nice one of the whole bunch. There's been no real shift from the vicious insults, accusations, and assumptions slung at me by the same people trying to act like we've been friends all this time.

Lucas comes back outside hauling a cooler.

"Sweet salvation, Saint," Carter says.

Lucas' biceps flex. He beams at his friends as they cheer.

Unbelievably, I'm relieved to see him because Carter steps away.

"Brought rations." Lucas drops the cooler beside the bench where Elena and I sit. He runs a hand through his hair as he stands. "Come and get it."

I grab my bag and shift away from the cooler before the vultures swoop in. The sky is really pretty right now, so I stroll to the end of the dock and sit down. Pulling my phone out, I take a few shots of the beautiful scenery.

I pick one out, edit it, and post it to Instagram with the caption *peaceful views tonight* along with a handful of hashtags. A few likes pop up.

This is nicer. I don't mind the raucous laughs and chatter over the music wafting in the air from a safe distance behind me as I sit alone.

It only lasts a short time before Lucas drops beside me.

"The party's back there."

"Not really my scene." I wet my lips and rub my palms against my knees. "Parties and I don't exactly have a great track record. I'll probably catch a ride home with Alec when he's ready to leave."

Lucas frowns and peers out at the lake. It reflects the purple and pink tones of the sky and the black silhouette of the trees and peaks.

"Don't leave yet." Lucas props his arm on his bent knee and

rubs his chin. He gives me a sidelong glance. "Come out on the boat."

"The boat?"

"Yeah. Just you, me, and Lancelot."

At my confused look he lets out a short laugh and whistles. The pug dog's nails clack against the dock as he bounds over with an adorable bark that sounds more like *bork*.

Lucas points at the dog leaning into his face, snuffling and licking his chin. "Lancelot."

That's adorable. My stomach unknots from the anxiety-induced cramps.

"Lancelot. Well, sir knight," I address the dog, giving him a scratch that makes him warble and wiggle his butt, "I suppose I can agree to a ride on your steed. Er, ship? What did knights call their boats?"

Lucas shrugs, chuckling. He watches me through his lashes, mouth pulled up in a lopsided curve. It's an unfairly handsome look on him.

"I don't really know. My Arthurian legend obsession only lasted long enough for me to name my dog."

"It's a good name."

"Come on."

Lucas climbs to his feet and offers me a hand up. Air catches in my throat when I look up at him, back-lit by the golden rays of sunset that catch his hair. I allow him to haul me up.

"Going out for a ride," Lucas calls to the group as he leads me into the boathouse.

The boat is beautiful, a cream color with tan cushion seats and chrome detailing. The steering wheel at the front is wrapped in white leather, surrounded by gleaming controls.

Lancelot jumps aboard after Lucas like they've done this a

thousand times. As Lucas starts the engine, I glance back at the dock.

"Coming, sweetheart?" Lucas has a hand out to me. "Let me show you my world."

"Is this the part where girls think you're smooth for quoting movies as you invite them aboard for a private make out sesh?"

"More like they're impressed because I have a boat. Now step onto the magic carpet."

"It's a boat."

"Then jump down the rabbit hole with me."

Lucas snatches my hand and tugs, catching me in his arms when I trip into the boat. I feel the pleased rumble coming from his chest. After a tense beat where we stare at each other, he sets me down and unmoors the boat.

Not knowing what to do with myself, I sink onto the cushioned bench, tucking my bag in my lap and hugging it.

It hits me that I'm going off alone with Lucas. Can I really trust him? He didn't hurt me when he stole me away for a joyride, but it wasn't a pleasant experience.

Maybe I'm some kind of crazy.

Maybe I'm kidding myself with my insistence on staying away when I keep running headlong into Lucas and all the dangers he represents.

Maybe...I'm trying to recreate what happened to me with Matt out of some misguided, subconscious effort to control my past and change it. Like fighting back.

But that won't change anything. My heart skips a beat when the engine purrs. If I want to get off the boat, now's my chance. I dig my fingers into my messenger bag and take measured breaths.

I don't get off the boat.

Lucas coils the rope, then sits at the wheel. Lancelot barks happily and hops on the captain's chair, squeezing behind Lucas.

They're both relaxed. It helps me loosen my claw-like hold on my bag and calm down from my brief mental spiral.

He navigates us onto the lake with little effort, looking completely at home. Once we clear the boathouse and coast out into deeper water several feet away from the shore and the dock, Lucas opens up the engine and we fly across the water.

An embarrassing squeak leaves me at the sudden speed and I grip the leather seat. The front of the boat cuts through the glassy surface of the water as Lucas takes us further away from his house. I watch his hair whip around.

The lake is huge, much bigger than I realized from looking at Google maps. There are dips into the bank as the whole lake curves around part of the mountain.

The worry that crashed over me slips away in starts and stops until the beauty of the lake soothes me into hypnotic wonder.

When Lucas slows down and I don't fear toppling from the boat, I take out my camera. For a while we're both quiet as I take pictures. The lake is even more beautiful from the middle of it all.

At the center of the lake, Lucas cuts the engine and plops next to me. I have a hawk in my viewfinder, tracking it as it arcs across the vivid sky. After I press the shutter, I sit back in my seat and take in the scenery.

"It's really pretty out here."

"Yeah."

"It must have been nice growing up with this as your backyard."

Lucas hums, absently playing with my hair. Lancelot leaps onto the bench and settles between us. I pet Lancelot's ears as Lucas stretches his arm behind me.

Everything about him seems to melt into a serene state out here. His legs fall open and his face loses the tension. I didn't realize it lingered around the sides of his mouth and the corners of his eyes until it dropped away.

I think this lake might be his happy place.

It's much more relaxing out here with the three of us rather than the party environment back at his house. My erratic demons—the memories that haunt me—retreat to the shadows of my mind.

We sit in a surprisingly comfortable silence as nature surrounds us, birds chirping in the trees, fish and frogs swimming in the water, a distant coyote calling early for the approaching dusk.

Lucas sinks his fingers in my hair and my eyelids flutter when he combs through the strands, massaging my scalp.

"What will you do after school?"

The question startles me out of a peaceful trance.

"College. With photography there're degrees, but I don't know what I want my focus to be. I like landscapes and the tranquility of waiting for the moment."

Lucas hums in acknowledgement, returning his hand to my hair. More thoughts spill forth before I've decided if it's okay to tell him or not.

"I also like taking pictures of people. But I don't think I want to direct them—fashion and studio portraits don't really speak to me. I enjoy watching and holding out for the right moment...the right emotion."

"So you'll try out a bunch of different things to find what feels like the right choice for you?"

I shrug. "I guess so. It'll be cool to intern with a news outlet to cover marches and protests, or maybe I can network with local wildlife photographers. Who knows, maybe I'll end up shooting for NatGeo."

A laugh leaves me in a huff at my ambition.

"Either that, or you could end up as a seasonal photographer for a mall Santa."

I smack Lucas in the chest without any heat. He snatches my hand and holds it to his lips.

"God, I hope not. The mall near my old house in Colorado Springs makes the photographers dress up like elves."

"I bet you'd look cute in red and white striped tights."

Lucas smirks and trails his eyes over me.

I shove at him and he curls his arms around my shoulders to hold me closer as he messes with my hair.

"Have you always taken pictures?"

Lucas tightens his hand in my hair for a moment after asking, then releases it along with a strained exhale.

"Well, not always. I've enjoyed pictures since I was a kid. My parents got me this toy disposable camera one year," I explain, shaking my head with a wry smile when I remember the abstract shots I came across when I packed up my room to prepare for our move. "But I only got into it more seriously in the last couple of years. It wasn't something I'd given much thought to, other than the camera app on my phone during family vacations or selfies. Then..."

I trail off for a second, not ready to fully admit to him how healing photography was for me after Matt and that party. Photography allowed me to remove myself from a situation while still experiencing it. I can capture what happens without being involved.

It's a safe barrier between me and the world around me.

Picking at the zipper on my jacket, I continue. "I got it more —why people love doing it. I prefer looking from the outside."

As long as I have a camera in my hand, I'll be happy.

I peek at Lucas in my periphery. His expression is closed off and inscrutable, but I discern the flash of pain in his eyes.

"What about you? I suppose you're off to make a name for yourself in football." I pat my camera on the cushion beside me. "You look good doing it. From a photographer's perspective."

Lucas doesn't answer. His jaw works and he opens his mouth like he has something to say, but then he blows out a breath and ruffles his hair. He's not as forthcoming about his future aspirations as I am.

"Yeah. My dad and I are taking a trip soon to visit University of Utah and University of Washington. He says he wants the best for me."

"Cool."

Lucas lifts a brow and looks at me from the corner of his eye. "They have impressive football programs."

"...Cool?"

His perplexed expression makes me crack up. I lose control of it quickly, gasping for air as my stomach muscles cramp. My laugh echoes across the peaceful surface of the lake and into the treetops.

It cuts off abruptly when Lucas leans over and kisses me. He cups my face, thumb brushing my cheek as his lips glide over mine. I loop my arms around his neck and part my lips for his tongue.

Unlike our other kisses that scorch the earth like wildfire, this one glows like a warm ember.

It's like he's trying to say something with the kiss that he couldn't put into words.

Lancelot barks, interrupting us by putting his little paws on my thigh.

"Oh, do you want some loving, too?" I ask after pulling away from Lucas.

I pet Lancelot as Lucas mutters. All I catch is *kidding me* and *jealous* as he rubs his mouth.

"Should we head back?" I suggest. "It's getting pretty dark."

Part of me is hesitant to give up this side of Lucas so soon. He's...different out here. Is this who he really is beneath the cruel bastard and the cocky quarterback?

"Are you afraid of the dark, sweetheart?" Lucas rasps the question against my ear, stirring my insides. "I'll show you the light. You don't have to worry."

"I'm not afraid."

I feel the curve of Lucas' mouth stretch against my lobe. His voice drops lower and it shudders through me when he says, "Then I'm not trying hard enough."

NINETEEN
LUCAS

As I'm passing the computer lab after the last bell of the day, I catch sight of Gemma alone, outlined in the artificial glow of the computer. Perfect, I was about to text her.

I redirect and duck into the lab. Enlarged photos fill the screen in an editing program. She must be working on an assignment.

Grabbing a rolling chair, I approach her. I drop onto it, straddling it backwards and fold my arms over the backrest.

Gemma ignores me and keeps working.

The corner of my mouth lifts. If she didn't learn her lesson about ignoring me last time, I'll gladly repeat the lesson. My attention drops to her green and white plaid skirt and my mind fills with images of making her come again.

I wanted to when I had her on my boat. Badly.

I prop my chin on my arms. "Are you going to the party this weekend?"

Gemma doesn't answer. I reach out and tickle her side, getting her to squeak and scoot out of range. She gives up trying to ignore me and flashes me a glare that's all bark and no bite.

"No."

She still won't surrender to my control. I can't say I'm mad at it. It's thrilling when she challenges me.

"No? That won't do. I think you mean yes."

"I'm serious."

"Nah, you're not."

"I am!"

Gemma huffs and returns her attention to the computer, clicking through her photos. There's a black and white of a building downtown. It's a favorite of mine. I've sketched it a few times. The high contrast in the photo highlights the sharp lines of the building.

"What will I do without my girl at my party?"

I thread my hands in her hair. It's not in a braid today, so I take advantage. She hums and tips her head into my hand for a second, enjoying the touch.

"I'll file it away that you like your hair played with. It'll make things fun later. What about hair pulling? That really gets me hard."

"Ugh." Gemma swats my hand away. "I'm *not* your girl."

I drop the playful act and sit up.

"You are."

When Gemma scoffs, I grab her chin and yank her face to meet mine. I look at her fiercely, grinding my jaw.

"I want you there. If you don't show up, I'm gonna be pissed."

There's nothing I can do to hold back the possessive growl

in my tone. I wouldn't bother, anyway. Gemma is mine. It's about damn time she stops fighting me on that fact.

"Sorry to disappoint." Gemma jerks out of my hold and taps a few keys on the keyboard. "You'll have to get over it."

With that, she grabs her stuff and leaves in a rush before I can untangle myself from the rolling chair. I stand there alone, breathing through the annoyance.

When the clock on the wall catches my attention, I head for practice.

She will learn she's mine. I'll make sure of it.

* * *

The lights on the field make my head throb. Or maybe that's the hit I took from the other team's massive douche on offense that plowed me over.

Carter is supposed to have my back, but he didn't catch the guy in time.

The cheerleaders rile up the crowd in the stands, Marissa leading her pack. I pace the sidelines and squirt my drink into my mouth, gasping as I gulp it down.

I'm done, but there's still two quarters to play. The marching band is winding down their performance on the field. I wish Coach would put in our reserve. Even my fingernails ache.

I'm stuck here playing the person everyone wants me to be.

Alec nods to me as he passes to sit on the bench.

I peer up at the stands and scan for Gemma. Coyote Girls hang as far as they can over the rails to shout to the Silver Lake High players. Proud parents, students, and local fans cheer us to victory. The one person I want to see is missing.

She never comes to the games. I don't expect to find her, but something in my body is calling out for her right now.

It might be my fucked up heart.

I have to suck it up, like she said earlier. I can't have everything I want.

"We've got this in the bag, cap." Carter slaps my back. "Sorry about that last play, bro. That dude is a fuckin' tank."

"Feels like it even more when he takes you down."

Carter chortles like I'm joking. I'm not.

I'm so tired. I wish I was at home with my sketchbook and Lancelot sitting on my feet.

Instead I'm stuck here, with everyone looking to me to bring it home. If I don't get us a win, we lose our chances at the championship playoffs. For every other dude on the team that goal is serious. It's in their eyes, the fierce need to win broiling beneath the surface. I see it when they look my way.

For me, I don't give a shit, but it's still weighing on my shoulders as the team captain.

I crave the heady relief of washing my hands of this and walking away. Something stops me and keeps me tethered every time I think I've worked up enough courage to pick what I want instead of what's expected of me.

This game used to be fun when I tossed the ball at the beach by the lake with my friends. I played because I had a good time. The weight of growing assumption for me to keep winning—to aim for impressing drafting scouts and go pro—slowly crushes me into the damp grass beneath my cleats.

No one cares what I want. They only see my potential because I'm good at the game. It sucks all the enjoyment out of it when there's pressure to make it my career.

What does it say about me that I've sometimes wished for a serious injury to take me out, to keep me from playing for good? But fate has been a kind asshole to me, leaving the decision in my hands. I just have to be strong enough.

I lean against the fence and Carter stands beside me, flirting with the Coyote Girls cooing at us above in the stands.

"Wave at the fans." Carter nudges me. "Look how adoring they are. Easy pickings for a post-game blowjob. Get your dick wet, man, you look like a fucking grim reaper right now."

I hide a grimace and give a half-hearted wave to the girls just so Carter will get off my ass. Gemma fills my head again. I flick a glance over the stands, despite knowing it's pointless. She's not here.

"Did you tap that sweet piece of ass yet? Mm, she's so fine."

"Just about." I cover my tight tone with a cocky laugh. "I've got her moaning all pretty for me."

"So where's the goods? Get that proof before someone else slides in and takes the pot from you." Carter waggles his eyebrows and pushes the sweaty hair back from his head. He lights up and grabs my jersey to tug me closer, like he has a secret. "Oh! I've got a great way to hide your phone so you can record it while you fuck her. I tried it out last weekend, worked like a charm. Remind me to show you after we win tonight." He flashes me a salacious smirk. It turns my stomach. "I swear, this chick squirted all over my dick."

I sincerely doubt that. I've seen first hand what Carter's like with girls.

"Yeah, man. Cool."

We used to hunt for frogs along the lake's edge, skip rocks, and scrape our knees on the trails. Somewhere along the way, I blinked and Carter changed from the kid I befriended in middle school.

"What's the deal? You're losing your touch. Usually you'd have pounded her and been done within a week. I heard Marissa complaining to Elena. She's getting all antsy that you're still avoiding her."

I have no idea what Marissa has to do with any of this.

Carter leans closer. "What's your next plan for taking that chick down a peg?"

I falter, searching for an answer I don't have. There are no other plans. I haven't thought about the bet I started in a while, too absorbed in Gemma. I don't care about destroying her anymore. I just want her.

My eyes cut to Alec on the bench. I suck on my teeth and endure the roll of guilt moving through my chest. I feel a little shitty talking about his sister with him right there. Hopefully he can't hear us.

"I'm going slow with her. Making her fall for me."

Carter guffaws. "Sick, brother. You're ruthless. You're not just going to break that prude, you're going to obliterate her. She'll never think twice about crossing you again."

A shadow of doubt punches me in the stomach. I started all this. This is my fault for turning my friends on her.

But I can't regret it.

Not when it drove Gemma into my arms.

She's mine now and I'm not letting her go.

The darkness runs deep in me. It's not just possessiveness over her. This is more than that.

I want to keep her to myself all the time. I wasn't kidding when I admitted to her I fantasized about watching her through her bedroom window.

"Yeah..." My jaw works and I push off the fence. "Come on, let's go over the next play with Coach before halftime ends."

Carter follows closely, grating on my mounting agitation.

I need everyone to back the hell off.

More importantly, I need Gemma. I'm restless as fuck and she's the only thing that'll cure it. She's like my drug and I'm taking hit after hit without control.

It scares me a little, how deep she's burrowed under my

skin and become my obsession. I thought I knew where I drew the line. When it comes to Gemma, I'm barreling across every one to get to her.

I throw myself into the rest of the game to get Gemma out of my head.

TWENTY
GEMMA

The tires crunch on the gravel as I pull up to Lucas' house. A distinct wave of déjà vu has me pausing next to a pearl white Escalade. The scene is just like before: people spilling onto the property from every crevice of the house—on the deck, the wraparound porch, all the way down to the dock.

No brave (crazy) skinny dippers this time, the chill of fall firmly settled over Ridgeview.

This whole week has been raining on and off. The ground is soggy when I get out of the car, the dampness lingering like an oppressive fog in the air. The wet chill seeps bone deep, wrapping around me like inescapable tendrils of ice.

It feels like the rain might pick up again at any second, the sky ominous and heavy with clouds, no stars in sight.

Despite how badass I often feel in my leather jacket, it was not the right choice of outerwear tonight. Shivering, I hug my body.

Thanks for making me get out of my cozy sweats, butthead.

This is the second party I've been sent to so I can drag Alec home.

I wait expectantly for the sick gurgle in my stomach, but it doesn't come on as strong as the first time I was here. I wonder if it has anything to do with the boat ride with Lucas that's been confusing me since it happened.

Pushing through the crowd of drunken party goers still isn't easy, upset stomach or not. I do a quick scan of the deck and come up empty on Operation: Alec Retrieval.

Everyone is celebrating the three day weekend.

Elena is playing beer pong with the same football player, his hands on her hips as he bounces to the hip-hop beat blasting from the sound system. She's killing it. The shot she sinks is sweet as hell.

"Gemma!" Elena spots me and bounds over, abandoning the game. "Jackson, it's all you for a bit, babe!"

The football player waves. "I've got this."

"I'm so glad you came!"

"Don't get too excited. I'm here to pick up Alec, that's all."

Elena gives me a dramatic pout. It won't change my mind.

"Have you seen him around?"

"Inside, I think. Or check the porch, he was getting close with Sasha Pierce a while ago."

I think that's the name of the girl that sat in his lap when we all hung out on Lucas' dock last week. The one he's been circling every time I see him.

"Cool. See you later. Good luck on your game."

Elena holds her arms high in the air like a cheer pose. "Jacks and I rule supreme." She thumps her chest and affects a deep dude-like voice. "Undefeated."

I snort and give her a high five before venturing into the house to search for Alec.

This time I find him in the living room dancing between two girls—one of them that cheerleader, Marissa. She's draped over his back, her manicured nails roaming his chest as he gazes up at the vaulted ceiling with glassy eyes. I don't see Sasha around, but Alec's face twists in a sour expression. He sways heavily from side to side, offbeat from the music.

"Are you *drunk*?" The accusatory words spill from me before I can process what I'm seeing.

He's worse for wear, more blasted than I've ever seen. I haven't touched drinking since the night with Matt, not interested in letting my guard down. But Alec has never gotten this sloppy.

He looks messed up as fuck.

"Alec."

Marissa wrinkles her nose at me, sneering, "Chill out. What are you, his mom?"

A heavy sigh hisses between my teeth.

"Can you not see he needs you two to hold him up right now?" I reach for Alec, but he lets out a belligerent slurred grunt and shoves me away. "Alec, what the fuck, dude? Mom's going to kill you. She's lenient, but this is too far."

"S'not," Alec mumbles, turning his glower on me. "G'way!"

"Okay. You need, like, so much water. And to lie down." I sniff the alcohol wafting off him. It seeps out of his pores with his sweat. "Ugh. And a damn shower. Why did you do this?"

Marissa and the other girl dig their claws in.

"Don't be such a prissy bitch," Marissa's friend snipes in a mean girl tone. She's like a carbon copy of Marissa, wearing a matching black leather miniskirt and a purple sweater. Their hair is even in the same high ponytail with a cheer bow. I decide to call her Marissa 2. She pinches my brother's cheek. "Alec's fine. Aren't you, baby?"

And *there's* the roil in my stomach I've been waiting for. My lip curls and I tug my brother away from them.

"If your definition of fine is unconscious and unable to consent!" The force of my own traumatic experience bleeds into my anger. The girls step back. "Go dance with someone else. I'm going to get my brother some help."

"Whatever," Marissa mutters. Most of her attention is on the guys in the corner where Lucas and his cohort hang around a keg. "Come on, Kel. There's better dick hunting over there."

Marissa and Marissa 2 hold hands and leave me to support all of Alec's weight when they push him into me. I grit my teeth and awkwardly maneuver him over to the couch. No one offers me a hand or does much to get out of my way.

"Need some help?"

I jump at Lucas' voice, not expecting him to materialize behind me when I just saw him across the room. I attempt to shrug, but it's impossible with my brother weighing me down.

"Here." Lucas takes Alec's other arm and together we get him settled on the couch. Alec groans. "Yeah, I hear you, buddy." Lucas pats Alec's shoulder. "I'll get him a water bottle."

"Thanks."

I fuss with Alec's hoodie, tugging it over his head to help cool him down.

"If you puke on me, you officially owe me for life."

Alec lets out a garbled moan. His face is flushed and he can't keep his eyes focused for too long. I mop the sweat from his brow with his sweatshirt.

"What did you get yourself into?"

Alec grumbles incoherent strings of words under his breath. Maybe in his head the rant makes sense, but all I hear is gibberish. I can't take him home like this. Mom and Dad will stop trusting us to be responsible and go back to the helicopter parent act.

Our parents will kill him, and then probably come for me.

Maybe Alec can crash here for the night. This house is huge, there must be plenty of empty bedrooms.

Once I make sure he's taken care of, I can get out of here and return to the three day Netflix marathon I have lined up.

Arms come around my waist and for a second I think it's Lucas, but my eyes land on him in the kitchen, retrieving a water bottle from the refrigerator.

My mind goes haywire as hot beer-scented breath covers the side of my neck.

"Hey, little Turner," Carter slurs. He's drunk, too. The acrid stink of his breath makes my spine go rigid. "You come to party with us?"

"Nope. Just helping my brother."

Carter rumbles something I can't decipher, too hyper aware of his hands pressing into my stomach. I pretend like I'm dancing to break free of his arms, but he tightens them around me and makes an encouraging sound.

"Yeah, girl. Show me what you've got."

Jitters thrum across every inch of my body, my skin crawling with Carter's hands on me. Hands that map the same path Matt's did. It sparks a weird sense memory and I gasp.

Carter mistakes it for one of pleasure and presses his half-hard dick against my ass, grinding on me.

"N-no," I wheeze.

My freak-out peaks in a visceral reaction when Carter tries to pop the button on my jeans. I sink my elbow into his gut, landing a good shot. He doubles over and my feet carry me away as tears blur my vision.

I can't breathe, even when I hit the cold, damp air outside. I don't stop running, the harsh echo of my pained panting loud in my own ears.

My natural instincts have me in a chokehold as I flee. I'm scarcely aware of what I'm doing until I'm speeding in my car down the road that leads out of Silver Lake Forest Estates. Tears roll down my face and strained gasps claw at my throat. My headlights cut through the deluge of rain that started back up when I was inside.

Escape, escape, escape, my brain screams at me.

God, I fucking left Alec there. He needed my help and I just *left*.

My knuckles hurt from how tight I grip the steering wheel. No matter how much I shout at myself to turn back because I'm overreacting, I can't turn around or slow down.

The car wobbles ominously as I take the next bend too fast. I suck in air and force myself to slow down so I don't die on the mountain roads in the pouring rain.

"Come on, Gemma," I coach myself in a ragged voice that is so strained it sounds foreign.

I ease off the gas, fighting against all of my muscles locked in place and shrieking to *get away*.

Around the next bend I slam on the brakes and emit a wild scream. A huge downed tree blocks my escape, its uprooted base reaching for me like gnarled fingers ready to trap me.

My eyes go painfully wide and I force my foot down harder to stop before I crash into the tree the CR-V careens toward.

"No, *shit*, no, no, no!"

The tires squeal, then spin out. I scream as the car skids in a violent fishtail, certain death right ahead of me. I'm either going to slam into the giant trunk of the tree or send the car careening over the slope of the mountain.

By some sick sense of luck, the wheels grind against the

gravel on the narrow shoulder and I'm jolted as the CR-V scrapes against a sapling, halting at last.

My chest rises and falls with my wheezing gasps as the sound of large raindrops relentlessly pound the hood in front of me, smoky fog swirling in my headlights.

I didn't die.

Holy. Fuck.

I sniffle so hard that my nose burns from the sharp breath and unclamp my hands from the wheel to wipe my eyes.

The adrenaline seems to leave me all at once. I start to cry harder, thunking my forehead against the wheel. My hands hurt from the death grip on the wheel. My heart beats so hard and fast that I'm actually a little worried I might be going into cardiac arrest.

I should call Mom and ask. She'd know as a nurse. But then I'd have to find my voice and I don't think that's happening any time soon. Sobs scratch my throat raw.

It takes a few minutes for me to get most of it out of my system, the explosion of emotion a combination of everything that happened in the last twenty minutes. Once I've calmed down a little, I swipe at my eyes and peer through the dull roar of rain.

There's a deluge of muddy water and debris sloshing across the road on either side of the tree. Fuck. A mudslide must have uprooted the tree.

The road is completely blocked. This is the only road out from Lucas' lake house.

That means everyone else is stranded, too.

On shaky legs, I get out and stumble like a newborn deer toward the tree that could've taken my life. The icy rain soaks my clothes in seconds, pelting me in big droplets. I blink through it, my lashes clumping. My hair plasters to my face when I try to shake the rain from my eyes.

At the edge of the stream, I stop, nervous about getting too close. It looks like the worst of the mudslide has already torn through the slope and across the road, but I don't want to chance it.

As I turn back to my car, I'm blinded by headlights whipping around the bend up the road. Fear grips me once more, the irrational thought that someone's come to hunt me down and finish what started back at the party paralyzes me.

The headlights are those bright blue halogen fuckers that feel like knives in your eyes when they hit you. I hold my hands up and squint as the car slows to a stop.

"Are you okay?"

The driver that shouts at me as he gets out is Lucas.

"I—yeah."

The rest of my words catch in my throat, impeded by the lump of emotion lodged there. I'm thankful Lucas is still a few feet away when I emit a whimper, trying to hold back more emotion bubbling over.

"Jesus, Gemma. What the hell made you drive off in the rain like that?" He closes the distance between us, holding a raincoat over his head like he rushed out of the party too fast to put it on. He tries to cover both of us with it and touches my face. "God, you scared the shit out of everyone. Don't you know how dangerous these roads can be?"

Lucas drove out in this torrential rain storm. For me.

My heart swells in my chest and it's hard to breathe for an entirely different reason.

He brushes the droplets and wet hair from my face. My lip gives a tremulous wobble, the impending threat that I might break apart again at any second looming over my head.

"Are you okay?"

I shrug, then nod mechanically, but my shuddery breath is

what he focuses on. Lucas peers over my shoulder at the downed tree.

"Looks like you're not going anywhere tonight."

"I want to go home." My voice is cringe-worthy, all petulant. I can't help it. I was just put through a traumatic experience and faced with a double whammy of unwanted sense memories followed by a near-miss car crash. "I wasn't supposed to be here."

"Come on." Lucas tugs at me. "You're going to catch a nasty cold. Let's go."

I stand my ground, my body locking up.

"No. I want to go home."

Logically, I can see I have no way to return to my house short of going all Bear Grylls and hiking down the mountain to the valley. Going back to Lucas' place means being warm and dry.

Yet I fight him as he tries to guide me to his car.

"No!"

Lucas stops and exhales. "Gemma. Get in the goddamn car."

"No! I want to go home right now! I have to!"

My irrational shouts are partially drowned out by the rain hammering the ground.

He scrubs a hand over his face. "I'm taking you home!"

"You're not! You're taking me back there! I don't want to!"

Nothing I'm saying makes any sense as I pound my fists against his chest in a fruitless effort to make him listen. It's like my mind is associating his house with my past, even though I know in my head that's not true. Everything in me bucks against the thought of going back there. Going back is bad.

An unimpressed expression takes over Lucas' face. He looks two seconds from being done with my bullshit.

"It's pissing rain, Gemma! It's not safe out here at night."

I wave my arms around. "It's a gated community! You have your own private security!"

"Get in the car," he repeats, pointing at his Range Rover. "If you don't get in on your own in the next minute, I'm going to make you."

A wild shout leaves me and I whirl around to run away. Lucas curses and grabs at me, but I slip free.

"Gemma, what the fuck?!"

He chases me. I pant as I scramble off, no idea what my plan is. The muddy water sloshes over my shoes and I take a leaping jump for the fallen tree, the bark scraping my palms with a rough sting.

A hand closes on my ankle and drags me back.

"Are you fucking insane?"

Lucas growls as he tries to wrangle me. I cry out, both in frustration and pain as freedom is stolen from me and my hands drag against the sharp bark. Lucas lets out a yell of surprise as he slips in the mud.

We go down in a crumpled heap, overbalanced by the weight of two drenched people. I catch his accidental elbow to my stomach in the fall, knocking the wind from my lungs. Lucas also hisses in pain, his fingers digging into my thigh. I think my knee landed on his balls.

Nudging me off him none too gently, Lucas lumbers to his feet. His face is set in a steely scowl. Wasting no time and offering me no choice, he hoists me over his shoulder in a fireman carry. I struggle feebly, mostly on principle, but whatever overcame me before is evaporating, logic setting back in.

Mortified, soaked to the bone, and covered in mud, Lucas gets me into his car. My burning palms throb from the scrapes. I stare out the window through the rain.

"What about my car?"

A muscle jumps in his jaw as he buckles my seatbelt with a

jerky movement. He covers me with the rain jacket, tucking it around me. "I'll take care of it."

He slams my door and gets in on the other side, shifting the car into gear. He whips us around without a word to me.

On the way back up the incline, he punches the controls on the dash to turn the heat on high. It helps with my shivering and chattering teeth. He also calls Devlin to come pick up my car, then reports the blocked road to the community's security personnel.

As we're about to reach his house, he cuts a sharp look my way. His face has become a mask that I can't penetrate.

"This time I guess I'm kidnapping you for real. I'm not letting you go."

I gulp and shift against the seat, my wet clothes heavy and giving me the weird sensation of being trapped.

When we arrive, he appears at my door before I've even undone my seatbelt. Most of the people that were outside huddle on the wraparound porch and have crowded into the house to keep out of the rain. I don't fight him when he takes me by the hand and leads me back into the house.

"Great news!" Lucas announces in a booming voice as he navigates through his house. He pauses on the stairs to address the party. "The road out's blocked. Let's keep this party going all night!"

Cheers erupt and the music pulses louder.

Lucas squeezes my hand and drags me upstairs. I don't see Alec on the couch anymore.

"Where's Alec?"

"Devlin helped me get him to a room right after I went to get him water. Devlin said he's sleeping it off. He'll be fine." He tosses a narrow-eyed glance over his shoulder. "I came downstairs to find you, but you weren't here."

I roll my lips between my teeth and avert my eyes. Lucas

leads me up two flights of stairs. We pass framed family photos on the wall that all feature Lucas smiling broadly on worldwide vacations, with Lancelot and Devlin, in his football gear. He was a cute kid.

At the landing, Lucas pauses. His shoulders twitch. In one smooth move, he pushes me against the wall and holds my face between his hands.

"Don't ever fucking scare me like that again."

I stare into his eyes, my heart thudding. I give him a slight nod.

Then he kisses me, crashing our lips together with a wild edge that I have no defense against.

TWENTY-ONE
GEMMA

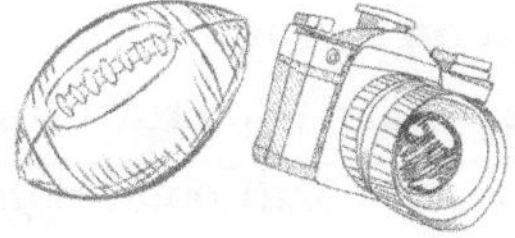

"As soon as it's warm, get in," Lucas instructs. "Can't have you catching pneumonia."

The bathroom connected to his room is like a hotel suite with marble floors, dark granite countertops with a glass bowl for a sink, and live edge wood shelves. He starts the shower and retrieves a first aid kit from a hidden cabinet. Lucas drops the soft case onto the counter and peels off his shirt, dropping it with a wet slap in front of the hamper.

I shift my weight. My palms are tender.

Lucas pauses and raises an eyebrow at me when he finds I haven't moved from the middle of the room.

"Did you get water in your ears?"

I shake my head.

Lucas points at the curtain. "Then get in the goddamn shower."

He turns his back on me again with a huff, muttering to himself. He doesn't appear to be leaving me alone in here. I follow him with hawk eyes as he sets a few fluffy gray towels on the rack beside the shower.

"Um..." My arms wrap around my middle when I have his attention. I can tell his patience is teetering on the edge of snapping. "Are you—Were you going to shower after me?"

A hot pulse spreads from my belly as he rakes his eyes over me, the protective concern overwritten by blatant desire.

"I'm not leaving until you get in the shower." He pops the button on his filthy jeans and shoves them off, displaying muscular thighs and curly golden leg hair. "Now get in. Or do you need me to take control again?"

"No." I bite my lip. "Can't you turn around or something?"

Lucas stalks across the bathroom, right up in my face. He exhales through his nose, then peels my jacket off. He yanks on the hem of my thin, damp sweater and it comes up over my head. My lips press together as I shiver in a black cotton bralette and ripped skinny jeans.

The only sound in the room is the hiss of the shower and our breaths as steam fills the room and we stare each other down.

"Boots next."

I swallow past the thickness of my tongue and toe out of my boots. His fingers go to my jeans. When I freeze, Lucas' calculating gaze moves over my face. He tips his head to the side, then turns around to lean against the wall.

"Hurry up."

Squinting at Lucas to make sure he doesn't peek, I wriggle out of the rest of my clothes. It's a little weird to stand naked while he's turned around. I cup an arm over my breasts and splay a hand in front of my vagina. I realize as I step into the shower this is totally pointless, but it helped in my head.

As soon as the hot water hits me I let out a faint moan of relief. It hits me then how the cold clings to my body.

Over the rush of the shower, I can hear Lucas moving around.

Is he seriously going to stay in the bathroom while I shower?

TWENTY-TWO
LUCAS

The white noise of the shower running calms me down, the lingering fear of seeing her hurt fading.

I take my time stripping out of my briefs, giving her a minute to warm up. My skin feels slimy after peeling off the dirty clothes, smears of mud and dead leaves stuck to my neck and hair. I grip the edges of the sink counter.

Gemma pisses me off so much, but at the same time I have never felt the icy grip of terror like that before.

When we were out in the rain and she was fighting me I just...shut down. I had no way to hold back my carnal need to control the situation—to control her. All I knew was that I needed to keep her safe. The best way to do that was to bring her home with me.

I might never let her leave, not until I'm satisfied she's safe.

There's a whisper at the back of my mind that the only thing keeping her safe is me. It's making me think up dangerous, crazy ideas.

A soundless laugh shakes my shoulders.

I really am some twisted king, keeping the kidnapped princess in a pretty cage.

My stomach clenches and I can't wait another second. I need to see her, feel her in my hands to know she's out of harm's way. I peel the curtain aside and climb into the shower with her.

"Wh—*Lucas*!"

Gemma's indignation and flustered fury greets me. It's adorable how her mouth pops open and closes, her brows flat over her green eyes. She scrambles to cover herself, snagging a small washcloth that hides nothing. Grimy water sluices off her body and swirls around the drain. There's a twig tangled in her hair.

My heart skips a beat as we stand there. I keep my eyes level with hers, but desire claws at me to look down and take her in.

Holding eye contact, I turn her around by the shoulders so she faces into the spray.

"Wash."

"But—"

"We're just showering. I'm not going to do anything to you. Relax."

Releasing a ragged noise and peering at me from the corner of her eye, she tentatively goes back to cleaning up. Once the stiff pinch in her shoulders eases, I grab the soap and reach over her shoulder to wet it. I catch the curve of her holding air in her cheeks from her profile and my lips twitch.

"There's a stick in your hair."

"Oh. Can you...?"

My fingers thread into her wet strands to free it. As I keep her distracted with stick removal, I swirl the soap bar against her back where she can't reach. She makes a small sound, but doesn't stop me from washing her.

The shower fills with the fresh scent. She's going to smell like me. That possessive thought tugs deep in my groin and I have to lock my jaw to keep from pinning her to the wall and grinding against her smooth skin.

Gemma relaxes for me, her head drooping forward as I massage her back. I take my time dragging my fingers all over her back, teasing close to the swell of her ass. Gemma's breath catches.

"Which one is the shampoo?"

"That one." I point it out and take it from her hands. "I'm doing it. Stay still and close your eyes so you don't get soap in them."

Squirting a dollop into my palm, I work her hair into a steady lather, going slower than I did with her back. Her breathing is uneven, but her body loosens.

Gemma falls into a quiet trance as I take care of her. Every minute my hands are on her, every fiber of my being sings with satisfaction.

After I finish, I direct her beneath the shower head to rinse.

"Turn around," I rumble against her ear when she pulls her head back.

Gemma snaps out of the relaxed trance.

Her hesitation is a palpable thing. I trace patterns over the curve of her shoulders with my fingertips. I stand close enough to feel the kiss of her flushed skin against my chest.

"Turn around and look at what you do to me."

Gemma spins to face me, holding my gaze with wide eyes. It takes her a few seconds. I can see the thoughts rippling across her expression as she works up the courage. Then her eyes dart down to take in my erection. They widen more and her lips part.

A gravelly chuckle leaves me.

"That's what you do to me, baby." I touch her chin. "Now, give me your hands."

Her eyes fly to my face. "I'm not jerking you off!"

Snorting, I circle my hand around my cock and give it a lazy pull.

"That's not what I meant."

Gemma watches my hand move on my dick, transfixed by the languid way I squeeze and stroke. She sucks her lower lip into her mouth, making the desire to put her on her knees and fuck her pouty lips roar to life. I can't hold back a slight groan. With one more tug, I release my dick.

"Give me your hands."

Gemma places her injured hands in mine and I turn them. I hold her attention as I carefully clean the scrapes. Gemma hisses when I wipe a deeper cut, but keeps a brave face. When I'm done, I kiss both of her hurt palms.

"My turn."

Gemma opens her mouth to argue with me. Once again, she assumes I'm only after one thing here. I'm not a mindless asshole, I can multitask.

I nudge her aside and step under the spray with a satisfied hum. My palms glide over my body as I quickly wash the muck away.

Gemma coughs and her glance falls away. I smirk and turn my face into the water, raking my fingers through my hair.

That's right, sweetheart. We're only biding time here.

Gemma will finally give in and all will be right with the

world. I'll prove once again that no one refuses me. More importantly, that *she* can't refuse me.

Gemma is the only one I care about making that point to anymore. She could only hold out for so long.

My mouth waters with the tantalizing taste of success. It hangs in the air, the sweet flavor of her impending submission to my control. I'm going to take it.

Once I'm clean, I step out of the shower.

"Stay in as long as you want. I'll put clothes out for you."

I kick at her dirty pile of clothes in the middle of the floor. After I dry off, I tug on a pair of briefs.

The water splashes against the tile as Gemma stands beneath the showerhead again. She hums and it draws my attention. The curtain is sheer. I can see her silhouette, the curve of her hips and tits as she runs her hands over her hair.

Blowing out a quiet exhale, I sit down on the closed toilet lid.

The shower shuts off a minute later.

"Can you hand me a towel?"

I rest my elbows on my knees. "Get out. They're right next to the shower."

"I'm naked," Gemma grumbles.

"I'm aware." I snort, imagining the expression on her face. "I've already seen. You're not going to surprise me. Hell, the curtain's practically see-through, so I can *still* see all of you. Every sexy inch."

An indignant little mutter comes from behind the curtain. Then Gemma gets out in a streak of bare skin, covering her body with her arms. Well, trying to.

I can still pretty much see everything. Covering her nipples doesn't change that I know what they look like hardened and speckled in droplets. I lick my lips at the desire spiking in my groin.

She gets a towel wrapped around herself, cheeks flaming and eyes avoiding me. I shake my head wryly and head for the door to my bedroom. I pause to wave at the pile of clothes on the sink.

"There's stuff to wear. Bring the first aid kit. I'll be in here."

The lock clicks once the door shuts.

"I've been able to pick that lock since I was twelve." Gemma's grouchy response is muffled. "Devlin and I were bored. We watched a YouTube video to learn."

"Stay outside!"

I hold my hands up in surrender, even though she can't see. I sit down on the floor and lean against the wall next to the bathroom door.

All Gemma has to wear are the clothes I gave her.

My insides flutter when she steps out of the bathroom with the first aid kit. My t-shirt hangs from her shoulders, exposing her collarbone. The boxers are like baggy shorts on her. She looks so good in my clothes.

She looks *mine*.

The wave of possessiveness that overtakes me is an unstoppable force.

"Shit," I groan. "Come here."

I clasp her wrist and drag her down to straddle my lap. She lands with a soft *oof*, legs splayed on either side of my body.

The first aid kit tumbles to the floor beside us, but neither of us move to get it. We're too wrapped up in each other.

A rumble builds in my chest. I want to do everything at once—kiss her, slide my hands up the sides of the boxers, fuck her.

"Lucas," she whispers after a tense beat.

I know she feels how hard I am. I love the little blush that creeps up her neck.

"You can't escape now, sweetheart. I'll lock you away in my tower."

Gemma's lashes flutter when I grind my cock against her. I go again when she doesn't protest, greedily gliding my palms everywhere, cupping her tit through the t-shirt. I breathe in her warm skin, getting a rush because she smells so good with my scent on her body.

A hush falls over us, blanketing the room in a bubble. The intense anger and fear I felt in the last hour, coupled with that shower with her, has me in a state of heady arousal.

We go slow like that, hips rocking sporadically. I skim my fingers up her legs and nuzzle into the crook of her neck. Gemma releases a breathy half-moan when I guide her hips down to meet the hard ridge of my cock through the thin barrier of clothes. I hold her there and rub against her clit.

Her mouth falls open and I lean up to capture it.

As she sinks her fingers into my damp hair, I feel like she's giving herself to me.

We grind on each other and make out with sloppy kisses. It's a slow build that's driving me crazy.

The world could go to shit outside the door and I wouldn't stop or care, as long as we keep going.

My hands squeeze her ass as I push against her. Gemma shudders above me. She's close to coming from this. Fuck, I am, too. She drives me wild. I grin against her mouth.

Be mine, I think.

"If we keep doing this, we're either going to need a second shower or I'm going to pull those boxers to the side and slide into your wet pussy."

Gemma stills. She's quiet for a long minute as I kiss her jaw.

"Don't," Gemma breathes.

A growl rips from me. "What?"

Why is she still saying no?

My cock throbs as she bucks against me, her body seeking the release she's denying herself. I clench my teeth and grip her hips tighter, grinding my cock harder against Gemma. She moans, panting against my neck.

"Please. I want to stop."

The heavy tension that blankets the room becomes suffocating as we both sit there, breathing harshly. I tumble her from my lap and she lands next to me on the floor. I crawl over her, caging her with my body.

Gemma's mouth tightens at the corners.

Ice slides down my spine. She still thinks I'm some kind of fucking rapist. It's written plainly on her face: she thinks I'll ignore her and take what I want anyway.

That's not me.

She flinches when I move, like she expects the worst. I glare at her as I grab the first aid kit.

"Show me your palms."

Gemma blinks, confusion shadowing her face. "You're not—?"

My whole face contorts and my nails dig into the area rug.

"No, I'm fucking not, Gemma! Jesus!"

Gemma's chest heaves, her lips mashing. Regret wavers on her face for a second. She turns her head to the side, unable to look at me as I straddle her and tend to her injured hands. It's a comical sight with my aching cock tenting my briefs. I apply ointment and climb to my feet.

I get dressed without paying attention, ending up in a pair of gray sweats and an old Rocky Mountain National Park shirt.

Without saying anything else, I leave the room. The door bangs behind me when I yank it shut. I stand outside in the hallway, flexing my hands.

Why does she still think the worst of me? Did I not save her damn life tonight?

I hang in the hallway, waiting for my erection to go away. The wild sounds of people having a good time drift upstairs.

I press my palms to the door frame and hang my head as I listen to Gemma rustle around the room. When it goes quiet, I assume she got in my bed to go to sleep.

TWENTY-THREE
GEMMA

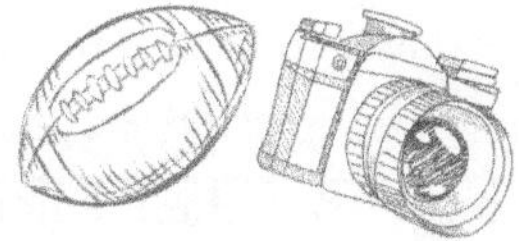

It's warm when I wake up to the sun peeking through tree branches outside the window.

My head swims for a second and I struggle through disorientation when I find myself in a strange bed and a room that isn't mine. The shelf of football trophies makes last night come back to me in a rush. I drag in air and flop against the blue sheets.

All of my muscles twinge in protest.

The sun is bright as it peeks over the horizon. The storm clouds driven away in the night.

Lancelot is curled against my thigh, snoring. A smile breaks free as I reach to stroke his back. He stretches and falls asleep again.

The other side of the bed is warm and unkempt, but empty.

A discarded Rocky Mountain State Park t-shirt drapes over the end of the bed.

I bite my lip. I remember waking up at one point when it was still dark. I don't know if it was one of those dreams that feel real or not, but strong arms surrounded me, holding me close against a solid bare chest.

Did Lucas sleep with me?

I'm still wearing everything he gave me last night. I slide my legs against the soft sheets and worry my lip with my teeth.

My body still prickles with an undercurrent of something. It's a restlessness that seeks satisfaction. Even the sheets against my skin feels nice.

Last night was a lot.

I don't know what made me stop. It felt good in the heat of the moment. A deep need settled in my gut and I kind of wanted to give into more. But then when Lucas voiced it...I don't know. It was like being in the storm again, rain dumping down on us.

Lancelot grouses when I get out of bed.

"I'd cuddle with you all day if I could, bud." I stretch my arms overhead and my spine realigns with a satisfying pop. A tender ache lingers in my body. I actually slept pretty great for the insane night I had. The bed is really comfortable. I could sleep longer, but not here. "I've got to get home."

I hover at the end of the bed for a minute. My clothes aren't on the bathroom floor, I can see the bare tile through the open door. I don't know if I should go downstairs in what I have on, or if I should try to find something else.

The mirror across the room catches my attention. I decide *hell yes* I need more clothes on right now. God, I don't even want to think about how I look wearing Lucas' oversized t-shirt and boxers.

Not only that, there are mild bruises visible on my thighs and arms.

My palms are still red, but not as sore as last night when the scrapes were fresh. I don't know which of the bruises are from trying to climb over the downed tree or from Lucas digging his fingers in my skin.

As I look for something to wear, I poke around his room. It's as big as the master bedroom at my house, with cedar accents and a rustic mountain style. The wood floors are mostly covered by a large gray and blue patterned plush area rug. The big window has a bench seat beneath it, where a couple of books have been left.

There's a desk next to the window, beneath the trophy-packed shelves. There are some sketch pads. I lean in to get a closer look at the Instax prints pinned to the cork board. In one Lucas is on his boat with Devlin and Connor Bishop. There are a few others—Lucas and Lancelot at the peak on a hike, Lucas and Marissa in their sports uniforms and on the beach at a lake.

A squirrelly feeling skitters through me. Frowning, I read the trophy plaques to distract myself. They all say Lucas Saint, quarterback, and the year. They date back to when he was a kid.

I find a big hoodie in the corner to pull on along with a pair of silver basketball shorts. I have to tie the drawstring tight and roll them a few times so they don't fall down. Most of the bruises are hidden. The hoodie comes almost to my knees and hangs over my hands, but it's warm and smells nice. Because I'm alone, I press the neckline to my nose and sniff, smiling.

Feeling a hundred percent better with more clothes on, I creep downstairs to raid the kitchen for coffee. The house is still and quiet.

I like mornings. The hush that stretches as the world wakes up is peaceful.

People sleep all over in puppy piles. I come off the bottom step and take in the remnants of the party. It's like a Titian painting of a bacchanal.

I tiptoe through the room and pause when I come around the corner to the open kitchen. Lucas is there, shirtless. He's the only other person up. He holds a steaming mug in front of his face as he watches me.

The world seems to hiccup to a stop around us as I stare back at him, my heart tripping over itself.

The aroma of fresh brewed coffee calls to me.

Gathering myself, I shuffle into the kitchen. Lucas' attention flicks down to his SLHS Coyotes hoodie I have on. His hoodie.

It's different when I have to face him wearing his clothes. Heat fills my face.

When I slip past him to look for a coffee mug, he plays with the ends of my hair.

My hunt for a mug stops when Lucas sets his cup down with a *clink* and corals me against the counter. I turn to face him. He plants his hands on either side of the granite, his forearms flexing as his head dips.

Lucas looks at me, eyes hooded, and lets out a rough, sleepy hum that pierces into my stomach and makes warmth pool there.

Between the hoodie and having Lucas close to me, his scent surrounds me. I'm lost in the foggy water with no way out. The only way forward is to cling to Lucas and hope he won't drown me.

The dream-memory that hovered on the edge of reality clarifies. He definitely held me in his arms last night.

"Morning," I say in a hush. "Uh, did you take my clothes?"

He grunts and presses his hips against mine, trapping me

against the counter. I'm pulled in opposite directions by my head and my heart.

"I like the way your lips pout when you're asleep."

He traces my mouth as he tells me this. That one small touch earns a throb between my legs.

The pounding of my heart rushes in my ears. My skin is still alive with that unsatisfied sensation and everything feels supercharged. It makes me a little dizzy.

"Are you mine?" Lucas asks in a low rumbling voice. "I want you to give all of yourself to me."

My breath leaves me so fast it scrapes at my throat. I feel like I'm locked in a tractor beam, drawing me closer and closer to kissing Lucas. I swallow.

This goes against my whole plan. I didn't know it would be so hard to fight Lucas. I didn't know he could affect me so much.

I picture it for a second, how his lips would descend over mine in another possessive onslaught if I gave in. If I was with Lucas, it would stop the ridiculous bullying. I'd be pulled into his circle.

Carter Burns couldn't mess with me because I'd be untouchable. Protected by Lucas.

I'd be his.

For that brief second, it makes me happy to imagine. Until reality sets in.

"No," I answer in a raspy whisper.

Lucas tenses, his thumb still swiping my lip. A muscle twitches in his cheek.

There's a wildness ebbing off of him in waves that puts me on edge. I don't know what he's going to do.

The high tension between us is sliced by the loud tone of the phone ringing.

Some people in the living room moan in grumbling protests

for the interruption to their sleep, dragging them to the surface to face their hangovers.

Lucas peels away from me to answer his phone and I'm left alone trying to calm the rabbity jump of my heartbeat.

His voice is deep and direct as he talks on the phone. I turn around and steal his half-finished coffee instead of finding a mug in the numerous cabinets. I fill the mug with the pot from the fancy coffee maker and raid his fridge for cream.

"Thanks. I'll send people out once you let me know it's safely cleared."

Lucas hangs up and reaches automatically for his mug, finding it in my hands instead as I take a sip. His eyes narrow. Wordlessly, he retrieves a new mug from the cabinet above the coffee maker and pours coffee, drinking it black.

"They're working on clearing the road. Someone will call when it's safe to drive on it again."

"So...everyone's stuck here until then?"

His mouth twitches.

"Yup." Lucas pops the 'p' and watches me over the rim of his mug as he drinks. "You're stranded here with me."

That Bear Grylls escape through the wilderness I thought of in the heat of the moment last night is looking pretty good right now.

TWENTY-FOUR
LUCAS

It takes around eight hours for the road to clear.

The novelty of the forced stranding wore off fast for most people. Except Devlin, who always hangs around until I need to kick him back across the lake.

At least when it's from a blizzard, there's the charm of fresh snow and snowball fights to keep busy.

Reception can be spotty in the mountains. The community has cell boosters, but I don't give out my WiFi to everyone that parties at my house.

Most people hung around my property all day in clumps. There were around fifty people stranded, hovering near those that had better reception to check in with their parents and entertain themselves with social media. A local hashtag trended: #SOSatSaints.

My Instagram feed was blowing up with a bunch of posts with the tag.

I didn't have enough food in the house to feed everyone. The boat was out of gas, too, so I couldn't go to Devlin's for more. We have a rowboat, but I hate that thing.

People were getting on my nerves. It was more intense to keep my mask in place in my own house when there wasn't a party going.

All I wanted was to go back to my room with Gemma, but she stayed out of sight along with her brother.

By the time they've taken care of the mudslide and downed tree, everyone peels off in a line of cars.

I'm glad to see them all go.

All except one person.

I snag Gemma around the waist when Alec says he's got everything. They're the last two people here. Even Devlin left.

She's still in my hoodie and shorts as the late afternoon sun cuts across the lake. We're on the back deck munching on the frozen pizza I shoved in the oven an hour ago. Alec snags another slice.

"That's getting old," Gemma shoots over her shoulder.

"Not to me." I drag her into my lap on the Adirondack chair and offer her a bite of my pizza. She sighs and accepts. "I think you should stay."

Alec's brows jump up. Gemma's follow suit. It's funny how they both have the same expressions sometimes.

"Um," Gemma drawls. "Crazy guy say what?"

She looks like the indignant meme of the guy blinking in disbelief.

"Stay here with me."

"Why?"

I mutter in her ear so Alec doesn't hear. "Because if you

don't, I'm just going to follow you home and drag you back here. I'm not ready to let you go. Keep your window unlocked for me, okay?"

Gemma punches my shoulder without much force. I dip my fingers into the pant leg of the basketball shorts and trace her skin.

When she shivers at my touch, the thrill of success buzzes on the tip of my tongue.

Gemma tries to disagree in silence and I answer her back with a face of my own. We have an entire conversation with nothing but our faces and hands.

"Wow." Alec has an accusatory undertone as he addresses us. "You guys have silent communication down. How long have you been fucking my sister, dude?"

"Alec!" Gemma struggles out of my lap, scowling at me when I won't let her go. I release her with my hands up. She charges into her brother's face, steering him back despite the height he has on her. She's a little spitfire and it makes an ember burn in my chest. "I am *not* sleeping with him. We've kissed."

That's not all of it, but I'm not going to admit that to her brother. I'm definitely not telling him about fingering her in the student lot. I already felt shitty about that conversation with Carter in front of Alec.

"After we got you to the room last night, Gemma took off." My attention slides to her for a second. I still want to know what the hell happened to put her in that state of terror. "I went after her in the rain. That's how we found out about the blocked road. Gemma almost crashed your car into it."

"You didn't tell me any of that," Alec says to Gemma, his hands on her shoulders. "Holy shit, are you okay?"

"I'm fine. It was—yeah. Lucas brought me back here."

Gemma quiets for a second, lost in thought. She brushes her hand over a bruise on her leg peeking out from the bottom of the shorts. She glances at me.

There it is. She doesn't know how to explain those to her family. I've got her.

I give her a subtle nod.

She frowns and squeezes her eyes shut. "Okay. Alec, tell Mom and Dad you dropped me off at Blair's for the weekend."

"What? Why?" Alec is out of our loop. "They'd lecture you about your lunatic driving, but as long as you're not hurt they won't be too hard on you." A foreboding flash of jealousy crosses his face. "Besides, they never yell at you anymore."

Interesting. Maybe that's why he first went along with us hounding Gemma. If I had a sister, I'm pretty sure I'd die for her before I let guys harass her the way the ones at Silver Lake High have.

"Just do it! Cover for me and I'll owe you one."

Alec pins Gemma with a suspicious look. He flicks it over to me. "If you hurt my sister, you're dead. You know that, right?"

I almost snort. Gemma has enough fire in her to crush my balls before Alec gets wind of anything. I'd never hurt her, anyway. At least not in any way she doesn't ask me to.

Gemma rolls her eyes and pushes him to the steps that lead down to the open yard.

"Okay, Mr. Misplaced Chivalry. Quit going through the motions and get out of here."

She leans in and mutters something to him I don't hear.

After Alec drives away, Gemma turns around. I pat my lap and she passes me to collapse into the other Adirondack chair.

"Give me more pizza." She fiddles with the hoodie strings and shifts in the seat. The sun reflects off the water below and paints her in golden hues. "I can't believe you. This feels like entrapment."

"You chose it."

"Only because you threatened to break into my window to kidnap me again, like the psycho monster you are."

"Critical damage." I hold a hand over my chest and pretend to die.

"Yeah, yeah. You're like a final boss. You never stay down."

We trade lighthearted bickering as the sun dips lower.

For the next two days, Gemma is mine.

* * *

We stay up late.

I haven't allowed her out of my sight all day, even when she went down to sit on the end of the dock to take photos after we finished the pizza. Lancelot follows her, leaning against her side.

I've been gradually chipping away at her wariness all night until she allows me to touch her freely. She let me check her scraped palms to apply more ointment. They're looking good, the redness fading with the healing abrasions. The bruises dotting her body will take more time, some of them an angry purple with yellow edges. There are finger shaped ones from where I grabbed her.

I made her late night pancakes. It's one of the few things I know how to cook. She sat on the counter with her legs dangling, kicking to the Spotify playlist I turned on in the background. My demanding little spitfire claimed every tiny pancake made from extra batter splattering in the pan when I poured. I slid between her open knees and fed her, teasing my fingers past her lips as I held eye contact.

She looked cute as hell perched on the countertop, wearing my hoodie, her honey-colored hair up in a messy bun. Blushing because she licked my fingers clean as I offered her baby pancakes.

A sense of rightness settles in my chest having her here. Like something's clicked into place that was missing.

It's past midnight now. We retreated to my bedroom after I chased her around the house, grinning at her protests followed by the gleam in her eye right before she darted out of reach. She liked the game as much as I did. She likes it when I hunt her down. I won when I picked her up and tossed her over my shoulder. She shrieked when I smacked her ass as I carted her to the stairs.

Gemma hasn't said anything about the sleeping situation. If she tries to argue about spending another night in my bed, she'll find herself tied to the bed posts with my school tie.

The mental image pulls heat into my groin. God, I love tying her up. It's the face she gives me, the stubborn jut of her chin.

After I set her down, I collapse on the floor in front of my TV and turn on the game system. She pads across the room barefoot and I snag her wrist to drag her into my lap.

Gemma twists to peer at me over her shoulder. "Do you have some fetish for me sitting in your lap?"

She's still wearing my clothes and it's driving me fucking wild. My arms snake around her waist, skimming underneath the hoodie to press into the warm skin of her stomach.

"You tell me." I trace patterns on her skin and her lashes flutter. I press my face to the back of her shoulder. "Call of Duty or Mario Kart?"

"Mario Kart. Prepare to have your ass kicked," Gemma crows. "I'm reigning champ in the Turner household."

"We'll see about that."

I hand her one of the controllers and get a game started. It turns out she knows what she's doing. She lays traps and gets boots that send my car spinning out.

"Oh, it's like that, huh?"

"You know it."

Gemma plays with her whole body, shifting in my lap as she follows the movements of her player.

It's. Fucking. Torture.

I decide I need to play dirty to win. I cage her in with my arms, leaning my chin over her shoulder as I swivel the toggle to steer my car into a speed boost.

"Damn it," Gemma mutters.

My lips curve and I aim to distract her by kissing the back of her neck. She squirms, making a faint sound.

"That's not fair."

"Who said I cared about fairness," I say against her skin. My tongue flicks her earlobe and she gasps. "I'll do whatever it takes to win."

Marissa never wanted to play anything with me. The closest she came to my game systems was sucking my dick while I half-heartedly played a Battlefield match.

This is making me horny. Gemma is absorbed in the game and hasn't snapped at me to stop touching her.

I'm getting into it, grazing my teeth at the juncture of her neck and shoulder as I peer up at the TV to keep track of things. My cock strains in my sweats and I press up against her ass.

She still crosses the finish line first.

I drag out a groan and toss my controller aside in favor of wrapping my arms around her waist.

"What?" Gemma scoffs. "You think girls don't play video games?"

"Nah, I know they do."

I lay another kiss on the back of her neck.

"Alec and I used to have limited time to play, so we pooled it together and bargained with our parents to stack how long we were allowed to have." Gemma tips her head back to rest on my shoulder. It gives me better access to attack her skin with my lips. A soft sound leaves her and her hands cover mine on her stomach. "We used to play a ton together. We'd strategize and take turns going up against big bosses."

"Cute." I nip at her skin. "Time to stop talking about your brother, though."

"Yeah."

I move against her ass and slip my fingers up the inside of the boxers to touch her thighs. She arches as heat builds between us. My touch roams over her body as she drops her guard.

I have her under my spell, commanding her pleasure.

"I want to make you come again." My voice is full of gravel and dark promise. "This time I want to make you scream for me."

Gemma shudders, spreading her legs when I nudge her knees to drop on either side of my lap. My hands dive beneath the waistband of the basketball shorts and give her what she needs, rubbing firmly. I waste no time, gliding my fingers over her slick folds and pressing one inside of her.

"Ah!" She nods as her back bows. "Okay. Yes."

I love having her body spread obediently for me, in my lap and at the mercy of how much I want to give her. I bite her neck, sucking the beginnings of a bruise into her skin as I sink my finger deeper.

"Oh god!"

"That's it, baby. Tell me all about it. Does that feel good?"

Gemma catches a strangled half-cry. I wrap my other hand

around her throat, tipping her head to me. My hand stills and she bucks against my wrist, silently begging for more.

"Don't hold back. It's just you and me here. Don't hide anything from me. I want it all."

Gemma's breath leaves her in a rush and she gives a tiny nod. I kiss her cheek.

"Good girl. Get up on the bed."

Gemma gets up, hesitantly perching on the edge of the bed. "Um."

I crawl across the room to her like I'm a big mountain cat on the prowl for prey. When I reach her, I force her legs apart and slide between them, kneeling on the floor.

Gemma's eyes are wide.

"You're going to scream for me, sweetheart."

I hook my fingers in the sides of the shorts and drag them down. She allows me to nudge her into place and settle between her legs. I hold her gaze for a minute, soaking in her evident desire. Then I drop my attention to her vagina. She's bare for me and it's glorious. I tease a light touch over her wet folds.

"Has anyone else ever tasted you here?"

A whimper sounds above me. I leer up at her. She shakes her head in response.

The all-consuming need to own every part of her, to erase every touch but my own rears up.

"Good. This," I cup her slowly, "is all mine. Now lie back so I can eat your pussy."

"Oh," Gemma breathes, biting her lip.

Her face is flaming red. It takes her a beat, but she does as I say. At the first touch of my lips on her, she pops up on her elbows to watch with unwavering alertness. I lick her in a long stroke and her lips part on a gasp. My eyes flash up to her as I lick and suck her pussy.

Gemma's legs part without resistance after that, widening to accommodate my shoulders. I hook her legs over them and drive her crazy with my mouth. I shove my hands beneath her and grasp her ass to give me leverage as I torture her clit.

It surprises me how she embraces her pleasure. She doesn't fight it like others try to, embarrassed about feeling good. Instead, Gemma rides the tide of it with abandon as I take her higher and higher.

She's stunning in every way.

Taking charge, claiming her pleasure, and bending her to submit feels like heaven as I rip her apart with my tongue.

I don't think she's aware of it when she starts to move, her hips rocking against my face in a carnal plea to give her what she needs. I squeeze her ass as I pleasure her with my mouth.

Gemma sounds wild, her moans and cries reaching a fever pitch that makes my cock throb. I love taking her apart like this. She claws at the bed, spreading her legs wider, begging in breathy groans for *slower* and *wait, more there, right there,* and *oh god, yes, harder*. I'm learning what she likes and the unbridled way she tells me what will draw her closer to orgasm feeds a fire inside me.

"Fuck, oh god, Lucas—I'm—I'm coming!"

Gemma arches from the bed with a sharp cry, bucking against my face. I flick my tongue and stroke her sides, pushing the hoodie higher so I can cup her tits as she comes in a mess of shaking limbs and hitching gasps. Her thighs clench around my head and I continue, pulling back to work her through it.

I slide two fingers into her pussy and her body seizes, legs tightening on my head and then spreading wider as I slowly pump them deeper, curling them. I hover my lips over her clit, catching my breath. Gemma's body trembles and I can tell another orgasm is building.

It comes on fast, the heave of her chest telling the closer she gets. Her pussy clenches on my fingers and I suck on her clit.

"Oh my god," Gemma moans as she shatters for me again.

I pull my fingers free and press my face into her stomach, out of breath and so fucking hard I'm a little dizzy. Her shaking hands bury in my hair, holding on as her body rides the waves of pleasure.

"God, god, god," she whispers in a tight, wrecked voice.

A lazy grin stretches across my face. "That's what I like to hear. You can call me that from now on."

Gemma swats my shoulder with no heat, her hand falling back to the bed. I lift to climb on the bed. I collapse beside her and toss my leg over her thighs, rutting my cock against her hip. Propping on an elbow, I lean over to give her a deep kiss.

I know she tastes herself on my tongue.

As we make out, I grab her wrist and drag her hand over my sweatpants on my erection. Gemma pushes my back to the bed and sits up. Her eyes are focused and she chews the corner of her lip. She bounces her gaze between my face and my crotch.

I cross my arms behind my head and let her figure it out.

Gemma peels my pants down and blinks at my cock. She saw it in the shower, but I like the determined tilt of her mouth. She wraps her fingers around it and I let out a sigh, my eyelids closing.

When her lips touch the tip, my eyes fly open. A groan rips from me.

Gemma looks perfect, her hair disheveled, green eyes bright, lips swollen as they kiss my cock. It takes everything not to slam into her mouth.

"Only if you want to." My words belie how much I want her mouth on my cock. "I'm not going to make you do it."

"I wouldn't offer if I wasn't into it. I want to," Gemma murmurs, then takes my cock into her mouth and sucks.

Fuck.

The wet heat of her mouth is sublime. I want to live in it forever.

I drag in air through my nose and rest a hand on the back of her head. My fingers dig at the elastic tie until her hair is loose for me to grip. I keep my word. I don't fuck her face at my pace, but I keep my fingers in her hair the whole time as she works my dick.

When she peeks at me through her lashes I groan, my hold tightening in her hair. She moans around my cock and it ignites a coil of fire.

"Shit, that's it, baby. I'm almost there." I trace her lips as they stretch around my cock and, fuck me, she parts them further to take it all—cock and fingers. "God, look at you. You going to swallow all my come when I fill your mouth?"

She nods.

My thighs start to shake as I tip over the edge and shoot into her mouth. I don't have time to warn her other than clenching my fist in her hair. She makes a startled noise when my come hits her tongue, but grabs my hips and swallows.

"Good girl," I rasp as my cock throbs.

My orgasm electrifies me, sparking across my skin in a blaze of white-hot pleasure.

Once I return to earth, I release a ragged exhale and grab Gemma, tugging her up my body. Our lips crash together as I roll her over, covering her body with mine. As we kiss, I strip her, only parting to drag our tops off.

When we're both naked, we collide like joining stars.

Nothing is between us, our skin sliding together. Her nipples harden against my chest and I hike her leg over my hip. I need all of her, the hunger far from sated.

The kiss is no longer me devouring her, but a rushing river that drowns both of us until we're destroyed.

I embrace the destruction Gemma brings.

Nothing feels better than this.

My cock hardens for another round and I glide the head against her folds. She goes so rigid I worry she might crack into jagged pieces.

Those pieces might never fit back together if I break her. The power to destroy and protect both sit in my hands, weighed on each side like scales.

"Wait." Gemma digs her nails into my shoulders and I grunt. "Wait, Lucas. I don't want to. I'm not ready for that."

I press my forehead against hers, growling as I move against her pussy for another minute.

"Lucas," Gemma says sharply.

"Relax. I'm not. You just feel so fucking good." After one last roll of my hips against her, I fall to the side. "When you do let me, you're in for it. I'm going to fuck your pussy so good."

"Confident," Gemma remarks as I peel back the covers.

She slides into bed as I go turn off the TV. I let Lancelot in the room, then duck into the bathroom to calm down. When I come back out, Gemma has Lancelot on his back, rubbing his belly.

My girl and my dog, together in my bed. It will suck when she has to go home. I wish I could keep her locked away in my room forever.

"You're making me jealous," I quip.

Gemma lifts her head and smirks. "Is that all it takes? Wow, you're fragile."

"Make it up to me. Give me head again. I haven't had enough of you tonight."

She snorts and addresses Lancelot. "Do you hear this guy?"

I slip into bed and draw her back against my chest after turning off the light. She's warm and her skin is soft. Lancelot moves to the bottom of the bed, circling a few times before laying down.

"Thanks," Gemma whispers.

I press my lips to her shoulder. "For what?"

"I thought you were crazy for making me stay here this weekend. But it hasn't been as bad as I thought. You can be fun to hang out with, even if you're a total dick at school to everyone who doesn't ask how high when you say jump."

I cup her breast and tuck her against me more comfortably, sliding a leg between hers. I could sleep tangled with her like this forever.

"You only think that because you don't know me. You're getting warmer, though."

"Well, you're not what I thought you were. Sorry for accusing you. You piss me off with your cocky attitude and over-possessive crap. But when it counts, you do know not to cross every line."

"Trust me, sweetheart," I smile into her hair as I whisper to her, "I want you begging me to fuck you. I only take what I know you want. And don't bother denying it, I know you're hot for me."

"I—" Gemma huffs. "Maybe. But you're not forgiven for stealing my first kiss."

The admission is a mulish whisper, but it couldn't be louder if Gemma blared it on a megaphone. *First kiss.*

Stunned arousal bolts up my spine at the admission. If I'm her first kiss and the first to taste her on my tongue, then other firsts await. My cock throbs as I rut against her ass, fantasies of fucking her virgin pussy filling my mind.

It stirs the beastly desire in me to own her in every way. It sounds as if I already have. My thoughts slip to the time I fingered her in the parking lot, how she always responds so beautifully and openly.

It'll stay that way. No one else gets Gemma.

She's mine. I'll claim each part of her and never let her go.

Gemma squirms into a more comfortable position, unaware of my racing thoughts. "You still piss me off, though."

"That's what makes it fun." I trace my fingertips down her body until they tease into the soft curls between her thighs. "But soon you'll stop fighting it. You'll give yourself to me. And when you do, you better prepare yourself."

TWENTY-FIVE
LUCAS

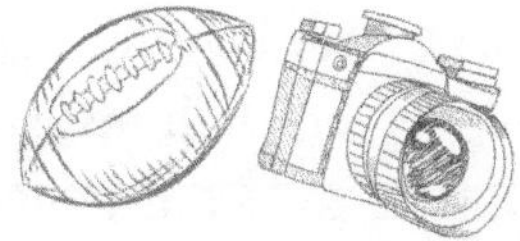

"Lucas, come here a sec," Dad calls out from his home office as I pass it on the landing.

I pause on the step with my late night cereal snack. He's cast in the orange glow of the lamp, files spread across his blotter as his reading glasses droop down his nose.

There's a framed signed jersey from the Broncos behind him—a gift from one of his firm's clients.

"I found flights for two weeks from now." Dad looks up over the rim of his glasses. His tie is abandoned on his briefcase, the top two buttons of his shirt undone. "We can go for a long weekend to Seattle. The Huskies have a game on Monday we can go see. Sound good?"

"Oh, uh." I scratch the back of my head and shrug, hovering in the doorway. "I guess."

Avoidance is going well for me. Now I'm out of rope. I have to make a choice soon.

My sketchbook sits open on my desk in my room, a half-finished concept in progress.

Dad sits up, removing his glasses. He motions me in with two fingers.

"What's on your mind?"

"It's nothing, Dad."

"Then where's your enthusiasm? Is it because you heard the Utes scouts would be at your next game?"

I blow out a breath. I didn't know that. Coach keeps us in the dark about that. He figures if we know about scouts, it'll shake our nerves and throw us off our groove. In his mind, we should play every game like we could impress a scout.

Dad gives me a sage nod, like my sigh confirms it. "I can check the available flights for Utah instead. You don't have to go to my alma mater just because I'm a fan of their team."

"Dad..."

He doesn't hear my weak protest, wiggling the wireless mouse to wake up the monitor. He slips his glasses back on and does that old person with technology face—a slight squint, head tipped back, lips parted and silently repeating the words on the screen.

I grip the cereal bowl harder. It's probably soggy now, ruining my late night treat. If you don't start eating cereal within the first few minutes after pouring the bowl, it turns into a mediocre, milk-soaked mess.

"Here!" Dad taps the screen enthusiastically. "Thursday night flight. We'll tour the campus on Friday."

I take a seat across from Dad, careful to nudge his files aside before I put my bowl down.

Once he was mad at me for a whole week when I was ten and spilled Gatorade on a motion of dismissal that cost him a client. I don't know if it's true that my accident lost him the case and made his client fire him, or if the DA simply had a stronger case, but from then on I've been cautious around his office. Even at eighteen, that habit lingers.

"Dad."

This time I gain his attention. I take a breath and leap.

"You're always telling me to follow my dreams."

"That's right." Dad smiles. "I want you to be proud of chasing down what you want."

Tugging on my earlobe, I go on. My insides ripple like a boat ignoring the no wake signs, disturbing the water with choppy waves.

"The thing is, Dad..." I swallow to wet my dry throat. "You encourage me to do that, but football isn't my dream."

There. I said it, plain as day. No take backs.

I drop my eyes and stare hard at the woodgrain of his desk. I hate that I can't look at him. It's like I'm barely brave enough to be honest about what I want. My heart feels like it'll rocket out of my chest. This is the first time I've voiced this aloud.

The application for Oak Ridge College has been filled in, hiding away in my desk drawer for months now.

Dad folds his fingers on the desk. "Go on."

My palms are clammy. I wipe them on my sweatpants. This is so much more difficult than I pictured when I went over how this conversation should go.

"It's the dream everyone else pushed on me. Everybody expects me to play football." I drag my fingers through my hair and tug. "I've been trying to tell you since summer. I don't want to keep playing. I don't even want to go for a sports scholarship."

When I gather the strength to lift my eyes, the remnants of a startled expression cloud Dad's face.

"Lucas," he says sadly. "I didn't realize your heart wasn't in the game, son."

My throat closes over with the foul taste of guilt. I look down at my lap, staring unseeingly at my fingers twisting around the drawstring on my pants.

If Dad lectures me about seeing things through and commitments, I don't know what I'll do. Admitting to him that his dream for me isn't the same one I have is challenging enough. I haven't told him what I want to study.

"I'm proud of you."

A soft sound tears from my lungs as my attention snaps up. Dad comes around the desk to squeeze my shoulder. The build up of anxiety sputters out like a sieve at the relief those words bring.

"You're—you are?"

"Of course. I'm proud you talked to me honestly. I always want you to follow your dreams and believe in yourself."

I feel like I could float to the ceiling because of the weight lifted from my shoulders. All the time I've been worrying about the assumptions thrown at me from all sides seems silly now.

"Thanks, Dad."

He gives my shoulder another squeeze and drops into his leather chair. He gathers his files with a thoughtful expression.

"Help me convince your mother to visit Seattle for a weekend. If you won't be playing, she'll be a tough cookie." He strokes his gray stubbled chin. "It was going to be easier to frame it as a trip to visit you and cheer you on."

My laugh echoes in the room. I've been anxious Dad would be weird about me having no interest in going to the same college he went to.

"That's up to you. Just balance it with a cool date night and she'll be down." I scoop up my soggy cereal and head for the door. "Night, Dad. Good luck on your case stuff."

Dad waves in acknowledgement as I slip out.

There's a huge rush that comes with a positive outcome from a long-term worry that's niggled at you. I can't wipe off my stupid smile.

In my room, I abandon the cereal bowl on my desk and grab my sketchbook.

Now the only problem is I can't make the excuse that everyone else is pressuring me to keep up with expectations.

I glance at the drawer where my application waits for me to submit it to the college of my dreams. I filled it out on a whim after spending hours virtually touring the campus and browsing the curriculum. Now that my chance to send in my portfolio is a reality, I have to decide if I want to stay in my uncomfortable comfort zone or not.

It's up to me to dig up the courage to choose what I want to do. If I can do that, I'll be who I am in my heart. The mask I constantly wear will fall away.

TWENTY-SIX
GEMMA

A couple of weeks pass, leaving me lost in a swirling whirlpool of conflicting feelings.

I thought I knew who Lucas was from that first stolen kiss at his party. I thought he was a mindless jock and a spoiled asshole only interested in fucking with as many girls as possible before going off on football scholarship.

He's proving me wrong, but can I forgive him for the tricks he's played on me? He threatened me, kidnapped me—twice—and I let him go down on me. Even returned the favor because the illicit hotness of the moment took over, stirring a need in me so strong I couldn't deny it.

Maybe that means there's something messed up with me for liking it in some twisted way. His filthy words have always had a way of getting to me.

Am I prepared to go from Lucas Saint's favorite target to jumping into bed with him? I don't know.

After Alec picked me up from that long weekend at Lucas' house, where we spent more time naked in his bed with our mouths on each other than dressed, I kept to myself at school to avoid Lucas. The weight of Alec's judging gaze as we left the lake house sent the oily guilt sliding over me as I trudged to the car, Lucas' hands glued to me.

There was no way to tell which bruises were from the night of the storm and which were from Lucas the rest of the hedonistic weekend.

Alec shed the protective brother act once I pried about his attitude on Friday and what made him drink so much.

Why should I feel bad about doing exactly what boys do? Lucas made me feel good. And he didn't press my boundaries again. Hooking up with him doesn't make me some whore and him a hero. Double standards are archaic bullshit.

The only thing wrong with the weekend was lying to my parents about where I was and what happened.

They believed me when I explained Blair and I took a hike and got caught in the storm on a trail. I kept my hair down to hide the hickeys dotting my neck, courtesy of Lucas. Those weren't the only ones he left on my skin.

Should I be more open with my parents? Maybe. Still, I can't bring myself to run the awkward gauntlet of *boy talk* with them.

Not only did I have Lucas to lie about, but the accident, too.

Lucas offered to pay for the scrape on the passenger side of the CR-V. He said Devlin had a guy that did good body work. I didn't want to owe him, but I also had no way to pay for the damage and I needed to hide it from my parents.

The kindnesses he offers paint a picture of a different

person than the one I skirt in the halls at school. I don't know which one is the real Lucas, but I know which one I prefer to be around.

The few times he sees me, he doesn't come after me like I expect. The hunter's look is back in his eyes, though. It's more intense now. I think he might be waiting for me to come to him this time.

I vow to focus on school and my photo project until I straighten out the tangled thoughts in my head.

* * *

I get back from my shoot after dark. Mom and Dad's cars are gone. Mom has a night shift at the hospital and Dad's gone camping for the weekend. There's an unfamiliar car in the driveway that must belong to one of Alec's friends.

"I'm home," I call as I come in the door.

"I ordered pizza," Alec yells.

It sounds like he's down in the basement where he's turned the finished space into his cave.

I swing by the kitchen to grab a lukewarm slice of pepperoni and nibble on it as I trek up the steps to my room. I elbow open the door, grunting as I sling my camera bag over my head and set it down by my desk. I turn around to grab the laptop from where I left it on my bed and freeze.

Lucas sits on the end of my bed in jeans and a black hoodie.

"Jesus Christ." I clutch at my chest where my heart skipped fifty beats at the unexpected sight of him. "You could've given me a heart attack. Why are you sitting all quiet in here?"

"I was waiting for you to get back. I haven't been here long. Maybe ten minutes."

He seems distracted. Quieter than usual. His attention flits around my room, taking it in.

"And you had to do that in my room?" I shove the rest of the pizza crust in my mouth. "Who let you in here?"

"Alec. I came to see him and he said I could wait up here for you."

My eyes narrow. My room is my sanctuary and I don't like people in it without my permission. Alec is dead.

The annoyance simmers away when Lucas shifts, playing with his hoodie pocket. It occurs to me that he appears less self-assured. It's what's off about him, tugging at my expectations and instincts.

I leave him be to retrieve my laptop and download my images from the shoot. There's a comfortable silence for a few minutes.

When Lucas speaks again, it makes me jump. It's not out of fear, but because I was absorbed in selecting images to add to my project.

"I like the bold lines in your photos."

The deepness of his voice washes over me with his proximity. He stands behind my desk chair, leaning over me to see the screen. His familiar woodsy scent envelopes me.

I'm a little taken aback that he understands some of the concepts of composition.

"Did you look that up online to say to me?"

"No, I already knew it." Lucas tugs gently on the end of my braid. "I like stuff like that."

A pleasant zing tingles from my stomach. I tip my head back to see him.

"I thought you were a football meathead."

Lucas stares at me with an open expression. "Actually, I want to study architecture at Oak Ridge College of the Arts."

My lips part and my stomach swoops. I was right. I don't know Lucas at all.

Every student and faculty member talks about Lucas Saint's pro prospects in football.

I just assumed...

Like everyone else does.

It's a really good school. I'm looking at it for their fine art degree in photography.

"They don't have football scholarships there."

Lucas is silent for a long stretch. He traces my nose from tip to bridge and cups my face.

"I know," he murmurs.

I feel like Lucas gave me a small piece of himself. I can see him better now that I have a key to unlock the door.

It's the guy he showed me on the boat, when it was just us and his pug dog.

This is someone I could like. Maybe even fall in love with.

An electric static fills the air.

I let Lucas encourage me out of the desk chair. He crowds me against the desk, framing my face with his hands before kissing me.

Kissing Lucas becomes a storm.

The thud of my heart resonates like rain in my ears, the insistence of his tongue the thunder that reverberates in my bones, our harsh breaths the strike of lightning illuminating what we need.

Lucas walks me across the room and we fall to the bed. He's all over me, a flurry of heat and lips and hands that peel me apart. He works my braid free.

My legs wrap around his waist and we grind against each other, the pleasure muffled by our clothes. I want to strip bare again, to feel his skin on mine once more with no barriers to hide from each other. Lucas must feel that need, too. He rucks my sweater up to lay kiss after kiss in a trail down my stomach until he reaches my jeans.

A rough noise leaves Lucas, his hot breath washing over my sensitive skin as he tugs my jeans down without unbuttoning them, taking my underwear with them. He follows the path with his lips, and then he descends in a rush of perfect wet heat.

"Yes," I sigh once his mouth is on me.

Lucas growls and in no time at all I'm a tight wire moments from snapping, his tongue inescapable as the heat builds in my belly.

It's like my body is attuned to his, primed to fall apart at a whisper from him.

Lucas strokes my folds and when he slides his fingers inside, I'm a goner. The mounting pressure explodes in a chorus of pleasure behind my closed eyes.

Then he's there, kissing me, tasting the muffled cries of my orgasm as it ripples through me in shock waves.

"That's it," he mutters into the kiss. "I love making you make those sounds. Did your pussy miss my mouth? I've been hungry to taste you again since the minute you left my place."

I reach down to palm his cock and he groans, attacking my mouth again.

We struggle out of the rest of our remaining clothes and it's like things slot into place when our naked skin glides together.

He enters me with his fingers again. My back arches from the bed and I ride them, rolling my hips with each stroke. My body is on fire and I'm not ready to stop.

I'm so wet that there's a squelch with each thrust.

"That feels really good," I gasp.

"Ready to come again? I'm not stopping until you're wrung out."

I bite my lip and nod. He gives me a completely feral look, like he won't be satisfied until I've disintegrated to nothing but dust.

"Tonight I'm making you mine for good. I want these fingers to be my cock buried in your body right now."

He curls them and a sound gets stuck in my throat as pleasure explodes outward. Lucas presses his forehead to mine. His hand stills and I claw at his arm.

"Don't stop."

"You know what you have to do." He kisses me once, brutal and filthy. "Beg."

My stomach tightens and flips.

Up until this point, I let him call the shots. He made me feel good and I didn't stop him from touching me. I've only initiated kisses and a few instances of oral when I was his weekend captive.

Lucas watches me with a penetrating gaze full of lust. His hand remains completely frozen, no matter how I circle my hips to get him to move. An agitated exhale leaves me and I lean my weight on my elbows.

He told me he wouldn't take it. That he wanted me to come willingly.

Blood rushes in my ear, my senses overwhelmed by how much I want to chase the orgasm I was close to.

Feeling good right now means giving in.

Lucas is waiting for me to jump off that cliff with him.

He removes his fingers and kisses me, whispering filthy encouragements and promises into my skin as he torments me. My heart races and I cling to him. He makes my body a live wire with wicked pleasures coursing through it.

Every time I get close, he stops until I'm blinking back tears of frustration. I'm teetering on the edge of the cliff.

All this time I've held back. But I'm done holding back.

I don't want my past to dictate how I live my life. I'm in charge. Lucas is offering me that right now.

I could cry and kiss him for that small kindness alone.

Somehow, he gets it. He knows that I need to make this choice for myself.

I jump off the cliff with Lucas into a free fall.

I want this.

"Please," I whisper as he brings me close again, hand between my legs as he sucks on my neck. "Please, Lucas. I need you."

"Tell me what you need, baby."

His voice is rugged and raw. He's feeling this as much as I am right now.

"I need you," I repeat. "I want you to fuck me."

"You do? Are you sure?" He leans up to grin smugly. "You don't sound sure."

"Yes!" I grab his hair and bring his lips to mine. "Yes, I want you. I want to come. Please fuck me."

We kiss and his fingers thread in my hair, tugging lightly to angle my head back.

"You beg so pretty, sweetheart." Lucas kisses my throat. "I'm going to mark your body all over. Even when my hickeys fade, you'll feel me there."

I shiver at his words. He kisses me again, then gets up to dig through his jeans. He comes back with a condom and a dirty smile.

Anticipation buzzes across my oversensitive skin, every inch tingling with a hungry need only Lucas can satisfy.

Lucas rips open the wrapper and rolls the condom down his cock. He sits against the pillows and pats his thigh.

"Come here, Gemma. You beg for my cock like that, you have to ride it to make yourself come."

My insides burst and heat floods my face. He knows exactly what he's doing to me. I kneel up on quaking thighs and straddle his hips. My hands rest on his shoulders as he strokes my sides.

"I've got you," he rumbles.

Nodding, I lick my lips. His thumb strokes over my ribs and he steadies me with a hand on my hip. I kiss him when he lines his cock up. When I inch down on his cock, he swallows my choked gasp.

He lets me set the pace and I go slow. There's an overwhelming sense of fullness and I don't think I've taken his entire cock yet.

A quiet groan hisses through Lucas' teeth and his hands skate everywhere, teasing my nipples and my clit with touches that are too soft, leaving me wanting more.

There's a pinch and a tightness with his cock filling me, stretching me. My chest heaves with my breath once I'm fully seated in his lap.

Lucas falls forward, face pressed to my chest and neck. His lips move on my skin and he massages my ass. I can feel his cock twitch inside me. It's a weirdly intoxicating feeling.

When Lucas shows me his face again, there's a wrinkle in his brow and his lips part. Darkness fills his eyes, the pupils blown wide.

He looks up at me like I'm some kind of goddess.

His salvation.

"Gemma." Lucas holds my waist. "Move. Make us both feel good."

"Who's begging now," I joke in a raspy murmur.

He swats my ass, then squeezes it. His mouth finds my neck and I drop my head back.

It doesn't feel as tight when I roll my hips. I lift up a little and his cock slides into me like it belongs there as I sink on it again. We fit together. I start slowly, concentrating on the new sensations and the intensity they illicit.

It starts to feel good, *more* in a level fingers didn't reach.

Sweat beads our skin as I go faster. Lucas makes a savage noise and drops his thumb to my clit.

"Come on my cock," Lucas demands against my ear. "I want to feel it. Come on, baby."

My hips move faster as Lucas drives me on.

When the build of heat becomes too much, I tip forward and bite Lucas' shoulder as I come with his cock buried deep inside me.

"Oh, god."

All at once, Lucas wraps his arm around me. With a growl, he flips our positions. I yelp as my back hits the bed. He pins my wrists above my head with one hand and lifts my leg, thrusting his cock back inside in a fluid movement. My gasp catches and I arch into him.

"Fuck," he groans. His grip flexes on my wrists. "You feel incredible."

I wrap my legs around him as he moves. The heat builds anew, the flames stoked by the words Lucas growls against my lips.

"You're mine, Gemma. Every inch. Your body, your mind, your heart."

He claims my mouth in a biting kiss. I clench on his cock and he snaps his hips, hitting a spot that lights my body up. He releases my wrists and my hands fly to his back, holding on as he fucks me.

"You'll belong to me forever," Lucas rumbles. He bites my neck hard enough to leave another mark. "No one else gets this —gets to have you. Only me."

"Y-yes," I gasp, partially because he drags a response from me and because I'm falling apart.

I can't keep my moans quiet, my insides breaking and building anew with each wave of pleasure pouring over me. I buck as he hits that spot again, wrenching another orgasm from me.

"That's it, baby."

Lucas' voice is barely recognizable as he loses himself in the throes of his own oblivion. The noise he muffles against my neck becomes a groan as his hips stutter and he drives his cock deep inside me.

For a minute, we're both still save for our panting as we try to catch our breath. The come down from having sex is ricocheting through my body. A soft sound escapes me and I hug his neck.

Lucas envelopes me in his embrace. He rolls to his side, bringing me with him. His cock slips out, which is a weird sensation, but I don't focus on it as he trails lazy kisses across my cheek.

"You were perfect," he mumbles in a sleepy voice.

He gets up to discard the condom, burying it in the trash basket by my desk.

I sit up and draw my knees to my chest. My vagina aches with an emptiness.

An odd vulnerability slips over me. "Stay a while?"

"Yeah."

Lucas returns to bed and pets my hair. He kisses my forehead and lays down, pulling me half on top of him.

It's nice, laying like this. He's sweet with me, massaging my shoulders and caressing my leg. It's unexpected how attentive he is, but it puts me at ease.

* * *

Lucas is still there when I come out of a content doze. I don't know how long I was out for, but he's asleep, too. With a soft smile, I get up to grab the throw blanket from the bottom of the bed and cover us with it as I snuggle against his side. In his sleep, he wraps his arms around me, holding me tight.

The next time I wake up, my room is dark and Lucas is gone. I have a t-shirt on and I'm beneath the covers. No underwear, though. I rub my eyes and check my phone. 3:42am.

There's a text from Lucas from after midnight.

He sent it with a picture of himself, the same open expression on his face from when he told me he wants to be an architect.

Lucas: Dream of me, sweetheart.

TWENTY-SEVEN
GEMMA

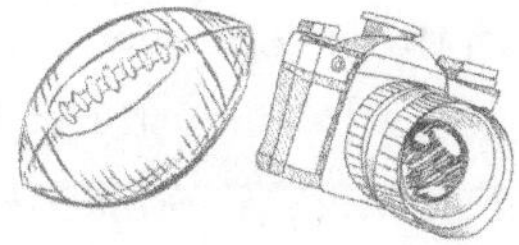

The weekend was a dream. Lucas texted me half-sweet-half-dirty one-liners on Sunday and selfies with Lancelot from a solo ride on the boat.

I'm riding on a giddy high, feeling like I can move on from my past and start on a fresh page.

But once I arrive at school everything crumbles to dust between my fingers.

I'm struck with confused mixed emotions. Should I expect things to change?

Are we dating?

Lucas and I didn't hash that out. I forgot to ask between our low-key flirty sexting rapport.

But sex means I'm his girlfriend, I think. He did say in that possessive gruff voice that I was his. I hope that means he's mine, too.

Walking through the parking lot with Alec carries a different connotation now. People that offer him high fives also greet me and ask to make plans to hang out. It leaves me on edge, tasting the crackle of something off in the air.

It's exactly what I told Alec would happen—the same dickheads that bullied me would flip their tune and act chummy towards me after I became Lucas' girlfriend. Officially.

It makes me uncomfortable.

We find Lucas and the others gathered around Devlin's shiny red sports car.

"Yeah, I wanted to get one last ride out of her for the season," Devlin says to one of the girls hanging around with skirts way shorter than dress code regulation. He winks at her. "They're calling for an early snowstorm. Will you come keep me warm? We can get snowed in and ice skate on the lake."

The girl coos with her friends. Two of them stand close to Lucas.

"We'll make a party out of it," Lucas adds, slinging an arm around the one on the left with bright red lipstick. "Blizzard Bash. That's what we'll call it. Start a hashtag."

Carter whoops.

Alec and I approach. I hang back a bit. Lucas' attention passes right over me. He doesn't welcome me with open arms like I'm his girlfriend or sling hatred at me.

It's like I'm invisible.

Wonderful. It's what I wanted all along. To be ignored and fly under the social radar.

And now I no longer need that.

"Hey man," Lucas greets, bumping fists with Alec.

"'Sup." Alec nods to the rest of the group. "What's this about a snowed in party? I'm down."

"I'm hoping we get a snow day," says one of the short skirts, twirling her hair as she leans into Lucas' side.

"We'll get drunk as fuck and go sledding." Lucas gives everyone a lazy grin as they cheer for his suggestion. "And a snowball tourney." He tips a salacious leer at the girl he has his arm around. "Hot toddies and hot tub time."

Devlin waggles his eyebrows and blows a kiss to the girl he was flirting with over his car. "My kind of party."

My lip curls. What the hell is this?

The Lucas Saint that visited my room on Saturday and told me about Oak Ridge College of the Arts and *this* douche are not the same people. The mask he wears at school is back in place. I was silly to think what we shared would make him change around his friends.

Lucas is still toying with me, happy to play possessive, but afraid to commit to more. I'm not having it.

"Count me out." I wrap my arms around myself. "I'm more of a movie marathon under a blanket sort of person during a snowstorm."

Lucas lifts a brow and cocks his head to the side.

"Suit yourself. I guess I'll need to find a few new cuddling partners. What about you, darling?" He addresses the girl batting her eyelashes at him as she presses her breasts into his side. "Yeah, you're down to keep me company, right?"

I bristle, gnashing my teeth. Lucas ignores the daggers I shoot his way.

"Of course, Lucas."

I almost gag at her breathy tone. Jesus. This is a school parking lot, not the set of a porno production.

You'd never know the difference with the syrup in her tone.

Lucas chuckles and walks off with his cohorts in tow, keeping his arm around the flirt's shoulders. I stay back from the group as they head for the steps to school.

Alec darts a concerned glance my way, but I ignore him.

Whipping out my phone, I let Lucas know that won't fly with me.

Gemma: What was that?

It doesn't take long for his response, my phone buzzing as I trudge to my locker.

Lucas: What?
Gemma: ??? Bimbo 1 and Bimbo 2 hanging on your arm? The cuddling? Sorry if I don't like parties, but don't think you can be a fucking manwhore and I'll be cool with it.
Lucas: Chill out, that's not what was happening. I was playing wingman. I can't help it if chicks flock to me. You'll have to deal.

My eyebrows fly up. This fucker...

Gemma: Don't act like you weren't eating up the attention. I won't be yours if it's a one way road.
Lucas: You are mine. It's cute you're jealous.

"Ugh!"

A few people glance at me curiously. I duck my head as I fume.

I don't like the fake Lucas he presents to everyone else. I thought he was letting me in, showing me he was someone else past all the bullshit. I can't get a read on him like this other than the neon sign declaring him a giant asshole.

* * *

Despite my anger in the morning, I take a seat next to Lucas on autopilot during lunch. Blair isn't in school today and I'm feeling stranded at sea amongst ruthless sharks. Blending in is better than painting a target on my back by sitting away from Lucas.

Everyone at the table looks at me like they know something I don't. There's that same sickening hunger for blood dancing in their gazes. It grates on my senses, like they're sticking me with needles to dissect me.

I've been on my guard ever since the start of school. Almost two months of daily heckling, lewd jokes, and stupid tricks aren't erased by an open conversation and the passion Lucas and I shared. It's a sharp contrast to the lackluster greeting this morning and our argument after.

Lucas is lost in a conversation with Carter about what they'll do if the playoff game this week is rescheduled. They gesture with their hands as they discuss the possibilities.

It's more of the fake Lucas. I can tell and he hasn't even addressed me yet.

The tight lines of tension around his eyes give it away. Those creases drop away when we're alone.

I wish I sat at my old table by the window. The other people at school have all been nice today, but I feel the chill in the air here. There's something coming. Anticipation is a live wire running a current down my spine.

I zone back into the conversation when I realize they've stopped talking about football. The topic changed to something I never wanted to hear Lucas talking about so brazenly in school.

Lucas fidgets, tugging on his ear. "Nah, man, you know I don't kiss and tell."

"You do, though," someone down the table says.

"It's for real. Lucas finally won the bet to fuck our resident prude. He really did, look," Carter boasts to Devlin, offering his phone. "Check this master with his after sex selfie."

Ice encases me from head to toe. *What?*

Carter's eyes flick to me as I sit rigidly beside Lucas.

Devlin does the same, his brows creasing. "You need to hit the gym, bro."

Lucas swats across the table for him. "Shut up, I lift plenty in the weight room."

The lemmings all laugh as I stew in humiliation. This has to be some nightmare.

"Can I see?" I swallow when they all turn their attention to me. It's like they forgot I was there. I clear my throat and fiddle with my fork. "I want to see it."

I set my jaw as Lucas lays his hand over the back of my neck, pinching to keep me complacent.

"You know what happened this weekend, sweetheart." His tone is light, but the warning is clear.

Oh, Lucas doesn't want me to see? I shoot him a mutinous glance. Too fucking bad.

If I'm going to be degraded, I'll damn well witness just how badly Lucas betrayed my trust. The ice capsule around me cracks with fissures. They see my brave face, but inside I'm screaming at the top of my lungs.

"Do I? I think I need photographic evidence as a reminder. I don't think it was that memorable without a little souvenir. You apparently thought so, too."

Lucas' eyes bounce between mine, shadowed with the danger my instincts predicted. His jaw clenches and he holds up his hands.

"Do what you want."

A glacial river floods my veins, crystalizing the blood flow as Devlin slides Carter's phone across to me with a frown.

Carter: Bro, where u at, I got tix for DJ Smokescrn tonight. U in?
Lucas: Bit busy here. [Fist emoji]
Carter: Right on, brother!!! [100 emoji] Finally plugged that whiny bitch up good with a sausage. Did she cry?

The conversation ends there. The words waver as my eyes blur with unshed tears. The sting slices me deep as I see what Lucas has done.

Lucas sent Carter a photo of us. We're in my bed. It's clear he's still naked as I sleep on his bare chest. I'm what keeps him modest in the photo, but the curve of my ass is visible at the bottom edge of the frame.

There's no question about how we got that way.

Carter slaps a wad of cash on the table. Several other people do the same. Devlin holds my wild gaze, frowning as he slips money from his wallet and adds it in.

Lucas lets out a forced bark of laughter that grates in my ears. I want to slap my hands over them to push everything out. Then slap him. *Hard.*

At first I don't understand, like I've watched a wreck happen from the sidelines. My mind is still lagging at the text message, unable to process what's going on here. When it clicks, my vision swims with dizziness and it takes a minute for me to realize that brittle wheezing noise is me struggling for air.

The doubt from earlier turns my insides to sludge as money exchanges hands.

"Pose with your winnings, dude," Carter instructs, holding up his phone. "I'm putting this in my Insta story. Hashtag playa gonna play."

Fissures spread across my heart like a frozen lake cracking, each new break audible only to me. People see me as this tough girl persona. They don't think they can hurt me because I don't let them.

But it hurts. It hurts so much.

Lucas made me believe he wanted me.

That was a lie.

None of his actions were sincere. I meant nothing to him. Just a bet to win for bragging rights.

All Lucas wanted with me was to use me.

Each new truth stabs a different point of my body, that cold dissection tray flaying me open for the world to see how gullible I was and how easy it was to shatter me.

I'm so angry at myself for falling for his tempting empty words after all the shit he put me through. Lucas is the worst kind of snake in the grass, his venom activating only when it will have the most lethal effect.

I'm a trophy to Lucas after all. A conquest and nothing more.

The hunter caught his prey and the game is over.

I jump when Lucas wraps his arm around my shoulder. My insides crawl as his lips graze my cheek.

"I was just a bet to you?" They go silent at the unbridled tone, my voice coarse and severe.

Deny it, I beg in my mind. *Be my Lucas. Tell me it's not real.*

"It was just for fun, sweetheart," Lucas mutters in a soothing tone. For everyone else's benefit he goes on. "It doesn't mean anything. Just guys being guys."

Too little too damn late, Lucas.

The anger and pain morph together to create a horrible torrent inside my chest.

"Guys being guys," I mutter. "Right."

Time to tap out. I can't sit through the rest of the period with him. I don't want to be near him another second.

As he receives praise for his success, I shove away from him with a grunt. In my scramble to get up from the table I trip, smacking into the linoleum.

A hush falls over the room. The vultures smell fresh meat to feast on. Here comes the lamb for sacrifice, hand delivered by their golden Saint.

My knee throbs as I drag myself up, scrubbing at my burning eyes. The ache runs deeper than a bruised knee.

My pride. My trust. My heart.

All of them bruised by Lucas and the brutal way he toyed with me.

"Gemma?" Lucas holds a hand out to me, hard lines etched on his face. There's a crack in his mask, but he won't let it fall. Through the crack, there's a hint of regret. Guilt, even. It's not enough. "Are you okay?"

How could I be?

"Yes," I snarl, turning a glower on him. His jaw tightens. "Leave me alone."

My feet carry me from the cafeteria. Each painful breath leaves my throat raw, like the scrape of nails slicing me open. I run for the bathroom.

It's empty. Small mercies.

I run the faucet and hold on to the sink with a white-knuckled grip.

I knew better. I should never have let myself get drawn into Lucas Saint's world. I can't fit myself in with the crowd.

It's better to watch from the outside. It protects me and my heart.

I bend down and splash cool water on my blotchy face. I look like hell in the mirror. The loose strands of my braid are wet, my eyes bloodshot, and my nose running.

Worst of all is the same betrayed look in my eyes from when I was sixteen.

I called it when I wrote those words on Lucas' windshield to get him back for everything.

Beautiful destroyer. That's what Lucas is. A plague on the heart, out for destruction for his own sick mind games.

TWENTY-EIGHT
LUCAS

Gemma isn't around the rest of the day.

When I chased her out of the cafeteria, she disappeared too fast for me to follow.

I didn't think Carter would need to be told not to spread the photo around. Things got out of control.

Once the topic came up, I didn't know how to shut it down. It's not something I've ever done before. My mask was slipping and it was a challenge to keep it from falling.

Laughing with my friends at lunch was the hardest thing I've ever done. It didn't feel good at Gemma's expense, not the way I'd fantasized about at the start of the year.

The tension hasn't left me since lunch.

It was stupid to think I could keep Gemma and my mask. The two don't go together. She sees through it.

I need a way to fix this. But I can't figure out how to explain to Gemma how things have changed since I set this in motion.

Scraping my fingers through my hair in last period, I send another text. Gemma has ignored all of my messages today. And she blocked me on her Instagram. I found that out when I went on to send her a DM.

Lucas: Babe, talk to me. Can I see you before practice?

I'm ready to cut out of class early to find her. God only knows what's going on in her head.

I sit up when three gray dots appear on the screen. They disappear and return twice. I tug on my earlobe as I wait for her response.

At the front of the room, my English teacher pauses her lesson to squint at me. I slouch in my desk in the back row and put the phone on my lap so she doesn't take it from me. She tips her chin up and keeps talking about nouns or analogies or whatever.

I tune the lesson out as I will Gemma to answer me.

At several long minutes, my phone vibrates on my thigh.

Gemma: Get one of your other girls to suck your dick today. Not feeling it. The others can have you.

My brow wrinkles. Other girls? Is this about those Coyote Girls from the parking lot this morning?

I grit my teeth. Damn it. That meant nothing. It was me being a wingman to Devlin. He was itching to get laid.

If anything, I kept up the act when Gemma showed because I was curious if she'd get jealous. I wanted to see her jealous over me, like I get anytime another guy even looks her way. Seeing her jealousy proves she needs me—*wants* me the way I want her.

Lucas: There are no other girls for me. Only you.

She replies immediately.

Gemma: Save it, your dick won't grow the more you lie. I'm done. Go away.

She can't keep me away.

Annoyed that I'm not getting through to her, I stuff my phone in my pocket.

She doesn't believe me. Fine. I won't plead my case to ears that don't give a shit to listen. She can cool off and I'll try later.

Your fault, coward, a voice niggles in the back of my head. I twist like I can physically escape the slithering thoughts.

It was easier when I hated her. When she didn't make me face the person I am and the one I pretend to be.

This all went sideways the minute I started to catch feelings for Gemma Turner.

My life would be cake if I simply put her in her place and moved on. Leave her for some other idiot to deal with, if he was brave enough to tame her.

Even thinking like this, my reaction is visceral. I swallow through the possessiveness that rears up. My mind screams *mine, mine, mine.*

Gemma's in my fucking veins. I can't get her out that easy.

Or let someone else have her.

My fists clench, the skin stretching over my knuckles.

The bell rings, cutting through my swirling thoughts. I gather my stuff and follow the rest of the class into the hall as our teacher shouts after us about a possible pop quiz.

Marissa finds me at my locker five minutes later as I'm stuffing books inside. Alarm bells go off in my head. I am not prepared for even more bullshit to cap off the day.

"Hey, baby," she says in a husky voice that carries across the hall as she approaches.

I sidestep the *baby* pet name. "I'm really not in the mood."

Undeterred, Marissa slips into my personal space, wedging between me and the locker. Her arms lock around my neck and she pouts at me.

Tensing, I snap, "Marissa, what the fuck?"

"Are you ready to come back to me? You know you've got it good when we're together. You can have this," she takes my hand and presses it to the front of her skirt, "anytime you want."

I open my mouth to tell her I'm never getting back with her. A strangled scoff to my left draws my attention.

Fuck. This can't be happening.

What karmic god did I piss off?

Alec and Gemma stand there, probably on their way out to their car. Gemma props her hands on her hips. She studies us with a hard expression, eyebrows raised.

"Not a liar, huh? Yeah. I thought so."

After she spits those words, she turns her back on me and rushes off.

"Goddamn it," I grit out. "Gemma, wait!"

"Why are you bothering with plain Jane when you have me?" Marissa's persistence crumbles my patience.

"Gemma! It's not what you think!" I shout. Marissa gets in my way as Gemma rounds the corner. I take her by the shoulders and move her aside. "Marissa, get the *fuck* out of the way!"

Marissa lets me go. She knows how to work a crowd in these halls. She'll only make a scene when it works in her favor.

I don't care about any of that, I only want to get to Gemma.

Alec stops me in my tracks with a hand on my arm, blocking me from following Gemma's hasty retreat. "That's enough. Leave my sister alone, man."

The protective challenge in his eyes puts a bitter taste in my mouth. I don't want to hurt Gemma. I'm worthy of protecting her. Or, I will be again, after I clear up the mess I made.

"Look, I just want to tal—"

"It looks like she's done talking to you. Back off."

With a shove, Alec releases me and stalks off in the same direction as Gemma. Stunned, I stand in the middle of the hall as people give me a wide berth. Their whispers fly freely as I try to make my legs move.

It's like I'm encased in cement, unable to drag myself to fall on my sword for Gemma—because that's what it will take to get her back.

I have to choose, my mask or the girl that holds my still-beating heart in her palms?

By the time I reach the parking lot, the silver CR-V is gone. I blow out a ragged breath, dropping my head back.

Flurries drop from the overcast sky.

This is why my life is easier when I play up what people want to see me as. If I shroud myself in my god-like persona as the golden king of Silver Lake High School, I don't have to deal with this fear and pain.

My phone vibrates itself off my desk later that night.

I tossed it there when I threw myself down after getting back from Gemma's house. Alec met me at the door and wouldn't let me in to plead my case.

I pull one of my earbuds free, disrupting the music

drowning out my thoughts as I sketch. Lancelot is curled up on the bench seat beneath the window.

None of it has been good, anyway. My head's too full of Gemma to focus on drawing concepts. I'm used to being naturally gifted with throwing a ball. My hands have never let me down like this before. It's scary to think I can have days so bad I can't draw.

Bending down to pick up the phone, I find a slew of missed texts. At first my heart jumps. But it's not Gemma. It's my cousin.

The last text catches my eye.

Devlin: This might be a problem.

Attached is a link to Instagram. Marissa's account. Wary, I open it.

It's a video post. I clench the phone in my grip so hard it might break.

The video shows a clip of a stupid mistake I made with Marissa when I thought I loved her.

We recorded ourselves once. A freaking sex tape. It was her idea.

In the clip, Marissa giggles as I kiss down her belly. I'm tagged in the post. Jesus. I scrub my face and read the caption.

@MightyRissa: Got my man back, bitches. [Lips emoji]

It's not the full video, thank fuck.

I'm dialing Marissa's number before I even process my dumbfounded anger.

She picks up on the second ring.

"Hey, babe." There's a sly smile in her voice. "Ready to grovel for that shit you pulled earlier? It's going to cost you."

I need to grovel, but it's not Marissa's mercy and forgiveness I need to earn.

"Marissa," I bark. "Cut the shit."

"You brought it on yourself for how you left me in the dust today!" She grumbles on the line. "I can't believe you'd chase after some nobody slut when I was standing—"

"Marissa, that's enough! Knock it off."

A vein pulses in my temple and I get up to stalk the length of my room in an agitated pace.

"You went too fucking far. I am *not* your boyfriend anymore. You decided that. You wanted a break. Posting this to make it look like we got back together is the most ridiculous shit you've ever done."

"Lucas—"

"No! I'm done, Marissa. I'm fucking finished! Don't test me again, or I'll rain hell on you so hard your reputation will be destroyed at school. Bishop collects everyone's dirty secrets and I won't hesitate to unleash yours to him with the order to put you on blast."

"Jesus, Lucas. What is your deal?"

"My *deal* is that I'm over playing this game with you. We've been done for a while. Whatever feelings I once had for you are gone. I thought we were friends, but you went and screwed that over, too."

I don't tell her she probably fucked me big time with explaining to Gemma. Marissa's actions in school were enough to make Gemma believe I was lying.

Marissa starts to speak, but I hang up and set her number to do not disturb so she can't bother me. I sink to my bed and hang my head between my hands.

Erupting from the mattress in a jolt of motion, I throw my fist with a yell. It crashes through the wall. Lancelot runs from the room with a shrieking pug warble. My chest heaves as I pant, the sudden instinct fading. I stare from the hole I left in the wall to my red, cracked knuckles.

Regret immediately settles in my gut. "Shit."

I flex my hand carefully. It doesn't feel broken. At least I threw a good punch. It'll bruise, but it seems fine. My wall on the other hand...not so much.

Thank god my parents are out on an overnight date in Denver.

"Fuck me," I groan.

I'll need to fix this before they see it. I grab a poster from the opposite wall and tack it over the damage to hide it. It'll do for now.

The need to hear Gemma's voice right now is inescapable. I dial and press the phone to my ear.

"Pick up, pick up..."

The line clicks and my heart stutters.

"This is Gemma. Leave a message and I'll hit you back." Her voice is a balm I don't deserve.

"I really fucked up," I tell the voicemail when the tone signals. I rub my forehead. "I wish I could do today over. I didn't mean to hurt you."

It's nowhere near satisfactory for an apology. Pitiful, in fact. My words flee, though, and I hang up. I dial again just to hear her voice.

My sketchbook sits open on my desk, but it feels wrong to make another attempt to use it.

I don't have to know the answer to the question running through my head when it comes to anything important in my life.

Am I good enough?

I'm pretty sure the answer is a fat fucking no.

TWENTY-NINE
GEMMA

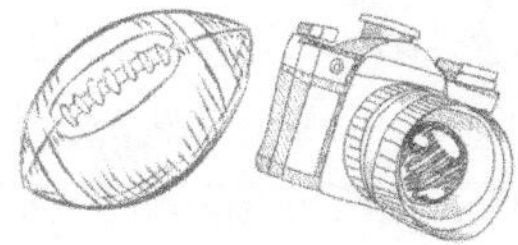

The bath I took with a scented bath bomb cleared my head.

"Everything okay, honey?" Mom asks, delivering a set of folded towels to the hall closet.

"Yeah. Of course."

I let out my hair from its bun and it falls around my shoulders. Mom steps forward and presses her hand to my face with a small frown.

"You look flushed. Your eyes are red. Are you coming down with a cold?"

I wave her off. "No, it's just the drop in temperature. I probably spent too long in the hot water. I promise, I'm fine."

Mom and I have never been the type of women to titter over crushes. Telling her vaguely about Matt was enough to put me off it. I'm not about to start now. I'll handle this on my own, too. Since moving here, my parents have seemed happy. I'm not going to kill that with my drama.

Besides, what's the point in telling her *yeah, I thought I had a boyfriend again, but oops, turns out he was a big jerkface liar, so that's over now*? Not my idea of a fun time.

"Want to order from the stack of takeout places we haven't tried yet?" She waggles her brows and it gets me to laugh. She loves takeout and has been on a mission to decide on a rotation of favorites. "I'm in the mood for curry. What about you?"

"Sure, Mom. Anything's good."

I check my phone when I pad into my room in a towel. There's a few Instagram likes on my latest post and a direct message.

Thinking it's a story share notification, I swipe to open it. I'm met with a message from an unfamiliar account.

I tap on the username to see the profile and my brow wrinkles. There's a thin bio, but the name says Devlin Murphy. His precious red car is in the first three posts. I go back to the message he sent me.

@DeviousDev: [eyes emoji].

That's the only explanation he gives, along with a post by another account. When I go to it, my heart plummets off a cliff edge.

Marissa's account.

Got my man back, bitches.

I watch the video clip three times. Each time Lucas kisses Marissa's stomach, my own twines into a tighter knot.

Take it in. Then pick yourself up.

I repeat my trusty mantra that got me through worse. The desired effect is lagging, like a magic spell that's run out of power.

I get dressed and curl up on my bed, an emptiness settled in my chest.

What did I expect?

Lucas is a cocky football player who swaggers around the school like the resident king.

He's not the guy with bigger dreams than people think he's capable of. He's not the guy that took care of me when I was freaked out and alone in the rain. He's not the same one that kissed me like I meant the world to him.

No. All of that was the world's oldest lie. One I fell for when I knew better.

As I lay there, I can't stir much anger at Marissa for going after what she wants. At least she's honest about it. She's been upfront this whole time that she planned to take Lucas back. Lucas is the one that lied to me and the one running straight to her.

Letting my guard down around Lucas was the wrong choice. Now I know not to make that mistake again.

Marissa and the rest of the school can have their self-important savior. I've had enough.

I'll protect myself the only way I've learned how. I'll stay safe on the other side of a camera lens. Getting involved means missing the bigger picture. It's only led to hurt and betrayal.

* * *

School sucks for a few days. The people that once labeled me a prude because I was angry about Lucas stealing my first kiss now have an active rumor mill to prove what a slut I am with the circulation of the selfie Lucas sent Carter.

Cute double standard, isn't it?

They're all absolute idiots.

Their bullshit isn't what gets to me. It's the twinge in my chest when I see Lucas in the halls.

Even when I've resolved to be strong, it's easier said than done. Controlling the longing call my heart gives when I see him is impossible.

My rotten heart hasn't accepted moving on from Lucas. Riotous little bastard.

Unfortunately, I have to endure it for the rest of the week. The snow that fell soon melted as the weather warmed. No snow days to get a minute's peace from Lucas. He glances my way, but as soon as he sees me a gate slams over his face, keeping me out of his true thoughts. Lucas sets his jaw, returning his attention to goofing around with Devlin and Connor.

I guess he didn't want to talk to me that badly. It was a gallant effort on his part to pretend for five minutes he was a decent human. It seems I was right to block his number.

The only upside is watching from afar as Lucas gives Carter the cold shoulder.

* * *

At home I can pretend everything's okay. Mom and Dad rope Alec and I into some Netflix original, a murder mystery that has all of us glued to the TV after dinner. When they both fall asleep on the couch, Alec and I head upstairs to go to our rooms.

"Hey." Alec pauses outside his door. He picks at the door-jamb. "Wait a sec."

"What?"

Alec follows me into my room. "Are you cool?"

"Cool about what?"

I grab a stack of square prints from the nightstand and

kneel on my bed to stick my new additions to the wall. The photos that have Lucas in them still sit in the drawer.

The bed shifts when Alec sits down.

"At school. The stuff with Lucas."

I shrug.

"He came by the other night. When you were crying in the bath. I wouldn't let him in." When I don't respond, Alec goes on. "Should I punch him?"

I peer at him over my shoulder. "Now why would you deck your friend, Alec?"

He chews on his lip, his face troubled.

"I've been a shitty brother."

"Alert the media," I deadpan.

"Seriously, Gem." He scoots closer and pokes my ankle as I return to my task. "I want to punch him every time I see him laughing with the guys. He treated you like shit and got away with it."

"Rich, popular, quarterback." I tick each one off on my fingers. "Privileged beyond belief. Basically an untouchable god amongst men."

"Okay, can you put the tough girl sarcasm on hold for five minutes? I want to know what will help you feel better. I've seen the way you still look at him."

My shoulders slump. "What makes you want to help now? You've been pretty hot and cold since we moved. I told you, Matt never asked—"

My voice cracks and I stop.

"I know," Alec says in a rush, voice gruff. "I know. I'm the worst for all of that. I should've believed you. I think..."

Abandoning my prints, I turn to face him. One hand is in his hair and his wide eyes stare at nothing.

"I didn't know how to handle it." He holds a palm up when I open my mouth to sling another snarky retort. "I know. It's not a good excuse. There aren't any valid excuses. Obviously things were worse for you, it actually happened to you. I didn't know what to say and I didn't want things to change. We all had fun together. He was my best friend. I didn't know how to flip to hating him overnight on your behalf."

A frown tugs at my lips. Alec lifts his tortured gaze to meet mine.

"I'm saying sorry now for being a dick about it. And for this year, since we moved." Alec scrubs his face. "I resented that we had to leave our home. I was ripped away from everyone. But it's cool here. I shouldn't have hated you for that."

Emotion bubbles over and closes my throat. I sniffle. Alec darts his eyes up.

"Oh god." He looks lost, but genuine. "Don't cry. Please."

I flap my hands as the tears flow. Alec wipes them away with his sleeve.

"Don't cry. It'll be okay."

A watery laugh leaves me. "Tough people cry, too."

"Yeah. You're right." He tugs me into his arms. "I'm sorry."

The tears run their course as I cling to Alec. I retreat with a gross snuffle, wiping my nose on my sleeve.

"It's fine." I knock my fist against his knee. It won't erase his actions and inactions, but he's apologizing now. "Thanks for saying sorry. And for realizing you're an ass."

Alec snorts.

"Yeah. I really am, Gem. God, when I saw you go through the same thing, only worse this time...it ate at me. But I was afraid."

"You didn't want them to lump you in with me after they accepted you?"

He shrugs. "I promise to do better now. I'll be a better brother."

Hearing him say that warms my heart. I missed him. We

had so many fun things only we shared, and when we moved here, they went away.

"Cool." I offer him a smile. "You know how you can really make it up to me?"

"Strawberry milkshake and fries?"

"Yes. Large fries. Maybe two large fries." I make grabby claw hands. "Gimme all the fries."

Alec snorts and shoves at me. "Want to go tonight?"

"Sure."

I roll from the bed to pull on a pair of jeans and find my jacket.

"You know, there's a party tonight." Alec gets up from the bed as I dig through my clothes. "The only way to show Saint you're not a fragile thing he broke is to show up."

"I don't know, Alec. Parties and I still aren't on speaking terms. I get all anxious in that kind of atmosphere."

"But you can show them you don't care about whatever they think of you. I've got your back."

"I already don't give a shit about them."

"I know, but they all think they got one over on you. Are you going to let them keep you down?"

I mull that over as I fold and refold the sweater I pulled out. He wouldn't expect me to show up to his party after I fought tooth and nail to avoid them.

"Okay. You're right."

Alec crows. "Nice. Meet me downstairs in twenty? I'll check on Mom and Dad and send them to bed."

"Deal."

As he leaves, I lay out a different outfit. One the old me would totally wear. It's going to be my armor tonight.

I am stronger than Lucas. Time to prove it to him.

THIRTY
LUCAS

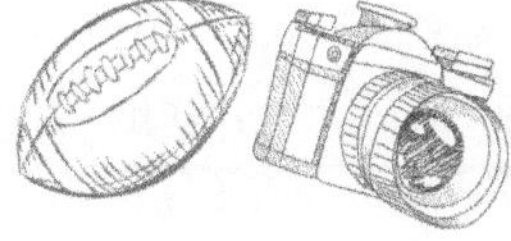

A weird mood has its claws in me as I set up bottles of alcohol on my kitchen island for the party.

If I'm honest, it's been a cloud hanging over me for days.

Gemma blocked my number when I tried to reach out again. I wanted to explain my side to her, but I don't know if she saw it before I couldn't get through to her anymore. I've taken to climbing the tree outside her window in the middle of the night to peer in on her in the faint glow of fairy lights strung over her bed.

It pisses me off that we apparently ended before we got started over another misunderstanding.

If she would just let me tell her the truth, this would all shake out differently.

Regret sits in my stomach like oil on top of water. I drew Gemma in the same way I drove her away.

There's only myself to blame. I'm the one that sent the photo to Carter, well aware of the chance he'd crow about it at school. I guess part of me was nostalgic for the guy I used to know.

Maybe if I was a better person, I wouldn't have done anything to hurt her. But I'm not a good person.

My thumb smooths the label over a bottle of whiskey that has a cool illustration.

I haven't been able to draw for days and it scares me. I feel like I'm cornered and the only way out is football. I threw out my application for Oak Ridge College, finally opening the drawer where I hid it.

I'm only good for one thing. It's time I accept that.

A knock sounds at the contemporary wall of glass panels on the deck. Carter stands there with a sheepish expression and what I assume is meant to be an *I'm sorry* six-pack. He's such a dick.

"I didn't invite you," I say as a greeting when I open the door.

"C'mon man, really? I said I was sorry. I don't know why you have your panties in a twist over some chick. But you do you, bro."

Devlin comes up the steps behind him. I roll my eyes, turning my back on Carter. He takes the frosty reception as an invitation to come in. They both follow me. Carter puts the six-pack in the fridge.

"Dev, turn on music." I want to get out of my own head.

He shoots me a finger gun and leaves me in the kitchen with Carter.

I crack open a beer and chug half of it. As soon as it hits my stomach, my body revolts. I keep it down—barely managing.

Maybe I'm too stressed to drink. That doesn't bode well for my plan to get wasted and numb. Bishop better bring the good weed tonight.

Carter hovers at the edge of my periphery. He needs to step back or I'll lose it.

As other people arrive, I brush off Carter.

The party quickly gets underway, the music cranking and plumes of acrid cigarette, weed, and vape smoke curling into the air from my back deck.

For a while, I throw myself into cheering for a game of beer bong. When it doesn't fill the hollowness in my stomach, I bum a cigarette from someone I've never spoken to and lean on the railing as I smoke.

Thunder rolls in the distance. Maybe it'll hail. It was sunny this morning, but an approaching storm hangs heavy in the air.

It matches my mood. No matter how much I try to enjoy the party, it's getting more difficult to be that guy.

I'm hanging with Devlin and Bishop when Carter lopes over to us. He's drunk. I've lost the slight buzz I was working on and haven't felt like another drink since the abandoned beer.

"Can't keep me down!" Carter rants incoherently. "Didn't want to miss out on the life of the party."

I can feel Devlin and Bishop looking for my reaction. My jaw aches from gnashing my teeth.

"Maybe take the party over there," Devlin suggests lightly. "Too much party in this corner. Not good for blood pressure."

Carter sidesteps Bishop's hand on his shoulder and the attempt to direct him away from me. Carter's arm lands around my shoulders. He leans in my face with beer breath.

Bishop whistles low. "Dead man walking."

"Lis'en. *Lis'en.*" Carter pokes my cheek, ignorant to the rising danger as my shoulders tense. "I only ask because we're friends. Bros."

"Yeah?" My tone is threatening. "I don't know, you haven't been a great *bro* recently."

"No, no," Carter goes on in complete drunken logic. "You finished with Gemma. So I can slide in now."

All the nerve endings in my body jump for a fight at his words. Carter comes critically close to meeting my fist in his face. It takes every scrap of restraint I have not to cold-cock him.

The Homecoming game is soon. And the championship game next month. If I fuck with Carter now, I'll still have to play nice with him and trust him to be my guard.

I exhale and walk away, only to halt in my tracks when Gemma and Alec walk through the door.

I go lightheaded for a minute. The room spins as the axis rights itself. She's here and she looks sinfully hot.

Gemma's wearing black leather pants and a slinky gold top with slits at the shoulders. Her hair frames her face. She has a confident expression as she stares down everyone who looks her way. Including me.

She's a walking temptation.

My mind goes blank except for a single blaring thought: *I screwed up.*

THIRTY-ONE
GEMMA

My bravado lasts five whole minutes once we arrive at the party.

What the hell am I doing?

People look me up and down, judgement plain as day in their eyes. I'm not welcome here. I feel it in the air as Alec nudges me in the house.

I battle against regret and the discomfort of being surrounded by loud music and flowing booze as people enjoy themselves with abandon.

Marissa shoots daggers at me from across the room, where she and Carter stand. She speaks in Carter's ear and a dopey grin crosses his face as he bobs his head in agreement. I feel sorry for her. The drama she thrives on in high school will leave her ill-prepared for real life when we graduate.

Alec leans in to be heard over the music. "You're strong, Gem. Show them all."

He pats me on the back and the regret slides away.

That's right. I came here to prove a point. I give him a firm nod.

I allow Alec to pull me in with the other dancers and after a few songs I get into wiping the floor with better dance moves than him. We laugh at his go-to move.

Elena joins us, wildly cheering, "Turner twins!"

"Hey, Elena!" Alec has a secret handshake with her. "Show us what you've got."

The three of us dance in a lopsided circle. Having a good time with them helps chase away the lingering effects of the party atmosphere on my psyche, holding the bad memories at bay as I make new ones.

A few brave guys approach, but Alec has my back. He stares them down and shoos them away when they try to dance up on me. I let go, focusing on enjoying myself. The music flows through me, lifting my spirits.

The only person at the party that hasn't directly acknowledged my presence after an hour is Lucas. But I can feel the weight of his gaze on me, trailing me every time I walk through the room.

He had his chance.

Take a good look, I tell him in my head. *This is my big fuck you to you.*

I take a break from dancing when I'm dying of thirst. I hesitate at the edge of the kitchen, where other students are heavy on their pouring with the alcohol on the island.

"Want one?" The guy brandishes a bottle of rum. "I make the best rum and cokes."

I shake my head. Slipping around the guy that offered me a drink, I dig through the fridge for a water bottle. There aren't any left. Lucas must have put them in one of the coolers I saw on the deck.

Sighing, I spin around. Lucas catches my attention. Marissa stands near him, looking like the cat with the cream. He's not talking to her, though. He seems lost in thought, an unhappy tilt to his mouth.

I decide to go back to find Alec and Elena, weaving through the people crowding to get into the kitchen. The party is packed.

Elena isn't where I last saw her. Neither is Alec. I frown and search for them. I think that's her out on the deck, talking to the football player she's always with. I grab a random person who's been dancing since we got there.

"Hey, have you seen Alec?"

The dude shrugs. "He said he had to take a piss."

"Thanks."

Without Alec and Elena distracting me, I feel on display. I take a post in the corner to people watch.

"Hey," Devlin says, propping on the wall next to me.

"What's up?"

"You seemed lonely."

He scans the room, grinning when his friend Connor does a handstand on the other side.

"Lucas didn't send you over here, did he?"

Devlin flicks a glance at me. "What if he did?"

"Tell him to go fuck himself. Ugh!" I grit my teeth and spin away. "He's too chickenshit to talk to me himself? Whatever. I don't even want to see him."

I start to leave, but pause when Devlin speaks again.

"Is that why you came here?"

"I came because it's a party. Half the school's here."

Devlin hums. "That's boring."

I blink, taken aback. "Well, I'm so sorry my entertainment factor dropped. I'll get right on that."

Brimming with annoyance, I stomp away. I need to take the edge off.

I stand back at the island staring down a bottle of vodka. My head fights my heart. I want to have a drink, but I can't make myself pour the shot. I wish Alec would come back. I'm ready to leave. I've been at the party long enough to prove my point.

A rough set of hands settle on my waist as a hard body pins me from behind. The rancid beer breath hits me before I turn my head.

"Hey, pretty," Carter slurs against my ear, his lips wet.

My skin crawls as I struggle to slide away. "Get off."

Carter either doesn't hear me or doesn't care. This is worse than the last couple of times he's tried to get with me like he has a free pass. His hands roam, palming my breasts. Anyone can see this happening.

"Get *off*," I spit. I'm trapped against the counter by his size and weight. My heartbeat thrums with a jitter. "Carter, stop!"

"You were easy for Saint. It's my turn to take you for a spin."

Is he drunk? There's a lethargic incoordination to his motions. Carter presses open-mouthed kisses to my neck that send disgust ricocheting through me.

He keeps mumbling against my skin. "He won the pot. I figure you owe me a turn. Been panting for my cock since school started. Know you want it."

I struggle against him when he grabs me, lifting me clear off the ground like some sick bridal ritual.

"No!"

Desperation sets in as I frantically search for my brother, for anyone, for *Lucas* to stop this.

No one pays attention to my obvious protests. Everyone's drunk and high, happy, having a good time with their friends and loud music. The only people around are the same lesser assholes on the outer fringes of the popular circle. The ones who bullied me at a snap of Lucas' fingers.

"Saddle up," someone says with a vicious laugh.

"Better wrap your dick up, Big C. You don't know where she's been."

How can I simultaneously be the school prude and the school bicycle? Yeah, you've got me there.

They don't see this for what it is. I'm obviously not consenting to jack shit here. But no, they slap Carter on the back for a good hunt, like I'm the prize he's won.

My teeth grind and my eyes lock with Lucas'. I open my mouth to call out for him, but the way his face contorts in anger makes me pause long enough for Carter to kiss me.

His mouth tastes sour when he forces his tongue past my lips.

I turn my head away from it with a broken cry. When he chases me for more, I bite him.

Carter manhandles me to a downstairs guest room. "You're mine tonight, sweetness."

The door closes behind us. I yell, kick, and flail. Carter is stronger than Lucas, his bigger muscles making it easy to hold me prisoner.

"Carter, let me fucking go!"

"Not a chance."

He tosses me onto the bed and drags me to the edge by a tight grasp on my ankle. I claw at the covers, pulling half of the bedding with me.

How could Lucas look at me like *he* was the one who was furious? How could he abandon me to his horrible friend?

"Alec!" I scream at the top of my lungs. "Help!"

"No one's coming, baby." Carter grabs my ass and I squirm to get away. "Be quiet. They can't hear you over the music. I want you to save those screams for when I split you open with my cock."

The panic taking over my body sears me from the inside out as I thrash.

"Someone! Please!"

Carter's right. No one is coming to save me. I have to save myself.

THIRTY-TWO
LUCAS

Ignoring Gemma for more than two seconds is an impossible feat. One I haven't accomplished all night.

My gaze keeps cutting back to her.

She looked good dancing, her arms overhead as EDM music pumped through the speakers. She came alive, shedding the guard she uses to keep everyone ten feet back at all times.

An invisible hook tugs at me, luring me to approach her.

At first I had half a mind to throw her out. But now that she's here and smiling, I want to rush up to her and hold her close. I want to spill my guts to her so she might look at me like that.

Watching as guys tried to move in on her burned like acid, sizzling and popping in my gut. My hands are getting sore from clenching my fists. Crescent shapes indent my palms from my blunt nails.

When she's out of my sight for a bit, I can't ignore the niggling at my instincts to find her.

I take a step away from my post in the corner, finally working up the balls to talk to her.

Marissa slides in front of me, blocking my path.

"What?" I spit.

I still haven't forgiven her for her petty Instagram post. As if I'd roll over and shove my dick back in her poisonous mouth because she posted it on social media? Fucking stupid.

She levels a cool look at me, stance full of attitude.

"Where are you off to? Aren't you having a good time?" She puts her hands on my chest. "We should go upstairs. I'll make you feel better."

I grab her upper arms in a too tight hold that makes her wince.

"What could possibly make you believe," I grit through my teeth, "I would be interested? How many times do I have to tell you I'm done?"

I release her with a shove. She stumbles back a step and rubs her arms. Her lip juts out petulantly. It works to get guys to do what she wants, but she can't control me like that anymore.

"If you don't get out of my face, Marissa, I'm making you leave the party."

"Just listen," she snaps. Her mouth curls into a cruel curve as she examines her nails. "I thought you'd need a shoulder to cry on. I saw your little Gemma yesterday in school. You might be hung up on her, but she's got it bad for Carter. She was going on and on about how much she wants to fu—"

My hand moves in a flash, wrapping around Marissa's throat. She cuts off with shock in her wide eyes.

"Jesus. You're pathetic," Marissa hisses, flattening her brows.

"Not as pathetic as you. I'm not believing your shit. You're being catty because you didn't get your way." I bring my face close to hers, growling, "Gemma isn't like you. She doesn't manipulate people."

Marissa's gaze flicks to the side. "Oh yeah? So what's that about?"

I let her go, turning in the direction indicated. Carter has Gemma in his arms.

A red haze slams over my vision, blood surging with a fiery rage at the sight of him kissing her neck. Her hands are on his chest, body arched.

No fucking way.

There's no way Gemma fooled me.

But I can't deny it looks exactly like Marissa said. My stomach knots itself and a tightness squeezes my chest.

He's all over her.

Gemma's gaze finds mine, like she wants to make sure I see before Carter kisses her.

My breathing is heavy, fraught with the tension of my rising anger.

Then she rips her mouth from Carter's with a cry that pierces through the haze. It's hard to hear over the heavy beat of EDM, but I make out the anguish crumpling her face. She's desperate and pleading, reaching out to grab hold of people as Carter hauls her away.

Fuck.

The scene rearranges, re-cast in the harsh light of the truth.

I search the room for Alec and Devlin as my veins freeze out the hot rush of anger.

"Hey!" Marissa yells when I push past her.

My heart pounds in time with the music, pulse speeding up as I urgently look for help.

It doesn't matter if Gemma hates me. I'm not going to leave her. She's getting my help whether she needs it or not.

Everything screams at me. I need to get Gemma away from Carter.

THIRTY-THREE
GEMMA

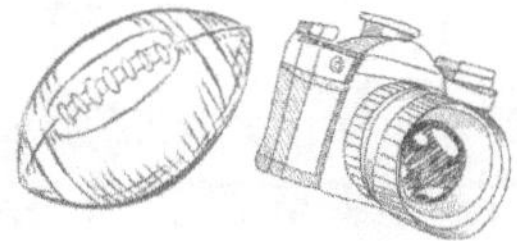

It's like last time all over again. Carter covers my back with his body.

Pained cries get stuck in my throat as Carter grinds on me. Tears burst forth like a wellspring.

"Please don't do this!"

Carter mumbles to himself, an incoherent string of words. He's too drunk for me to reason with.

His hands mesh with Matt's in my head as he touches me, my assault in the past converging with the one currently playing out.

I'm barely able to draw air into my lungs as I hyperventilate. Panic collides with the awful memories of Matt, leaving me almost catatonic.

I have to do something! If I don't save myself, no one else will. Alec is out there and has no idea I'm in trouble. Again.

It takes a monumental effort, but as Carter tugs uselessly at the waistband of my tight leather pants from behind, I bring my breathing under control. My throat is sore from screaming. I clench my fists in the covers, thinking I might be able to confuse Carter for a split second by covering his drunk ass with them.

My opportunity comes when Carter grunts and flips me over. I bounce on the mattress, rolling into action without waiting. I drive my knee towards his groin.

"Augh!" Carter shouts, crumpling over the edge of the bed.

This is my chance!

I scramble in a twisted mess of bedding to get away. Then he grabs me again.

"No!"

My pulse rockets out of control. My chance to get away slips through my fingers as Carter pins me to the bed. It's difficult to breathe with his entire weight crushing me.

"Bitch!" Carter snarls.

It must have been a glancing blow to his balls. Frustration slithers down my spine. I blink back more tears.

Carter slides his hands beneath my shirt and bra, going so roughly the shirt rips at the seams. He digs his fingers into my breasts until it hurts. I whimper pitifully as tears stream down my cheeks.

His breath coasts over my face. "You're gonna wish y'didn't pull that shit. Lucas likes his girls to play rough. But I like it when they *take it*."

A silent sob wracks my body, precious air hissing between my clenched teeth.

Dread fills me. This isn't like what happened with Matt. This is so much worse.

He pinches my nipples savagely, beady black eyes pinned

on me, watching the way my face twists in pain and horror.

I turn my head away. I can't look at Carter anymore. I close my eyes for a brief respite, wondering if it's true what some articles say about the mind's ability to shut off in extreme trauma situations. Maybe I'll get a mental panic room to block it all out.

That would be lucky.

It's sick that thoughts like that cross my mind.

Carter mistreats my breasts and drags his gross lips on my neck. I jerk, unable to sit there and take it, no matter the threat he poses.

It's crystal clear to me now. Lucas is nothing like this. A rapist. My heart cracks open, the contents leaking onto the floor as I wish for Lucas to show up. He would never hurt me the way Carter is about to. The worst mind games Lucas plays don't cut as deeply as this.

But even if he's not the perilous monster Carter is, Lucas isn't here to protect me.

I want him here. I want Lucas' strong arms and gentle touch. I would give anything for Lucas to kidnap me right now. I'd gladly enter his cage and sing like a pretty canary.

If only he'd come for me. If only I hadn't protected my heart by slamming walls around myself. For what? My pride? Look where that's gotten me.

The tears burn my cheeks and sting my eyes, hot as they glide down my cheeks in a continuous river. My entire body stiffens as Carter fumbles to get my leather pants down.

I can't decide if it's a small blessing that I wore them tonight. They're keeping him from raping me, but also prolonging the waves of torture as Carter gets frustrated and bites my neck.

A bang sounds in the room, making Carter and I startle violently. It's the door hitting the wall hard enough to leave a dent as Lucas storms in. Alec and Devlin follow behind him.

"Get the hell off of her, Burns, or I'll fucking kill you!" Lucas roars.

The relieved sob that spills from my lips isn't human.

He's here. He came. Somehow he knew I needed him.

Carter is ripped off me. I curl up in a protective ball, my body so tense I'm shivering. I flinch at the sound of fists hitting flesh and the sick grunts Carter makes as Lucas punches him.

"She wanted it!" Carter moans. "Askin' for it dressed like that!"

"Are you really trying to justify why you would do this, fucker?" Lucas' voice is almost unrecognizable, filled with an unmoored rage. "You assaulted her! You were going to rape her!"

His fists fly until Carter's face is swollen and red, bleeding from the lip and a cut above his eye. Lucas doesn't stop attacking him, savage in his punches. It should terrify me. But I'm not scared of Lucas. The violence in him on my behalf speaks to something deep inside me.

Alec and Devlin help me up from the bed with gentle, slow movements.

Alec takes point, keeping his hands where I can see them before gathering my hands in his. His face is lined with brittle tension, probably beating himself up for leaving me alone.

I shake my head, trying to convey it wasn't his fault.

Alec hands me the keys. I clutch them to my chest like a lifeline. They mean freedom. A weapon of self defense. Control.

"You keep these. We'll go in a minute." His voice is soft, at odds with the sounds of Lucas tearing into Carter behind him. "Are you okay?"

I nod stiltedly, taking raw gulps of air. He takes my hands in his again and presses his forehead to them.

"I'm sorry, Gem. It'll be okay now. You're safe."

Alec gets up and tries to push Lucas aside, but he's too far gone in the violent storm of his protective fury. He has to drag Lucas away with Devlin's help. Lucas stumbles aside, panting. Alec stands frozen over Carter for a second. Then in a burst of movement, he punches Carter in the stomach.

"Don't ever come near my sister again! You hear me?"

Lucas flexes his bloody hands, poised to jump back in. His eyes are dangerous, the set of his jaw enraged. He swings his gaze at me and it takes a beat for the shadows to fly away.

"Do you want to press charges?" His voice is hard. He can barely keep himself in check. "My dad can help."

It takes me a minute to find my voice, my tongue sluggish. My body is still on high alert as I sit up and hug myself.

"No. I just want it to go away."

Lucas furrows his brow, but nods. He turns back to Carter, grabbing him by the collar to drag him up.

"If you ever touch Gemma again, talk to her—fuck, if you even *look* her way," Lucas gets in his face, "I will come after you. I will end you."

I find it ironic that Lucas can offer me his dad's lawyer services in one breath and turn around to threaten Carter in the next.

Carter's sports a puffy eye that'll turn into a black bruise later. His head lurches when he nods in acknowledgement.

All at once, I'm overcome by the need to get out of the room, fight-or-flight kicking in.

I slip away as the guys show off their testosterone. The music is too loud, the laughter grating. I have to get out of the house.

My stomach threatens to revisit my dinner as I stumble onto the mostly empty deck, the rain chasing everyone inside. It's not enough. I have to leave. Right now.

The nausea intensifies as I hobble down the steps to the

yard. Lightning flashes in the sky, followed by the rumble of thunder.

Rain pelts me, the frigid droplets snaking down my neck into my ripped shirt. I shudder.

In my head, the haunting memories of Matt coalesce with what just went down in a sickening amalgam. I get to the car and wilt against the side as I struggle through dry heaves.

I scrub at the slimy feeling on my skin. It doesn't go away. I want to get as far away from Carter as possible. I rip open the door and hop in the CR-V, starting the ignition with shaking hands. Every shadow, every creaking tree limb, every echo of rainfall makes my heart falter.

I check my mirrors for my demons fifty times before I peel out.

I thought I had built my walls back up after Matt. I thought I was strong. But my fight-or-flight mode skews hard in flight's direction.

The thunderstorm makes me jumpy as I drive down the winding mountain road. Each booming clap makes my heart skip a beat. I hope there isn't another road blockage like last time.

I shriek when the wheel fights me, control flung from my hands for several heart-stopping seconds as the car fishtails on the slick road.

I regain control and tears blur my vision.

Headlights appear in the rearview mirror.

My eyes snap up to check the reflection as my body goes cold, the icy prickle rushing across my nerve endings.

I'm sick to my stomach, in a chokehold from my fear.

Carter is coming after me.

I floor it. He can't have me.

THIRTY-FOUR
LUCAS

The second I finish directing Devlin to throw Carter and Marissa out, I turn to find Gemma missing.

She vanished.

An ice cold fist breaks through my chest to strangle my heart as I rush through the party, chasing after her with Carter's blood on my sore knuckles.

My fury hasn't abated. Carter deserves more than a beating for touching Gemma. I seethe with the need for revenge, a bloodthirsty focus blaring in my head. It'll have to wait. Gemma is my first priority.

"You looking for the sad girl?"

I pause my edgy scan of the rain-soaked deck. There's a lone smoker huddled under the overhang, a cigarette dangling between his fingers.

"Yeah."

The smoker nods to the steps. "Tore off, like, five minutes ago."

"Fuck."

I'm already taking the steps two at a time as I barrel down them. I pat my pocket, sending out thanks to whatever force is listening when I feel the outline of my keys. I don't have time to grab Alec or the others.

As I throw myself into the car and kick it into gear, I press a hand to the pounding beat in my chest. My heart hasn't fully calmed from the last thirty minutes. As soon as I ensure Gemma's safety from one situation, she goes and dives into another.

"Damn it, Gemma."

I grip the wheel and click my wipers on the faster setting. I hope I'm not too late. The last time she took off on the unfamiliar road in the rain, it was a close call. That's not a fate she can escape twice.

It's hard to regulate my speed when my anxiety climbs. I know better, and yet I'm still flying around the bends quicker than I should.

Fear curdles in my gut.

Please let me catch up. Let her be safe.

Sweet relief spreads as soon as I spot the taillights of the CR-V.

"There you are!"

Gemma doesn't slow down, though. She speeds up. I curse and follow her. I lay on the horn to get her attention, thinking she might not realize it's me. It makes things worse.

Her car swerves, careening around the curve in the road too quickly.

"No! Gemma!"

A flash of lightning blinds me for a second.

The CR-V whips around, tires losing traction on the wet road. I suck in a breath and slam on the breaks as the CR-V finishes spinning out. We're lined up for a head on collision.

I'll go from her savior to the one that takes her life. My foot crushes the brake pedal. I'm too scared to speak, pleading in my head.

The CR-V skids to a stop, the whole car rocking with the force. Gemma did it, she stopped!

My elation shatters when I see the car still rocking. I manage to fully brake a few feet away. The Range Rover is barely in park before I sprint from the car.

The back wheel of the CR-V teeters off the edge of the road, dangling over the muddy slope with no traction. It's too close for comfort.

"Gemma!" My lungs burn with the force of my scream.

I reach the CR-V and wrench the door open in a flurry of movement, blood smearing over my hand as the rain batters me. I reach in to cut the engine, then pull her from the car into the pouring rain.

She's lucky. Another few inches and her car might have overbalanced to slide down the incline. I think we're in the clear.

Lightning illuminates us, highlighting her broken face. My heart clenches.

"Gemma." I tuck her against my body. "You're okay. You're fine."

She trembles all over. I hold her tight as we're battered by rain. The thunder makes her jump.

"You broke your promise." I press my lips to the top of her head. "You promised to never scare me like that again. Then you did the same fucking thing."

Gemma starts to cry, burying hiccuping gasps against my

chest. I crush her body against mine, needing to envelope her in security. I'll protect her.

Even if I don't deserve her.

"Shh, sweetheart." I stroke her hair. Words spill forth. I'm powerless to stop the confessions flowing out me. "I'm so sorry, Gemma. About everything. I should've fought harder. Spoken up. Protected you better. I never should've hurt you. I don't want to do that. I only want to make you happy. I want you to smile always."

Her hands burrow in my shirt, clinging to the material. I cup her face and tilt her head to see her eyes.

"I'll always keep you safe now."

Gemma nods, her face a painting of torment that spears my heart. With my unbloodied hand, I swipe the rain and tears away. Gemma's lip wobbles and she stares up at me with big green eyes.

I kiss her, my lips a soft press against hers as I cradle her face like it's fragile.

I know she's not fragile. She's strong. Fierce.

The girl who snuck up on me, who challenged me, who made me face the mask I've worn for so long.

Gemma is the only soul that's ever sung in complete harmony with mine. I love her.

THIRTY-FIVE
GEMMA

The perilous patter of my heart gradually slows the tighter Lucas holds me.

Lucas soothes all the pain wrecking my heart and mind. His mouth moves soft and slow.

Everything falls away as we kiss.

We part on a breath, his forehead pressed to mine. His thumbs swipe over my cheeks in a light brush.

"Lucas," I whisper.

"I care about you so much it scares me." His confession isn't complete. He has more to pour out. "Tell me what you need. If you want me to get up in front of the whole school and tell the truth, I will."

A soggy chuckle leaves me.

"I'm serious." Lucas rests his lips on my forehead. "I'll

explain that nothing happened with Marissa. I've only been with you since September." He pulls back to meet my eyes with a serious look. "That video is old. From when we dated."

"I'm sorry, too." I blow out a breath and tuck my hands around his waist, burrowing into his body for warmth. One of his arms wraps around me and it feels right. "I was so dead set on believing what I thought of you in my head that I jumped to conclusions. It was easier, because it gave me an excuse to go back to where I was comfortable."

A sad look crosses his face.

"I know. It's a downer, but my life has been easier to deal with when I stay on the outside. Like photography. My pride makes me push people away. It was the only way I knew how to safeguard myself. If I believed the worst, I could go back to being on the outside by myself, where nothing could hurt me."

"I don't want anything to hurt you again."

Lucas gives me a kiss that's over too quickly.

"That's improbable. What are you going to do, follow me around for the rest of my life and encase me in bubble wrap? Punch everything that ever crosses me?"

"I want to try. I only want to make things right. If that means you never want to speak to me again, well," Lucas frowns, but forges on, "I'll understand. I'll make it happen. And no one will bother you or mess with you ever again."

I tilt my head to the side, studying his contrite expression. I see the real Lucas—*my* Lucas. Not the fake one that pretends for the school, hiding himself from all of them.

"And if I want you to mess with me? I kind of like fighting with you."

Lucas blinks, then relaxes. His expression shifts into a mix of relief and happiness.

"I like fighting with you, too, sweetheart."

"It's pretty fun."

Lucas releases a breath. "Gemma."

The lightning silhouettes the trees overhead and for a second the brightness makes him look like his namesake, an otherworldly saint. His gaze is intent.

"The only girl for me is you. I've never wanted anyone the way I want you."

"Oh."

Hearing him say it like that makes my pulse stutter and my stomach swoop. My unruly heart runs laps.

"You're in my veins. You course through me, give me life." He brings his face close to mine, the warmth of his breath fluttering over my mouth. "You're the first person I told about architecture. I want you to be the first person I tell all of my dreams and fears to."

A swell of emotion builds in my chest. I stare at him, speechless.

"I swear nothing will ever hurt you again. I'll make sure of it." Lucas cups my cheek. I hold my hand over his, tracing his battered knuckles. "Will you be mine, Gemma? If you can forgive me and accept me, will you let me love you the way you deserve?"

Since the first encounter with Lucas he has demanded everything of me.

Stolen firsts from me without mercy.

Held me in his control.

He took what he wanted. He tried to command my loyalty in the past.

This isn't that.

It's Lucas asking me. He offers his heart on a platter, if I'll have it. I can tell if I say no, he would accept it.

"Yes."

I gasp as his mouth covers mine in a searing kiss. The gentle tentativeness is burned away in a rush of heat that has me clawing to get closer to him. Raindrops speckle us and the thunder matches the sounds we make as our kiss becomes a storm of its own.

A phoenix soars in my body, the white-hot flames rising from the ashes of the demons that haunted me to overwrite new memories, strengthening me.

My broken heart heals in that moment as I fuse my soul to Lucas' with a kiss.

A shiver runs down my spine as we part. I don't know whether it's from an epic kiss or the chilling rain.

"We should probably get out of here. You'll get sick." He leads me to his Range Rover, the heat of the interior a warm embrace. He helps me into the passenger seat and gets a blanket from the back to bundle me, carefully tucking the edges around my body. "Can I kidnap you for old time's sake? I'll keep you warm and feed you. You can hog Lancelot for companionship."

"You're a dork." I shake my head, smiling.

Lucas winks and shuts the door. He stands beneath the low-hanging bough of a pine tree as he talks on his phone.

When he gets in, he reaches across to take my hand. "Community security will get your car and bring it up to my place. I'd have Dev do it, but he's busy at the house."

I nod as Lucas turns us around and drives up the road. I occupy myself by brushing the pads of my fingers over his knuckles. The skin doesn't feel broken, it's only stained by the blood of someone that tried to hurt me. This is the second time he's taken me back after a rainy rescue mission. I squeeze his hand and flash him a smile when he returns it.

The rain begins to die down. Cars pass us on the road, coming down from Lucas' place. As we pull in more than half are gone.

"Where's the fire?"

"Who cares, I'm not in a party mood. Are you?"

"Not really."

We get out and find Devlin, Alec, and Connor herding people into his SUV. Lancelot dances around their feet, barking at the commotion. When we walk up, Lancelot abandons them to circle around us, sitting on my shoes.

"Did you get it done?" Lucas asks Devlin cryptically.

"Yeah. They put up a fight, but Connor's got blackmail on Burns that shut him up. Once we threw him and Marissa out, it ended the party." Devlin holds up a finger. "But not to worry. I am generously opening my house to those too drunk to go home. A few other people that live here are doing the same."

Lucas lifts his brows. "That's unlike you."

"You can thank me later." Devlin shrugs and glances at me. "We didn't want you guys to come back to a raging party."

"Thanks," I say.

People groan as they trudge out of the house.

Alec comes over. "Are you okay?"

"Yeah," I assure him.

Alec breathes in relief. "Good." He hugs me. "Do you want me to take you home?"

I shake my head. "I'm staying here."

My hand finds Lucas' and I thread our fingers together.

"Okay. I'll crash at Devlin's after I drive everyone over there."

"This way—yes you, too. Come on."

Connor waves like he's guiding a plane, directing people to the line of running cars with open doors. The foggy headlights of swanky brands make it look like a mismatched caterpillar of expensive proportions.

Devlin sees my confused expression and gestures to the cars as people pile in. "Drunk shuttle service."

There's a tug on my hand.

"Come on." Lucas nods to the deck.

I follow him up. Lancelot runs inside, pads across the room, and flops into a cushy bed. The house empties and we have the place to ourselves.

* * *

Steam fills the bathroom.

Lucas asks before taking off my ripped shirt, voice deep.

It's funny how the first time I was in this room I felt on high alert. Now I feel safe and at ease.

"It's okay. I trust you."

He sways into me, dropping feathery kisses on my cheek.

Lucas peels my ruined shirt over my head and watches my face for any protest before unclasping my bra. He hugs me. My breasts press to his bare chest. His skin is warm.

He spends a few minutes massaging my back until the rigidness bleeds out of me. I melt against him with a faint sound.

"I've got you, baby. Let me erase all your hurts."

We finish undressing, both of us cracking up as we struggle with the leather pants that melded to my body after the rain. The burst of humor feels good. Lucas kneels at my feet to yank them down until I'm free, mouthing at my thigh as he exposes it.

The kiss of the shower when we step in is heaven. I tip my head back and Lucas supports my weight from behind. The hot water washes over my skin in a cascade I embrace.

I lift his hand and clean the blood until the water runs clear, then bring it against my lips to nuzzle it. The skin is red and tender, likely to bruise.

Lucas turns me in his arms and I wrap around him. Steam cloaks us as the water beats down on my back.

"This isn't the first time," I whisper against his chest.

His embrace tightens, but he remains quiet. I tip all of my secrets out, ready to give Lucas my whole heart.

"I was sixteen. He was...Alec's best friend. We've known him since we were kids. We were all at a party. Matt and I had been flirting a lot. I was crushing on him hard."

There's a rumble in Lucas' chest. His hands flex on my back.

"I thought Matt was going to ask me out. That's why I went into the room with him, away from the party. The cheap beer went to my head. I didn't realize until—" At the hitch in my breath, Lucas crushes me to him. It gives me the anchor I need to go on. "He never kissed me. He only held me down and tried to—"

The last of my sentence is cut off when Lucas tips my head up and seals his lips to mine. His shoulders shake and I press my fingers into them to bring him back to me. He pants against my mouth.

"No one will ever hurt you again. Will you let me take care of you?"

I hum and snake my arms around his neck.

"Can I—?" Lucas glides his palm down to my hip. "I want to make you feel good."

"Yes. Please."

My hold on his neck tightens as his fingers burn paths across my skin. He kisses my neck as his fingers delve between my legs. He traces every path where I was tarnished and hurt, marking me his all over again.

My shallow breaths become low moans as I buck against his fingers.

Lucas murmurs encouragement against my neck. He sinks to his knees, propping one of my legs up to give him better access. He devours me with a slow, methodical focus that drives me mad.

The pleasure soars, pulsing in my clit. My cries echo off the tile as I hold on to his hair, my thighs shuddering.

Then I peel apart at the seams, the ache bursting like shimmering starlight.

Lucas stands, putting me back together with a deep kiss.

"I need more."

He pauses, studying me through heavy-lidded eyes. "Are you okay to keep going? We don't have to do anything you don't want to do."

I can see the shadow of his cock jutting.

"Please, Lucas." I'm alight with the tingles only Lucas can bring on. I dig my fingers into his hair. My voice is a husky rasp. "I want you to make me forget. I only want to know your touch."

Lucas groans and kisses me again.

He turns off the shower and lifts me up, bracing a palm beneath my ass. I wrap my legs around him as he takes his time stepping from the shower so we don't overbalance. The whole time, his lips never leave mine.

He lumbers into the bedroom, pausing to retrieve a condom from his nightstand.

As Lucas settles me in his lap, time seems to slow, syncing to our breaths. The beads of water cool on our skin. I trace them, mesmerized as they roll from his shoulders, down his pecs and over his stomach. He rolls the condom on and caresses my hip.

"Take what you need from me, sweetheart." Lucas cradles me in his arms as I straddle him. He swoops in for a kiss, threading his fingers in my damp hair. "Don't stop until you feel good. Then do it all over again."

I inhale as I sink down, welcoming the sensation of

connecting to Lucas. We rock together in a sedate rhythm. Lucas strokes up and down my back.

His lips part. I trace the corners of his mouth, following with my lips.

We are two pieces that fit together, unbreakable as a sailor's knot. We are joined beneath the stars, surrounded by love as we float to the sky together on waves of perfect pleasure.

I do as Lucas told me, owning my body. I take a page from his book and bring myself to the edge over and over until I can't any longer.

When I reach that peak, Lucas holds me close, taking over. He whispers to me as we chase our release together. We tremble and quake as we tip over into oblivion.

Lucas presses soft kisses to my shoulder as he shifts us into bed, taking care of me. He draws me into his arms and my palm finds his chest, covering his heartbeat as I drift into a peaceful sleep.

* * *

Two weeks later, the party music has me bouncing and rocking.

Being at Lucas' house is becoming a staple, which comes with a party most weekends when his parents go out of town.

The party doesn't bring me the same grief. I have my boyfriend, my friends, and my brother around.

"I challenge you to a dance off." Alec points at me and executes a disco move that's at odds with the music. "Winner gets bragging rights and control of the Netflix account for a month."

A bright laugh escapes me as I twirl with flare. "Oh, Alec. It is *so* on."

He makes a solid effort. Elena hollers and fist pumps for him.

Alec catches the eye of that pretty girl he's been waltzing around for weeks. He winks at her and she waves.

I blow him out of the water when I end my turn with a split. Everyone around us cheers and I hold my arms overhead.

"What! Oh, come on." Alec tries to rally the crowd judging our battle. "Half the girls here can do a split!"

"No go, dude," Elena laments. "My girl killed it."

I grin at her. "Enjoy hours of travel documentaries."

Alec groans dramatically.

I slip away from the dancers to find Blair. She's my official party buddy tonight, and it took a lot of convincing for her to come. She has a drink and stands by Lancelot.

"I see you've met the dog."

Blair glances down at him. "Dogs are better than people."

I chuckle. "No argument there."

Her attention floats past my shoulder. I turn to find Devlin glaring at her. I roll my eyes.

"Don't let him bother you. You're welcome here."

"These people never accepted me before."

"Well, let's change that. They're not all bad."

Blair shrugs. She gestures to Lancelot. "As long as I can hang out with this cute, perfect guy I found, I'm cool to stay."

"I'm glad you're here," I tell her with a big smile.

I'm slowly learning that joining in isn't the death sentence I once feared. It worked for a while to shield myself, but I feel more like myself than ever, now that I've stopped keeping everyone at arm's length.

I still won't give the jerks that bullied me the time of day, but Lucas and his closest friends accept me. Anyone that has given me a problem in the last couple of weeks gets my teeth, along with my brother and Lucas flanking me.

No one crosses me now. I'm not the weak prude they labeled me as. I never was.

I jump when hands grab my hips. I'm spun around and warm lips collide with mine in the best kind of déjà vu. The forest-fresh scent hits my nose. I smile into the familiar kiss with Lucas.

He runs his fingers through my hair as his tongue teases me. I open for him, my toes curling as he stakes his claim in front of everyone.

People howl like coyotes all around us.

I tuck my hands into his back pockets in a mirror of the first time he kissed me. He chuckles against my mouth as I squeeze his ass.

I claim Lucas right back. I'm his and he's mine. We belong to each other.

EPILOGUE

GEMMA

The marching band gets the crowd pumped from their section in the stands at the Homecoming game. I get swept into the excitement, jumping up and down when the team spills onto the field.

"Who knew you were such a maniac fan," Devlin teases, elbowing me.

He and Connor found me in the stands and joined me.

I shoot him a sly look. "I used to be on pep squad."

His brows hike up. "I would have never guessed that."

"What's wrong with my level of pep?"

Devlin snorts at my sarcasm.

Officially, I'm here to take photos of the game for Ms. Huang and the school newspaper. My camera hangs around my neck as I clap for the band.

When Alec and Lucas' names are introduced by the announcer, along with their positions, I cheer.

There's a thrill of being surrounded by hundreds of other

people yelling, music thrumming, and love filling your heart as you support your team.

All of my support today is for Alec and Lucas.

His eyes zero in on me as the team comes to the bench. Alec slaps him on the shoulder.

The look on Lucas' face is worth everything. It splits into a huge, prideful grin. He shoots a fist overhead, pointing right at me. I wave back.

I'm wearing his number. Devlin got me his alternate jersey. *Saint* is broadcast from my back in block letters so everyone knows.

I lift my camera to capture his face in time, snapping the shutter.

There's a notable player missing as the game gets underway. A different guy plays the position previously held by Carter Burns. He's off the team.

Lucas got his dad to help me pro bono when I changed my mind, determined to make sure Carter could never attack anyone again. I pressed charges with Mr. Saint's guidance. Carter got five years in jail. Everyone will know he's a predator.

This time I battled my fear and told Mom and Dad everything, even the truth about Matt. Mom cried and hugged me close as Dad touched my shoulder. It felt good to be honest with them.

Lucas' parents and mine sit higher in the stands, with the other team parents.

The game is close. I end up swatting Devlin half the time as our guys drive the ball to the end zone down to the wire. There's only a few minutes left, the timer running out fast. The other team is ahead. The Coyotes need this play to take the game.

My trigger finger is on fire as I capture shot after shot. As usual, Lucas hogs the spotlight in my photos. I can't help it—his grace when he throws the ball is unparalleled.

It'll be fun to make him throw the ball in a field for a photo project I have in mind for my portfolio. We're going hiking this weekend and he said he knows the perfect spot.

Lucas sends the ball spiraling through the air and it sails straight to Alec, who cuts across to an open position with wings on his feet.

We shout ourselves hoarse as Alec sprints to make the touchdown. The buzzer announces the end of the fourth quarter seconds after Alec passes into the end zone. He slams the ball into the turf and his teammates tackle him. The stands go wild.

A voice on the loudspeaker calls it. "Coyotes win over the Bulldogs 28 to 26!"

The marching band explodes into a celebratory song as the players on the field celebrate their win.

I cup my hands as I see number 14 and number 19 head for the bench, trailed by the rest of the team. "Go Lucas! Go Alec!"

Lucas hauls himself over the fence, heading for the bleachers. He sprints up to me, a grinning, sweaty mess.

"Congratulations!"

Other people around us in the stands echo my sentiments.

"I had my lucky charm in the stands." Lucas takes my camera and tucks it into my bag. He lifts me, arms around my waist. "Couldn't lose if I tried. Not when you were up here wearing my number. It looks good on you."

"How's it feel to play your last game?"

"Fucking awesome." He tilts his head. "But I'll still play for fun. As long as I don't have to join an official team."

He plans to hand over his position to the reserve player. When he told me, he said it was time to pass the torch for the championship game. He wants to give the chance to someone that works hard and has their heart in fighting for the win.

"How are you planning to celebrate?"

Lucas smirks. "First, this."

He kisses me, the heat of it making me melt in his arms.

A camera phone shutter sounds in my ear. We part and find Devlin shaking his head with a wry expression.

"I'm updating your contact info in my phone. You're both always fused at the face. It's the photo I'll show the police if you go missing."

Lucas cocks his head. "Real funny."

Connor snorts and wrangles Devlin. They head out with the other people flowing from the stands. Lucas picks up my bag and takes my hand, leading me back to the bench where he collects his things.

He tosses me a cheeky look.

"What is it?"

"I was just thinking how I was right."

"About what?"

Lucas stops our trek toward the school. He pins me with a fierce look.

"I told you by Homecoming you'd be mine."

I roll my eyes and shove at him playfully. Lucas gathers me to him and gives me a toe-curling kiss that makes my heart flutter.

He's not wrong.

EPILOGUE

LUCAS

4 Years Later

Heat pulls in my stomach as I creep up on a familiar, unsuspecting figure from behind. Gemma waits on the quad, our usual meeting place on Thursdays before we grab dinner. As soon as I spotted her, the irresistible urge to play a possessive prank reared up.

Four years of being together and I still can't get enough of her.

Her blonde hair is half-down, a tiny bun knotted on top of her head. Snug skinny jeans hug her ass as she cants her hip to the side.

Tossing a quick glance around to ensure there's no one near, I prowl closer.

She's not expecting me for another twenty minutes, but my 3pm art history class let out early.

I smirk. This never gets old.

Gemma is absorbed in her phone, oblivious as I loom behind her.

I snatch her around the waist and lift, relishing her yelp. I cover her eyes with one hand as I wrangle her toward my Range Rover parked in the nearby lot for students.

"H-*hey*!" Gemma flails like a rag doll when her feet leave the ground, her defenses kicking in first. "Get off!"

An electric thrill zaps through me at the way she squirms in my hold. The excitement climbs, making me hustle her across the parking lot at a faster clip.

I have to get her to the car before anyone sees. The last time we played our kidnapping game a few months back, an overzealous freshman got the wrong idea and reported me to campus security thinking I was actually trying to hurt my girlfriend.

Explaining to security in a cramped office beneath fluorescent lights that we were messing around—plus Gemma's wide-eyed embarrassment as she clutched her trench coat closed over the risqué outfit she wore beneath, preserving her modesty—damn near killed the mood.

I haven't kidnapped her in public view with the risk of witnesses since then.

That self-defense class she takes twice a week has honed her instincts. The wind is knocked from my lungs for a moment when her elbow jabs me in a tender spot. I keep hold of her, hiking her up higher by hooking a loop in her jeans. A delicious yelp escapes her.

C'mon, baby, I think in amusement. *Who else knows how to toss you around the way you like?*

She snaps her teeth and kicks my shin, earning a pained grunt from me. I keep my mouth clamped shut, not ready to give away who her captor is if she hasn't figured it out yet.

Gemma turns into dead weight just as we reach the car,

indicating I have seconds to pull this off before she wails me with the back of her head to take me by surprise. It's a defensive maneuver she's practiced with me before. I'm not about to let her whack me with the full force of her skull. The familiar tone of the lock disengaging makes awareness shift in her muscles.

"Babe?" Gemma's voice carries hesitant suspicion. Her head turns beneath my palm covering her eyes. I don't hold her as tightly now that she's stopped struggling, allowing her free range. Her nose tucks against my neck as she inhales. "Damn it, Lucas. Dickhead."

The warmth she infuses in the word *dickhead* expands in my chest. A chuckle rolls from me as I get the passenger door open.

"Not fucking funny."

"*Totally* fucking funny, sweetheart. You know I love catching you whenever I want. You can't run from me. It'll never grow old."

My palm slips from her eyes to skim over her front, tucking beneath her loose white t-shirt to touch her stomach.

"Will, too," she sasses as I get her into the car. Her arms cross over her chest, fingers drumming on her bicep. A mutinous pinch tightens her mouth as her gaze slides over my body, stronger and broader than when we first met thanks to the days I hit the gym. "If you were a real kidnapper, I would've taken you down."

I bite back a smile. She's more pissed that she didn't get a good enough shot in than annoyed I started our game back up. A flare of heat seeps in at the edges of her annoyance.

My grin breaks free. I tuck a piece of her hair behind her ear, rubbing at my sternum where she caught me with her sharp elbow. "Absolutely, baby. You're my tough girl."

I lean in and kiss her gorgeous stubborn pout. After a

minute, Gemma parts her lips and lets me in. Her hands loop around my neck, fingers threading through my hair.

That never gets old either. A happy sigh slips out of me as I press my forehead to hers.

"Did you cut out of class early?" Gemma peeks up at me through her lashes.

"Mhm." I drop another kiss on her nose. "I've got a surprise for you, too. It's lucky the professor let us out early, we'll make it in time for sunset."

Gemma lights up at that. She loves the golden rays of late afternoon before the day dips into night.

"What kind of surprise? I only have two lenses on me, a fifty and an eighty-five."

I swing around to the other side of the car, dumping my backpack in the second row.

Pulling out on the main road, I slide on a pair of sunglasses and flash Gemma a confident smirk. "The best kind of surprise. Sit tight, captive."

"Oh, so it's like that?" Gemma releases a breathy laugh and props her elbow on the window. "This better be some date night."

My lips quirk higher. "It's definitely like that." I reach across the console to snag her hand, bringing it to my lips. "I'll take good care of you tonight, sweetheart."

As I take us toward our destination, I don't tell her what awaits us. The lease agreement burns a hole in my back pocket and my stomach feels like it's on a roller coaster.

We've worked hard to chase our individual dreams since graduating high school, working hard on our degrees—her in photography and me in architectural design. Lately I've been itching to go for bigger goals on my list.

* * *

"This one goes in the kitchen," Gemma directs, waving at a big box labeled with her looping handwriting. "And that one has mostly photos."

My gaze zeroes in on the box labeled *photography*. Tingles shoot across my nerve endings. Fresh sweat beads on my neck, but it's not entirely from moving our things inside. I rip my attention from the box and focus on Gemma.

She paces the stack of moving boxes with a determined tilt to her mouth as Lancelot winds around her feet.

Wispy hair sticks out from her braid as she scurries around everything we have left to bring inside. Lancelot follows her loyally, bounding back to me every so often with an elated bark. She ditched her jean jacket after an hour, cheeks pink with exertion because she refuses to let me do all the heavy lifting.

Stubborn little thing. I can't help the way I track her. She's beautiful. And she's moving in with me.

My girl, my dog, and me. Together for good, at long last.

I wanted to hire movers, but Gemma wouldn't hear it.

"*Can your brain even fathom the value of my combined photo gear, Richy McRich-butt? A lot. It's a-freaking-lot. All paid for on my own. No way am I letting movers touch it.*"

My amused exasperation didn't go over so well. She didn't care that I could easily buy her new gear if movers fucked with it. Gemma waved her hands around until she pounced on me, making me promise we would move in together on our own for the safety of her photo equipment and for the memory. How was I supposed to refuse when she was straddling me? It's an impossible feat.

We've been at this a while.

I swear I've moved fifty boxes, but over half remain on the resident terrace awaiting the trip to the apartment. It surprises me how two people can accumulate so much stuff when moving into the same place.

Spring break lasts four more days. Gemma plans to have us unpacked in two. Something about forming diligent habits and not turning into her parents.

"You've got it, my liege." I heft the kitchen box and whistle for Lancelot. "Be back in a few for the photo box if it's too heavy for you."

"I can do it." Gemma flexes her cute little bicep.

The determination only lasts so long before Gemma is distracted by the view of the boulder-dotted hillside our new apartment overlooks. It's cast in the orange wash of late afternoon light.

Gemma's itching to get her camera out, I can tell. My girl can't resist the tug at her creativity calling her to capture the world around her.

Fond warmth travels through me, mixing with the jitters fluttering in my gut. We need to get all the boxes inside so she can find what I hid in her photo box.

Moving in with Gemma has been on my mind since we graduated Silver Lake High School. I've needed her to be close enough to hold at all times, but she was adamant we wait. When I brought her here under the guise of a date night with a signed lease in my back pocket, the view sold her.

I thought bringing her to an apartment that would be ours one way or another was nerve-wracking, but move in day has amplified my anxiousness to make that date night look like no sweat.

Taking a breath to reel myself in from speeding through the plan and fucking up, I remind myself that everything will be fine.

Lancelot and I head for the sleek elevator, riding up to our new home as I take in the view through the glass walls. The old guy's energy is waning and I suspect he's heading off for a nap in his bed where the sun cuts across the living room to provide him a perfect sun spot once we enter.

Our apartment is on the top floor with an open floor plan, west-facing kitchen and a sleek balcony. Big windows provide natural light that Gemma's been raving about. The architectural lines drew me to the building near campus immediately. I've been eyeing it since we started our first semester at Oak Ridge College of the Arts.

Now it's our home. A space we'll grow into and make ours. My gaze flicks to Gemma as she enters the door, cheeks puffed with air while she carries the photo box.

"Here, babe." I scoop it from her.

One hidden item makes the box feel far heavier than a collection of photos. The urge to skip the plan and drop to my knee now is strong. I fight the powerful cascade and hustle back outside to get the rest of our things.

Twenty minutes later I'm drained as I drop on the couch beside Gemma.

"I'm skipping leg day tomorrow."

Gemma snorts at my lament, the corner of her mouth curling. "Uh, please. The elevator did all the work."

Instead of answering, I shift to lay my head on her lap, burrowing my face into her stomach. The sunlight fades into a faint orange-purple as it dips behind the ridgeline. Gemma's fingers find my hair, carding it in a way that makes me groan in relaxed content.

Best of all? I don't have to say goodbye to Gemma at the end of the night or after a weekend. For the last couple of years we've been splitting our time between my old dorm room, her parents' house where she commutes from, and my place at the lake. While it felt like we were never separated for long, this time it's official.

We live together.

My arms tuck around Gemma in a hug.

"Think your wimpy jelly arms can hold up a level tonight?" Gemma pulls on my hair, sending an answering pulse of heat tugging at my dick. "I want to do the photos first and decorate the room around them. Like our own private gallery."

The hushed joy in her voice pours through my chest like liquid gold, more valuable than precious jewels.

A jittery flutter follows.

The photos.

"Jelly arms? I can go all night." To prove it, I stand and hoist Gemma over my shoulder, smacking her ass. "I'll hold you up against the wall while I take you apart."

Gemma laughs, her hands splaying on my lower back for balance. She smacks me back in retaliation and grabs a handful of my ass. A small shriek leaves her when I whip us around.

"Lucas! Let me down!"

"Get used to it, sweetheart. You signed up to live with me and I've got lost time to make up for." My palm skims up the back of her thigh, fingers teasing between her legs. "You're all mine."

My meaning encompasses so much more than what my words convey. I mean *there's something big in that box* and *I'm ready to put a goddamn ring on it because I want the world to know you're my devotion.*

Gemma arches as best she can in her position against my hand. I set her down, meeting her heated look with a matching one of my own.

"Hold that thought." I retrieve the box labeled *photography* with a quiet, shaky breath.

Unaware of my inner turmoil, Gemma scoots to the edge of the couch and breaks into the box. She peers briefly at each framed photo as she pulls it out, setting them beside her and on the coffee table.

"Remember this day?"

It's from our anniversary last year, a selfie we took on the boat in the middle of the lake, both of us bundled from the morning chill.

I hum and take the picture from her. My thumb smooths over the print.

Out comes photos of Lancelot, strung together Instax prints from our senior year at Silver Lake High School, breathtaking landscapes from after she moved to Ridgeview. Our memories spread before us.

Lancelot snores in his bed, knocked out to the world. Each minute ticking by feels like an eternity.

Gemma stills and pulls her bottom lip between her teeth. She frowns, brow furrowed as her hand hesitates midair with the next photo in her grasp. My heart jumps into my throat. I don't know what to do with my hands, twitching them in small jerky movements before dropping them at my side and pinching my sweatpants.

Gemma pulls out the framed photo she took of me smiling at the last football game I played in senior year. She spares a fond smile as she sets the print of me with others from school, then focuses on the small velvet box I hid beneath that photo.

"Is this yours?"

My throat is dry when I swallow. I remain quiet, watching her work it out when she pops the lid open. A sharp gasp leaves her when she reveals the ring.

I've looked at it so many times I have it memorized—a sparkling cushion cut peach gemstone nestled at the center of a rose gold halo of stones. I told the designer to make it look like a bright sun, because Gemma is my light.

"Holy shit," Gemma whispers.

Licking my lips, I perch next to her. "You're the only one who sees my dreams and helps me believe in them." Gemma swings her shocked gaze to me as I continue in a raspy voice, loosely wrapping my fingers around her wrist, thumb stroking her pulse point. "I want to be that person for you, too."

"What's happening right now?" Gemma breathes, possibly too stunned to say anything else.

We're both sticky with dried sweat from hauling moving boxes all afternoon. Instead of a fancy dinner, we're dressed in gym clothes. The dog is snoring as the sunlight fades into a blanket of dusk.

This moment couldn't feel more perfect than it does right now. Somehow the nerves that have plagued me all day ebb away as I take in her expression.

I love Gemma more than I ever have. The feeling grows bigger by the day.

"I gave you my heart a long time ago." I meet her gaze with steady intensity. "It's yours, Gemma."

She holds her breath, then releases a shuddery exhale as moisture makes her eyes shine. My heart thuds with a heavy beat, each pulse of life chanting how deep my devotion for her runs.

"I once said I'd make you mine forever. I want that promise to come true." Cupping her hands, I slide off the couch to kneel before her. Gemma's eyes go wider. I wait a beat, wetting my lips. "Marry me?"

Gemma is quiet for a long stretch of seconds that are agonizing to outlast.

She'll say yes, won't she? It never occurred to me she might refuse me. She hasn't refused me in years.

"Yes." It's a breathless gasp. "Yes, Lucas. *Yes*! Oh my god!"

Gemma trembles as I let out a relieved laugh, gathering her to me in a bear hug. We part long enough for me to slide the engagement ring onto her finger. She admires it, tilting it side to side.

"It's really beautiful."

"I'm glad you like it. It's how I think of you."

Gemma darts her eyes up to meet mine, a look of warmth and awe on her face. "Lucas..."

"You're my sunshine, sweetheart."

Gemma looks to the ring again. After a moment she whispers. "Holy shit, we're getting married."

Excitement and elation overwhelm me at once. I shoot up, swinging her in my arms as our lips connect in a searing kiss.

My tongue slides against hers as she wraps her arms around my neck. One of us is mumbling *I love you* over and over between kisses, but I can't tell whether it's her or me. Lancelot wakes up, giving us a pug stink eye before he trots off toward the bedroom.

I lose myself in kissing Gemma, walking her backwards until I can rest some of her weight against the wall, making good on my vow.

Those dreams of mine are closer in reach. I'm living with Gemma and she'll become my wife. I can't describe the bubbling emotion welling up inside me, but it's addictive.

We come together in another kiss, Gemma's hips rolling against me. A sinful growl leaves me as I rake my hand up the back of her thigh, hiking it higher. Gemma tosses her head back on a gasp.

"I think we should get started on marking this place ours," I say against her skin, licking a stripe up her neck. "Let's start with in here."

"Marking?" Gemma lets out a low moan when I suck on a sensitive patch of skin. "You're such a caveman."

"Urg," I mock-grunt against the side of her face, thrusting my erection against her. She laughs, then releases a needy cry that drives me wild. I work her shirt up and over her head, leaving her in a strappy bralette. "Sexy woman, *mine.*"

"Stop, I can't—*ah*—take you seriously when you do the caveman voice, too."

Together we work her leggings down until she kicks them free. With one hand braced beneath her ass, I adjust her into a comfortable hold. I pause long enough to grind against her pussy as her legs wrap around my waist. God, she makes me so crazy.

"You're marrying me," I murmur against her mouth.

"Mm, locking it down." Gemma arches. "Fuck, come on. I need you."

"Yeah?" I slip my sweatpants down far enough to pull my cock out, rubbing against her underwear. "This what you need, baby?"

"Hell yes. Always."

"Always." I kiss her while tugging her underwear to the side, driving my cock into her on a smooth glide. Together we tense and moan. She's wet and ready for me. "Fucking *always*."

I pull out and snap back into perfect heat enveloping my cock. Gemma digs her nails into my shoulders as I work up to a faster pace, hitting her at an angle that makes her scream.

"You feel so good." Keeping one arm around her waist for support, I move from squeezing her ass to burying a hand in her hair, tugging to control the angle of her head.

Gemma's mouth drops open, her neck a beautiful curve. This is what I give her. Permission to lose control, because I've always got what she needs. *Always*.

I give her hair another domineering tug, a growl ripping from me as I fuck her against the wall. My thighs burn, but I won't stop for shit while she's claiming her pleasure from the way I take care of her.

"Oh god!" Gemma's nails rake my arm as she drags across it to squeeze my forearm, silently begging for more.

"Yeah, baby? You need me to take control?" My hips pump in time with my words.

"Please," she moans.

"*Fuuuck,*" I drag out on a long breath.

Her pussy clenches and I'm a damn near goner. I hang on for a little longer, enough to move my hand to grasp her throat. A flush fills her face, darkness flooding those beautiful green eyes. She tips over the edge, squeezing my cock like a vice as she shudders in my arms. I'm right there with her, tensing and driving deep inside as my cock pulses through my orgasm.

When the burn in my thighs and abs are too much, I stumble back. Gemma leans heavily against the wall, grinning at me in a daze. I collapse on the floor in a tangle of sweatpants.

Pointing up at Gemma, I give her a cocky half-smile. "Don't think we're done. I just need to catch my breath, then we're taking this to the bedroom. I'm eating your pussy next."

Gemma laughs and crawls over to straddle me. My hands find her hips, thumbs brushing her bare sides.

"How about a nap first?"

I blow out a sated sigh. "Yeah. Lancelot has the right idea."

We pull off our sweaty clothes and clean up in the bathroom. After, we wind up naked and entangled on the couch as the stars begin to dot the sky. Gemma rests her head on my chest. My cock wakes back up, but we're in no rush.

I play with Gemma's left hand, tracing her palm. She holds up the ring to admire it again.

"It really is beautiful," she murmurs. "I love it."

I kiss the top of her head and wrap her in my arms. "I can't believe you'll be my wife. I'm gonna marry the *shit* out of you."

She snorts. "Yeah, you are. Ditto."

We started that first time I kissed Gemma, mistaking her for someone else. I've needed no one but her. From then on, she has been in my heart. I've belonged to her in the same way she is mine.

I stretch and settle back down with Gemma comfortably draped over my body.

Our next adventure is beginning to unfold.

We're only getting started, I think as I skim my hand over her belly. Gemma pops her head up, expression matching mine. It's full of promise and ideas for the future.

Our future.

Thank you so much for reading WICKED SAINT! The Sinners and Saints series continues in Devlin and Blair's book, TEMPTING DEVIL.

THANK YOU + WHAT'S NEXT?

Need more Sinners and Saints series right now? Have theories about which characters will feature next? Want exclusive previews of the next book? Join other readers in Veronica Eden's Reader Garden on Facebook!

Join: BIT.LY/VERONICAFBGROUP

Are you a newsletter subscriber? By subscribing, you can download a special bonus scenes for the Sinners and Saints series.

Sign up to download it here:

VERONICAEDENAUTHOR.COM/BONUS-CONTENT

ACKNOWLEDGMENTS

I want to thank you, readers, for reading this book! It means the world to me that you supported my work. I wouldn't be here without you! I hope you enjoyed your read! I'm really excited to bring you more from this series!

Thanks to my husband for being you! He doesn't read these, but he's my biggest supporter. He keeps me fed and watered while I'm in the writer cave, and doesn't complain when I fling myself out of bed at odd hours with an idea to frantically scribble down.

To my beta readers, thank you from the bottom of my heart! Y'all blew me away with your above and beyond dedication, attention to detail, and consideration of the characters and the storyline! You've helped me so much! You're a dream team and I'm so glad I met each of you! Your time and hard work are much appreciated!

As always, I want to send a big shout out of love to my writing hags, the best bunch around! I always cherish your support and encouragement of my writing, no matter where my heart eyes and the muse take me. Every book I publish is thanks to you guys.

Special thank you to Gwen Martin for always being around throughout my writing process, for endless hours of chat, for flailing with me as I plotted, for never blinking when I come to you with a new genre obsession or plot idea, for reading early previews, and for genuinely being a fan. I'm really glad we get to share a virtual office space on the days we can't get together in person for writer work days!

Tempting Devil

Sinners and Saints Book 2

Available Now

* * *

BLAIR

I SOLD MY SOUL TO THE DEVIL.

Hard times prove who's a survivor and who's not. Me? I'm a survivor.

The plan was perfect: steal one of his cars for a payout to set us up for life. All while getting back at him for tormenting me from the moment I first stepped foot in stuck up Silver Lake High School.

But he caught me red-handed. What's worse, a jail sentence or becoming the devil's favorite toy?

My devious monster made me an offer I couldn't refuse. Now I'm selling everything to him. Even my soul.

DEVLIN

THE SECRET TO BEING CAREFREE IS LOVE NOTHING.

The puppets are fooled into believing my game of pretend. But the way she looks at me has always pierced beneath my skin. Like she *knows*. She's a gutter rat—how could she possibly understand?

I vowed to break her. When I catch her stealing my car, it's clear she hasn't learned her lesson. She won't escape my wrath again.

Ready to play a game, little thief? The rules are simple: my way is law.

One-Click: bit.ly/DevilSAS
Add to Goodreads TBR: bit.ly/GRtemptingdevil
Sign Up for Updates: bit.ly/veronicaedenmail

TEMPTING DEVIL PREVIEW

BLAIR

Being here is necessary, I remind myself while crouching between the trees, scoping out my target. *It's all part of the perfect plan.*

Silver Lake Forest Estates has always made me feel out of place. Tonight's no different, even as I lurk in the shadows. My friend Gemma Turner dragged me to this community of mansions often last year for parties at her boyfriend's house on the other side of the lake. Maybe the sense of not belonging comes from being surrounded by people with so much privilege it bleeds from their ears, compared to what I have. Maybe it's that I can always feel Devlin Murphy judging my presence.

Either way, there's never been a question about it. I'm definitely not welcome here.

Now I'm staking out a place I never thought I'd willingly go: my enemy's house.

The weather has been mild for early September in Ridgeview, but I'm dressed in all black to blend in with the night. Sweat dampens the armpits of my faded long-sleeve t-shirt after hiking to my hiding place, where I have a clear view to the giant gate guarding the house. I don't know if it's from the anxious anticipation coursing through me or that I'm overheating in the outfit I scraped together for tonight from the second-hand shop. Probably both.

If Devlin catches me on his property, he'll live up to that big bad name of his. He's known as the notorious dark devil of Silver Lake High School, both for his looks and his lethal attack on the soccer field.

Douchebag devil. I hate him more than any of the jerks at my school.

One week into senior year and he's already cashing in on making my life hell once again. He cooled off a little last year after Gemma started dating his cousin and king of the school, Lucas Saint. It didn't stop him from sniping at me every chance he got, though. It just made him get more creative.

With Lucas and Gemma off at Oak Ridge College of the Arts, the high school has become Devlin Murphy and Connor Bishop's kingdom, the evil duo ruling over us with iron fists.

Today, Devlin and his soccer buddies baited me with dollar bills on fishing wire, hunting for my desperation. His vicious sneer burned my insides with acidic hatred. The most depressing part? We need money so badly that I almost gave into their cruel trap to add a few more dollars to our meager savings.

Survival always outweighs pride when it comes down to it.

A warm breeze moves the branches overhead, the creaking limbs the soundtrack to my illicit troublemaking.

The plan is to break in and take one of the things he loves most.

From what I can tell, Devlin has at least five cars—expensive ones. These aren't your typical economy class cars. It's about four more than the average person needs.

A car heist goes a little further than my usual song and

dance. *More like miles further.* The corner of my mouth lifts without a trace of humor as the thought crosses my mind.

Devlin Murphy deserves it.

The bastard's had it coming since freshman year. I've endured his brand of tormenting bullshit for too long.

A twig snaps with a muffled sound beneath my shoes as I shift my weight. I tighten my ponytail to keep my hair out of my face while I work, flicking my gaze up to the stars dotting the sky above the evergreens. It's dark enough I think.

Time to get moving if I'm going to pull this off. No more stalling, dancing on the line of will I or won't I.

There is no will or won't tonight—only *have to* and *no choice.*

I blow out a breath and rub my fingertips together. My shoulders are too tense. Needing to loosen up, I give them a little shake.

The isolated house looming before me is a mix of modern contemporary style with luxe cabin touches—large windows, metal framework, white-washed concrete, and the aesthetic comforts of an oversized mountain cabin.

Cabin is being coy. This is a legit mountain mansion. The biggest in the private community of Ridgeview's own brand of royalty.

It comes off as arrogant and out of place. The house's jutting lines sprawl out like it's their right, juxtaposed against nature as the trees fight to stand their ground.

Because money gives you everything. It opens any door. Nature doesn't get to say no to money.

My mouth twists in bitter contempt as my nails dig into the bark of a tree trunk beside me. I stand and keep to the shadows.

Adrenaline tingles in my fingertips with the first step I've taken in over an hour, the sharp pricks jumping along my awareness and contorting my stomach.

No one is around. Devlin's house is spread far from the neighbors, the most remote property I've seen here. Still, I don't let my guard drop.

A flash of light makes my heart trip over itself—*headlights! Security patrol?*—and I duck behind a cluster of boulders. It moves off into the tree line, turning away from Devlin's house. I breathe out a relieved sigh and creep closer to the house.

Funny how a private community for the most elite of Ridgeview doesn't expect unwelcome intruders to walk right in, assuming guests and residents only pass through the security kiosk at the gate. Dusk settled as I hiked from the road, slipping between the homes unseen, tracing the path I mapped out to get to Devlin's house on Google Maps at the library.

A bitten-off snort leaves me. I peek around to check if the coast is clear and dart by a skinny sapling. A little farther and I'll be past the point of no return.

If the sport schedule bulletin on the school website was right, Devlin should be at soccer practice until 8pm. That gives me at least forty-five minutes to work under the cover of night. His Range Rover was in the student lot today, three spaces down from the rust bucket 2001 Corolla that gets me from point A to B.

The plan races through my head on repeat: *get in unnoticed, disable the GPS tracking system according to the YouTube tutorial, drive off like a fucking boss, watch that dick's fury from afar in school...*

I move my hand over my hips, checking the pouch hooked through my belt loops. Inside is everything I'll need for this plan.

The sense of preparedness, calculating every move, is born out of faking it until I make it. It's not like I've ever committed a crime this serious before.

My wheelhouse is petty theft—earning the stupid sticky

fingers name the devil of Silver Lake High taunts me with by shoplifting what I can't afford and picking pockets when necessary.

The corners of my mouth tighten. Devlin Murphy has no idea what it's like to constantly stress about money.

Robin Hood steals from the rich, right? Well, the wealthy snobs of this town are the ones teaching me brutal lessons in survival, so I'm returning the favor.

I've long since let go of any moral guilt hanging over my head for being a survivor.

Pausing my approach to the house, I bite my lip. The undeniable consequences of what I'm here to do scroll through my head like a marquee. Devlin has more than enough money to bury me and then go after Mom. Hell, he could probably *kill* me for touching his cars and get away with it.

That crazy look that haunts his eyes when they're on me...

A shudder shakes my body. Yeah, he's messed up enough to murder someone. No doubt about it.

You're stalling. "Ugh."

I force my feet to move.

This is a big score for me, bigger than I've ever taken on. I'm not stealing cheap mascara, taking an extra carton of milk, or snagging a hundred bucks from spoiled classmates that don't notice they're short when their no-limit credit cards make up the difference.

No, this is a real crime. High risk, higher reward. The *go-to-jail-if-caught* kind.

My stomach turns over as I hesitate in the darkness.

If I get caught, Mom won't make it on her own. Maybe I should have done this at the end of junior year, before I turned eighteen in June. I tug on the end of my ponytail and chew on my lip again.

There's no other way. This is the only thing I could think of to get the money we need fast. It's a better idea than robbing a bank.

If I have to become a vigilante, repurposing some useless extra wealth to those more needy—me and my mom—then so be it. Getting back at Devlin is the cherry on top of this sour sundae.

Moving from shadow to shadow toward my goal, my resolve strengthens. It gives me the false sense of bravery I need to take this leap from my comfort zone.

I stop along the waist-high stone wall that forms a perimeter around Devlin's property line. Everything about his house screams elite, down to the cold iron gate cutting the property off from the road that turns into the circular driveway.

"A gate for the biggest house inside a gated community," I mumble to myself, shaking my head as I hop onto the stone wall and swing my legs over.

I drop off the wall into a crouch in case the community's private security patrol comes this way. My footsteps are light and quick.

The same honed focus falls over me that I feel when I'm about to pick someone's pocket or swipe something at the store. Steady breathing, exuding the confidence that nothing is wrong, and blending like I belong are the ways I get away with what I do.

This is no different. Even though my heart skips a beat at every unfamiliar sound. I keep my cool mask in place as I reach the garage.

It's a sub-level entry from the house, the circular drive sloping down an incline to the four large black garage doors flanked by industrial style lamps. Tossing a quick glance at the main house, I dig my homemade set of lock picks from the pouch of tools on my belt and slide on a pair of driving gloves.

They're not quite badass cat burglar leather gloves, but they were in the fifty cent bin in a thrift shop.

My expression melts into surprise when I grab the handle of the side entrance door, freezing as it turns. It's not locked.

Swinging my astonished gaze back and forth for another check of my surroundings, I slip inside, closing the door behind me.

Other than the foreboding entrance, Devlin's security is appalling. The keys aren't even in a lockbox. They're proudly displayed on the wall by the door, with tiny spotlights beneath the logos of each car brand.

Fucking rich people.

Their arrogance grates on my nerves. While they live with the constant expectation that they can have everything they want, Mom and I struggle to keep our heads above water. These pampered assholes are so trusting of their huge gates and private security to do the heavy lifting.

I'm offended it was so easy to get in here as I tuck my lock picks back into my zipper pouch of supplies.

The air inside the garage is cool and artificial, like there's a fancy temperature regulation system at work. Each car is parked diagonally in its own spot with an overhead light illuminating its sleek features. There are more than the five cars I've seen Devlin use—every high-end model I've ever heard of and some I don't recognize. It's like I've walked into a museum where car nuts would drool over makes and models they only dream of setting eyes on. The excessiveness of this collection turns my stomach, and a quiet scoff falls from my parted lips.

There are so many that my eyes blur and my temple throbs as I try to do the math in my head to add up the value surrounding me. I don't know what some of these retail for, but the ones I do are easily upwards of seventy grand. This entire room could wipe out the debt that hangs like a poisonous fog over Mom's head in one swoop.

It's not fucking fair.

But this is the cruelty of the world.

My hands clench into fists, the material of the gloves creaking the harder I squeeze. Dad taught me all about this harsh world at a young age before he took off.

Another collection notice from one of his gambling debts sits heavy in my pocket, the crumbled mail stuffed there after reading it made my eyes sting and a sickening panic surge on my way out of the trailer to execute this plan. The only choice was to take it with me. I couldn't leave it for Mom to find. Each one breaks her spirit a little more, no matter how strong she tries to be for the both of us. I'm the strong one and soon she won't have to worry.

I take a quick stroll down the row of cars on the left, sneering at a garish yellow Lamborghini, a gunmetal gray Audi, a shimmering pearl-colored Mercedes-Benz GLS, and a sleek black Escalade. The other side of the garage is just as bad with a vintage Mustang and vehicles that look more like futuristic flying cars.

For a moment I'm struck by indecision. I didn't realize he had this many cars. It's safer to take one of the more nondescript ones I've never seen him use. It'll be easier to move something common rather than the high profile cars. My gaze flits back and forth, considering the options.

I have to be smart about my choice.

Mom's voice still echoes in my mind when I overheard her last week, pleading on the phone for a loan she applied for. It fell through, the slimy scum of a loan officer unsympathetic to her quavering voice as she explained to him what our situation was if we didn't get that money. He didn't care, like all men.

Like *Dad.* Once again reminding me why I can't trust any of them.

My throat thickens at the memory and I screw my eyes shut. I don't have time for this. I need to act now.

At the end of the row in a prominent position is a car that makes me fume as soon as I spot it.

The red Porsche.

Devlin's prized ride. Possibly the only thing he loves in this world more than himself. I've seen him practically make out with it in the school lot while his groupies watch and giggle. They probably hope he'll fuck them in the cramped back seat, but I've never seen him give any of his hookups a lift when he drives it.

The gleaming red car is a beacon, drawing me a few steps closer. I tap my fingers against my legs. The sweet satisfaction of taking something precious from Devlin sings in my blood. My indecision vanishes, obliterated by the chance of getting the ultimate revenge on him.

Stalking back to the mahogany display box on the wall, I snatch the key fob beneath the shiny Porsche logo. A smirk curls the corners of my mouth when I admire the empty space left behind.

"Karma's a bitch, Murphy."

Spinning on my heel, I hurry over to the Porsche. The door opens without hitting the button on the fob. Even the cars are barely protected, left unlocked.

I huff in angry amusement, muttering as I slide behind the wheel. "Is that big gate supposed to keep you safe? Think again, asshole."

After adjusting the seat forward from Devlin's height, I push the keyless ignition. The engine purrs to life, sending power racing through me as I grip the wheel. A subtle rumbling vibration stirs through my thighs and I bite my lip. *Damn,* this is a nice car. My eyes crinkle with my smile. Now the driving gloves are more appropriate.

I'm searching around for a way to trigger the garage door to open from inside the car, figuring with Devlin's wealth he's probably the type to have something like that in all of his cars. My gloved fingers fumble over the visor and scan the touchscreen.

Then a shadowy figure moves in my periphery, blocking light from the window.

Within seconds my perfect plan crumbles before my eyes as my body pulses with the overpowering wrongness of someone being there. I jump when the door flies open a beat later, sucking in a strangled gasp as I fly into motion.

"No!" The shout leaves me in a garbled rush as I try to get away.

"Oh, I don't think so," Devlin snaps in a deadly voice. "Get back here!"

A strong hand with long fingers clamps over my wrist, stopping my wide-eyed scramble across the center console to escape. My heart drops into my stomach, every hair on my body standing on end. Fuck!

I kick with all my might, landing a solid hit against his torso. Devlin grunts angrily, but I can't break out of his hold.

He yanks on my wrist, dragging me from the car. I'm met with an angry snarl as he towers over me. "What the fuck are you doing?"

Devlin's face is etched in anger, thick brows furrowed and his damp black hair curling across his forehead, hanging into his eyes. A muscle jumps in his chiseled jaw, sending my instincts into fight-or-flight mode.

Shit, shit, shit. My heart beats in time with my racing thoughts. He was here the whole time—but the Range Rover!

It's not here. I dart my gaze around to confirm that. He's not supposed to be home yet.

Devlin shakes me, demanding my full attention as he leans into my face. His lip curls, giving me a glimpse of his perfect white teeth. With a grunt, he shoves me out of the way, pausing long enough to reach in the car to cut the engine without releasing his hold on me. I barely have time to consider if I can escape before he's in my face again.

I am so fucked.

"You are in way over your head, you thieving bitch," he seethes, tightening his grip on my wrist until it's painful. With his other hand, he digs his fingers into my upper arm. "You'll pay for this."

Every muscle in my body tenses with the need to run.

For the first time in years, I've been caught in the act. And now I'll face the consequences at the hands of someone that hates my guts as much as I hate his. Devlin Murphy, my bully.

I should've taken my chances robbing a bank instead.

ABOUT THE AUTHOR

STAY UP ALL NIGHT FALLING IN LOVE

Veronica Eden is a USA Today and International bestselling author of romances with spitfire heroines, irresistible heroes, and edgy twists.

She loves exploring complicated feelings, magical worlds, epic adventures, and the bond of characters that embrace *us against the world.* She has always been drawn to gruff bad boys, clever villains, and the twisty-turns of morally gray decisions. She is a sucker for a deliciously devilish antihero, and sometimes rolls on the dark side to let the villain get the girl. When not writing, she can be found soaking up sunshine at the beach, snuggling in a pile with her untamed pack of animals (her husband, dog and cats), and surrounding herself with as many plants as she can get her hands on.

* * *

CONTACT + FOLLOW

Email: veronicaedenauthor@gmail.com
Website: http://veronicaedenauthor.com
FB Reader Group: bit.ly/veronicafbgroup
Amazon: amazon.com/author/veronicaeden

facebook.com/veronicaedenauthor
instagram.com/veronicaedenauthor
twitter.com/vedenauthor
pinterest.com/veronicaedenauthor
bookbub.com/profile/veronica-eden
goodreads.com/veronicaedenauthor

ALSO BY VERONICA EDEN

Sign up for the mailing list to get first access and ARC opportunities! **Follow Veronica on BookBub** for new release alerts!

DARK ROMANCE

Sinners and Saints Series

Wicked Saint

Tempting Devil

Ruthless Bishop

Savage Wilder

Sinners and Saints: The Complete Series

Crowned Crows Series

Crowned Crows of Thorne Point

Loyalty in the Shadows

A Fractured Reign

The Kings of Ruin

Standalone

Unmasked Heart

Devil on the Lake

REVERSE HAREM ROMANCE

Standalone

Hell Gate

More Than Bargained

CONTEMPORARY ROMANCE

Standalone

Jingle Wars

The Devil You Know

Haze

CPSIA information can be obtained
at www.ICGtesting.com
Printed in the USA
BVHW041323210123
656723BV00004B/867

9 781957 134123